Secrets Revealed

Book 3 of the Secrets Series

By Amy M. Ward and Olivia Cayenne

Secrets Revealed

Book 3 of the Secrets Series

Copyright © Amy M. Ward & Olivia Cayenne

This is the work of fiction. Any resemblance to real persons or entities is strictly coincidental.

Cover art by Covers by Christian

Other works by Amy M. Ward & Olivia Cayenne:

Secrets Above

Secrets Below

Other works by Amy M. Ward:

Myra: Changed – A Short Story (Part 1 of the Myra: Everlasting Series)

Dear Secrets Keepers,

If you have made it this far into the Secrets Series, then you have probably eagerly awaited the release of Secrets Revealed. Which also means that you probably skipped this page altogether. No hard feelings. We understand.

Secrets Revealed is set to be a roller coaster of emotions for you. It was for us as we wrote it. We worked really hard to try and give Lia and Lukan some resolution. They have endured so much already but sometimes with great change comes great pain.

Although Secrets Revealed is the end of the story for Lia and Lukan, the story of Terra Convex and Grayson is far from over. In fact, we have already begun working on Long Ago Secrets. We are going to travel back in time, ninety years, and tell you the story of the Langston Virus. We will follow along as certain characters fight to survive in a world that is dying around them due to the virus. You will discover just how Grayson was rebuilt and be introduced to key people that entered into Terra Convex.

First, enjoy a little more time with Lia, Lukan, and their closest friends as they work towards revealing secrets from the past that will hopefully ensure a brighter future.

Much Love,

Amy M. Ward & Olivia Cayenne

Please feel free to send us your comments, questions, or fan art!

wardsarewriters@gmail.com

www.facebook.com/wardsarewriters/

Twitter: @wardsarewriters

Website: wardsarewriters.com

Chapter 1

Lia

My eyes, burning with hot tears of anguish over the death of my mother, have a difficult time focusing. My breath catches in my throat as I realize that I am not alone with my pain. He stands over me, on the other side of the window. The young man that I believe to be Lukan stares down at me with one wide eye. His other eye appears to be covered. I have a hard time making out his features through my tears and with the sun shining brightly behind him. What I am able to discern, though, is a boy about my age with dark shoulder-length hair. His clothing is much different than mine. My attire is bland and without color. Lukan's clothing seems to have a personality all its own. Colors, patterns, and textures melded together in a way that makes it seem as though there is a story to be told with each article.

We stare at each other through the window for several seconds. Lukan seems just as startled to see me as I am him. I continue to wipe the tears from my face as I try to formulate a plan to communicate with him. I am certain the boy from the outside world is here to save me from this world of misery. I can see his wide eye narrow as he takes in the sight below his feet.

How pitiful I must look, laying on the floor, face wet with tears of mourning and desperation. I have imagined being able to see Lukan since the day I saw the bloody handprints. That day seems like ages ago now. I imagine that when he left the arrow, and the flowers, his image of me was much different than the sobbing girl he sees now.

Suddenly, Lukan falls to his knees and places his hands on the glass. When he does, I am able to see his face much more clearly. I know that I should find the fact that he only has one eye worrisome; however, the thing about him that bothers me the most is that it appears he is covered in blood. So much blood on his clothing and hands. It also seems that he has been crying. What has happened, in his world, to cause him the pain that is so obvious on his tear-streaked face?

Lukan's mouth begins to move, and his face is consumed by a look of desperation. He is trying to say something to me, but the glass is too thick. I unable hear his words. I can only sit and stare at him, shaking my head.

Sitting up now, I watch as Lukan tries to communicate with me. The longer I watch him shouting into the glass, the more unnerved I become. Taking my eyes off Lukan, I scan the small room in search of a way to communicate with him. Tearing an empty sheet of parchment paper from my mother's journal, I reach my finger into some muck on a nearby pipe and write the only thing that comes to mind.

HELP

I hold the paper up as high as I can reach, desperate for Lukan to see. His mouth quits moving immediately. He stares at the word for a long time. I lower the paper back down to my lap. Lukan shakes his head slowly, and a look of sadness passes over his face.

I look away as my tears begin to fall once again. The realization of my situation tumbles over me with tremendous weight. Lukan cannot help me. Nobody can help me. More importantly, I cannot help the people of Terra Convex. We are doomed to this living tomb for eternity.

Above me, Lukan begins to pound on the window, startling me from my despair. Looking up once more, I can see that he is pointing and mouthing a word. I shake my head to communicate that I do not understand what he is trying to communicate. He is obviously becoming aggravated. I'm surprised at how much emotion he can convey with just the one eye.

He stands and walks away from the window. I fear that he has abandoned his communication with me and a wave of anxiety rushes over me. Seconds later, he returns with dirty fingers. Stiffness begins to settle into my neck; still, I continue to stare up at him. With a mud-covered finger, he continues to try to communicate with me. He writes out one simple word.

ROOD

Even though the word he writes with his finger is backward, I know that he is trying to tell me to go to the hatch door. So Lukan knows about the hatch. Apparently, Lukan knows more about Terra Convex than I had realized. I wonder if he knows that the metal door is locked, with a combination that I do not know. He seems adamant that I go there, so I reluctantly stand and walk over to the door that leads to the hallway. Looking back at the window, I see that Lukan is already gone. Obviously, headed towards the hatch. Hoping against hope that he knows a way in, I also make my way to the only way in or out of Terra Convex.

Lukan

Although I had hoped to see Lia, I hadn't expected to. We stare at each other for several seconds. Lia's tear-streaked face is a mixture of misery and astonishment. I imagine the look on her face is much like my own. Matching Lia's movements, I wipe my face dry of the tears that I thought would never cease.

I am curious as to what has caused her so much anguish. The image of the chimney, belching up the horrid stench of death, scratches at the back of my mind. I try to ignore the irritation it causes, but I can't help but wonder if the chimney of death is the cause of her turmoil.

Now that I have actually made eye contact with the girl from the underground world, I seem to be at a loss for what to do besides stand above her and stare awkwardly. Her eyes are probably a lovely shade of blue when she isn't crying. At this moment, though, they are blood-shot and charged with torment. Even while witnessing Lia's anguish, I am still confident that there is safety for Grayson on the other side of this window. There has to be.

Lia's eyes grow wider with every second that she stares up at me. I can only imagine what a frightful sight I must be to her. A one-eyed boy. Face and hands smeared with dirt, sweat, tears, and the blood of the girl I love. Looking down at my clothes, I can see that there are rips and tears that are the result of running through the forest without regard to the trees, bushes, and briars that attempted to hold me back.

Suddenly feeling that time is slipping away for Grayson, I fall to my knees and place my hands on the glass. I hope she can see the desperation on my face and let me in. If I can just explain the events that led me here, I know that she will have pity on me and then, hopefully, my people. In my mind, I can see the large metal door opening. Lia is just inside, beckoning me into her world with a smile and a welcoming wave of her hand.

The door is the key. It is the gateway to the survival of my community. With great desperation, I tell Lia to go to the door. I point and say the word repeatedly. She only sits and stares at me. She shakes her head, and I realize that the glass is too thick for me to be heard beyond it. I grow increasingly unnerved by the whole ordeal, but I am determined to communicate with her.

Lia begins to look around the small room. She seems to be searching for something. Why does she not go to the door? Surely, she must know of its existence. Suddenly, Lia tears a sheet of parchment paper from the book in which she has been clinging. She reaches behind the pipes that are closest to her and begins to smudge her fingers across the paper. When she holds up the paper, my hopes shatter.

HELP

I stare at the word for a long time. When I first saw her, I could tell that she was going through something dire. It hadn't occurred to me that her situation might actually be something she needed help escaping. Shaking my head slowly, I regretfully try to convey to her that I have no help to give. Lia lowers the paper back to her lap and her tears resume.

I am surprised by the burden I feel for this stranger. Her despair floods over me with tremendous weight. I feel guilty for giving Lia hope. Perhaps my guilt is because I wasn't able to help Merritt when she needed me the most. More importantly, if I am unable to get into the door, I cannot help the people of Grayson. We are doomed to a life of servitude and torture at the hands of the Howlers.

The significance of the situation - the situation Lia and I share - becomes too much for me. In anger and frustration, I strike the window. Lia flinches and looks up at me once more. I yell into the window and point in the direction of the metal door. Lia merely shakes her head. She obviously doesn't understand what I am trying to convey. I become increasingly aggravated.

Another thought occurs to me, and I stand and walk away from the window. I find a patch of dirt nearby and spit into it until it becomes mud. Dipping my fingers into it, I quickly return to the window and try a different type of communication. With dirty fingers, I hastily write one simple word on the glass.

DOOR

Looking down on the word, and Lia beyond, I immediately realize that the word she is looking up at is ROOD. Still, she seems to understand the meaning. With a noticeable look of dejection, Lia slowly stands and walks over to the only door in the tiny room. This seems like progress, and I race away from the window and toward the large metal door that represents my salvation.

Chapter 2

Lia

With a heavy heart, I stare at the hatch door. There is no way for me to open it. I don't know the code. Tears stream down my cheeks as I listen to Lukan on the other side, the free side, trying to get in. If he knew what evil lies on the dark side of the hatch, he wouldn't be trying to open it. He would certainly run away and never return.

Lukan continues to pound on the door. Turning my back to it, I lean against it and slide down to the cold hard floor. I cover my ears with my hands and sob. The image of my mother's battered body comes hauntingly into my mind. I told Matlok that I would be back for her. More than anything, I want to be able to bury her in the earth. Outside, where the sun can shine down on her grave, growing beautiful flowers from the place where death lays.The thought of her body being burned unceremoniously and without any thought of her beauty or grace, makes my stomach twist into knots.

As I ponder this, I realize that the pounding on the other side of the door has ceased and I am left in stillness once again. Standing, I place my ear to the cold metal, tentatively. Of course, I hear nothing. Lukan, apparently, has given up on me. Has given up on Terra Convex.

I can't blame him. He has no reason to want to get in here.

Turning from the door, I make my way back to the window. I am in no rush to get back to the empty room. I imagine Lukan is returning to his home now, trying to forget the pitiful girl on the other side of the window.

The complete darkness of the corridor seems to help sort my thoughts out. I think about my sister. I wonder if Matlok has told her the news of the death of our mother yet. My heart goes out to my sister's husband. I am thankful for the position he holds as an Enforcer. His job made it possible for me to see my mother, to hold her as her life faded from her eyes. If not for Matlok, she would have died alone in that horrid place.

Not alone.

For the first time since entering that tomb of the dying, the image of those with outstretched arms and moans of despair begins to snake its way up my spine and embed itself into a memory that I will never be able to be free from. I don't want to be free from it. I believe that if I allow myself to become immersed in the memory of their anguish, then hopefully, I will begin to pay for my disobedience and curiosity. Because of this belief, I concentrate on the faces that I was forced to step over as I slowly made my way to my mother. In the pitch blackness of this corridor, it is easy for me to remember the wrinkled hands of the discarded elderly that reached out to me. A tremendous guilt floods over me.

By the time I reach for the door that leads to my secret place, I am sobbing once again. I pause at the door, trying to compose myself, hoping that Lukan will be back at the window with a plan. As I open the door, I am shocked to find Axel leaning against the pipes with his hand covering his face. He looks up, startled but relieved to see me.

Axel and I rush to each other. He wraps his arms around me and buries his face in my hair. I can feel his body tremble and I realize that he is crying silently. He must know about the death of my mother. News travels fast in this underground world.

Axel's silent tears seem to stifle mine. I will learn to live with my own grief; I cannot bear the grief of this sweet man that holds my heart. He never had the pleasure of knowing my mother. Even though she raised me, I am aware that I never realized what a pleasure it was for me to know her. This thought is almost too much for my fragile emotions. I feel myself breaking once again.

"I'm so sorry," Axel manages. He is still clinging to me, but he is leaning back so he can look into my eyes. His strong but gentle hand cradles the back of my head tenderly. I am unable to match his gaze. I allow my eyes to look above him, to the empty window.

Axel follows my gaze up to the window, curiously.

"Lukan was there," I say quietly. The despair I hear in my own voice is unsettling.

Returning his eyes back to me, Axel's hold on me loosens a bit. He stares at me questioningly.

I release him and point up at the window. "He was standing right there."

Axel's eyes follow my finger up to the window. Of course, there is nothing for him to see that he hasn't seen before. A sunny, cloudless sky. The tops of trees are swaying gently in the wind. There is no Lukan above us. There is no salvation.

With tremendous despair, I take the two steps it takes to walk over to the pipes, and I lean against them with a heavy sigh. Axel joins me. As I stare at the concrete below my feet, I can feel his eyes on me. I'm sure he is wondering what else is going to have to happen before I truly snap.

The silence becomes too much for me. "I don't suppose you know the code to the hatch, do you?" I look up at him and attempt a grin.

"No. I'm sorry," Axel responds quietly. His eyes do not leave me, and I begin to feel irritated that he continues to stare.

With a huff, I ask, "What *can* you tell me about the hatch?"

The aggravation in my voice causes Axel to flinch just a bit, and I give him an apologetic look. He ponders my question for only a second before answering.

"I know that it is made out of thick metal and that it requires a code that only two people in Terra Convex know. My boss and the president." He tries to match the snarkiness in his voice to mine. His heart is too pure for snarkiness, though. "When the windows need to be cleaned, my boss gains a new code from DePriest. When the task is complete, the code is changed. The president is always aware when somebody is above ground." Axel shrugs his shoulders as if to say there is nothing more to say about the hatch.

"So, to get the door open, I will need to get to the president," I say, contemplating his words.

"Lia..."

I turn on him sharply. "What? What? Tell me, Axel. What is it? What am I supposed to do now? My mother is dead. I can either live like a victim, or I can do something. So, tell me what am I supposed to do?" I am breathing heavily, trying to control my emotions, but failing miserably.

Axel is quiet for several seconds. Finally, he replies calmly, "For now, you can tell me what you know about Lukan."

I stare at him, realizing that I am attacking the wrong person. Axel is my ally. He holds my heart and yet I am taking my frustrations out on him. Ashamed of my outburst, I feel as though I can't do anything right lately. My shame weighs heavily on me.

Shaking my head, I look away. Quietly, I attempt to make amends, "I'm sorry, Axel. I-I've had the worst day of my life." My voice trembles and tears threaten once more. I try to give him a weak smile, though.

With a kind smile, Axel reaches his arm around my waist and gently draws me close to his side. "I know. You have had the worst day imaginable." He kisses the top of my head. "No need for apologies. There will be time for planning."

I consider this for a moment before I reply, "No. I don't have time to formulate a plan. I told Matlok that I would be back for my mother's body. I want to bury her outside. I might have said it purely from emotion, but I just couldn't bear the thought of her body being burned. Still can't."

"Burned?" Axel asks with a hint of disgust in his voice.

With a lump in my throat, I explain the horrors of the Isolation Chamber. Axel looks at me with wide eyes as he tries to understand what I am telling him. He doesn't want to believe that the government disregards the life of the elderly, disabled, injured, or sick. In our time of learning, we have never been taught anything about the Isolation Chamber. I wonder if Mrs.

Bermingham even knows that such a vile place exists in our underground world.

"No food? No water?" Axel asks in astonishment.

With a sour taste in my mouth, I shake my head. "When the government decides that a person is too weak to be a productive member of Terra Convex, they are taken there to die. People that are found guilty of whatever ridiculous crime they have been accused of, well, they are beaten and tortured. Then, stripped of their clothes and their dignity, they are left there to die."

Axel ponders this, and I can see his face contort as the realization of how dire our situation inside Terra Convex really is.

"It's a death chamber," Axel finally says quietly. I can only nod in agreement. "How is it that nobody has ever known about this? How can they have kept something like this quiet for ninety years?"

I don't have an answer for him, so I merely shake my head. Axel's eyes narrow and his hand comes up to a strand of my hair that has decided to fall out of place and is covering my eye. He gently places it back behind my ear.

"I hate that you had to go into that place. I hate that you had to see any of that." Axel conveys quietly.

I feel my chin begin to quiver and the lump return to my throat as I look into his eyes. The tremendous amount of affection in his voice is soothing in a way that brings tears to my eyes, once again. Nevertheless, the memory of what I experienced, what the doomed are still experiencing, haunts me and a shiver snakes up my spine.

Sensing the downward spiral of my emotions once more, Axel changes the subject with a small smile. "So, tell me about Lukan."

I think about this for a moment before I answer. "Well, he looks like he is about my age. His clothing was odd. His hair was about as long as yours but straighter. The most interesting thing that I noticed...one of his eyes seemed to be covered. It was hard to see his features because I was looking into the sun." I pause as I try to remember all the details of seeing Lukan for the first time. "He seemed upset. Seemed like he wanted in as much as I wanted out."

"What do you mean?" Axel asked, perplexed.

"I think he was crying. Or had been. He actually seemed desperate to communicate with me. He knows where the hatch is, but he couldn't get in."

Axel is quiet, and he looks up through the window. I know he is pondering everything I have told him. I know he wishes he could have seen Lukan. The silence is unnerving to me. With nothing to talk about, my mind goes back to my mother. It's almost as if I can still feel her lifeless body, beaten and battered, in my arms and against my chest.

I am thankful when Axel interrupts my gloomy thoughts.

"It makes me wonder," he says slowly, bringing his gaze back to me. "What's above us that has Lukan so upset that he is desperate to get in?"

Lukan

With growing exasperation, I stare at the metal door. There is no way for me to open it from out here. I am relying solely on Lia. She should have been here by now. Should have it open already. My annoyance with the whole situation turns to anger, and I begin to beat on the door with my fists. My nerves are frayed, and I start to think that maybe I have lost my mind to madness.

Pounding.

Pounding.

I do not stop pounding until I see that my hands are bleeding. Looking down at my wounded fists, I find myself welcoming the pain. Somehow, the physical pain and dripping blood, make me realize that I can feel something other than inner turmoil.

Still, Lia does not come. The door remains closed tight. Grayson remains in the grips of the Howlers. Merritt remains dead. My life continues to be consumed with guilt and torment.

Breathlessly, with bruised and bloodied fists, I stare at the metal door. In my nightmare, it had seemed much more frightening. Gazing at it now, I do not see it as something scary. Now, I see it as my enemy. Just something else in this world of torment that is meant to chip away at what little sanity I have left.

"Lukan?"

Startled, I turn around quickly. I am astonished to see Helix standing at the top of the concrete steps. The sun is shining behind him, making it difficult for me to see his face. With his thick fur, he appears eerily like a Howler. I have no fear of this man, though. I know it is Helix by his voice. His distinct voice, deep and husky, is one of my favorite things about the strange Wanderer. Usually, when he speaks, his voice has a soothing effect. Even when he isn't speaking, his presence provides comfort. I doubt I will find any comfort in Helix's presence on this day. Or any days to follow.

"Lukan?" Helix repeats.

I do not doubt that he knows I am here. The man has a keen sense of, well, everything. Except for sight. That was stolen from him in a horrific manner when he was a child. His sight, along with his childhood, was snatched away from him by the Howlers. Because of his blindness, he can hear sounds and smell odors better than anyone in the land. I am certain that he only repeats my name in case I didn't hear him the first time.

"How did you find me, Helix?" I ask with a bit more annoyance in my voice than I intended. It isn't that I am actually irritated with my friend; it's just that the weight of the day is beginning to feel like a knot between my shoulders, and the pain I feel from the loss of my friend burns inside my chest.

"Come up here. The stairs make me nervous." I find his statement strange. Helix has never expressed concern with his blindness. Repeatedly, he has surprised me with his sure-footedness, and calm, as he had made his way through the forest. As a self-proclaimed Wanderer, Helix has traversed many miles in a completely black world, with little trouble.

Another thought occurs to me. How does he even know there are stairs? That man's ability to see without sight is almost eery.

Exasperated, I shake my head, even though he cannot see the action. "Not right now. I'm in the middle of something."

"It sounds like you are in the middle of an incredible battle with something metallic, Lukan, and you are losing. Stop the nonsense and join me."

That explains how he knew I was here - the pounding I was giving to the metal door during my fit of rage.

I look back at the door and then up at Helix again. Even with most of his face covered with cloth, it is easy for me to see the concern he has for me. He holds his staff in one hand. His other hand reaches for me. Reluctantly, I decide to humor my friend. With one last look at the door, I turn and make my way up the steps to where Helix is waiting patiently. When I get to the top, I do not stop. I push past his outstretched arm and begin walking back towards the window.

"Lukan, wait." Helix beckons from behind me. For the first time since I met him, I can hear something that sounds a lot like desperation in his voice. Even engulfed in my anger and turmoil, the sound of it halts me.

"Where are we going?" Helix asks when he catches up to me.

"I am going to the window. Lia might be there." I answer matter-of-factly.

"Lia?" Helix is confused. He knows of the girl on the other side of the window. He was with me when I found her name written on parchment. We had both assumed that it was her name and that she had left it there for me to see. She was trying to communicate.

"I saw her there earlier. That's why I was at the door."

"What do you mean? Why were you at the door?" His voice grumbles from deep in his belly.

With a huff of annoyance, I answer rather curtly, "It's a long story, Helix."

I turn to walk away, but Helix gently places his hand on my arm, stopping me. I turn around quickly, anger brimming. The look of compassion that is on his face causes me to pause, though.

"We have time for a long story, Lukan," Helix says calmly, releasing my arm.

The despair that I cling to begins to feel the soothing effects of his voice. I look at him for several seconds, contemplating his words. His face does not change.

"Do we have time, Helix? Do we?" I ask quietly. "I have to find someplace safe for my family, for Grayson, before the Howlers hurt anyone else like they did..." I cannot finish. The image of Merritt floods into my mind. The feeling of her battered body in my arms gives me a feeling of weakness. She wasn't just hurt; she was murdered. I stare at Helix with a wide eye. My legs seem to lose their ability to work, and I nearly fall. As if Helix can sense my waning strength, he reaches his hand out and steadies me.

With a slight tilt of his head and a quiet, deep voice, Helix responds, "Because of that, we have time. You must take time before what happens next."

His words confuse me. "What do you mean, Helix? What happens next?"

I can hear his groaning start in his belly and work its way up his throat as a confident smile spreads across his face. "What happens next is the end of the Howlers and the beginning of your new life. First, you must take the time to say goodbye to the pain and the hate. Only then, will you be able to forge a plan of action."

His words, said with a passion that I wish I could match, find their mark inside me. I consider his words. Although Helix cannot see me, I find myself nodding slowly. He still holds my arm as if he is afraid I might fall. I place a shaky hand on top of his with gratitude and quietly say, "Okay, Helix. Thank you."

Helix continues to smile. "You're welcome, my friend. Now, tell me about Lia."

Chapter 3

Lia

"I have an idea," Darcy says with wide, excited eyes.

Axel, Darcy, and I have been sitting under the window for what seems like hours. In the two weeks since my mother was tortured and killed, the mood in Terra Convex has been on a steady downward spiral. Two weeks since her death. In ways, the time has gone by swiftly; in other ways, it has crawled. It's only been one week since Matlok, my sister's husband, finally had the nerve to tell me that my mother's body had indeed been cremated. Nothing remains of the first person that ever loved me. Nothing except for the ashes. I had so wanted to bury her under the tree that sways above my secret window.

"They did a comprehensive cleaning of the Chamber," Matlok explained with disgust in his voice. "It seems almost as if..." He couldn't meet my eyes. I prodded him, and he finally continued. "Almost as if they are preparing for something and they need that space." There was no need for him to explain further. We all know what the government is preparing for.

Us.

They continue to search for us. Continue to threaten the citizens of Terra Convex to turn us over. The rest of the community lives in utter fear of Leadership. My friends and I live in defiance.

The government calls us Agitators. When they broadcast their threats over the intercom system, condemning the Agitators and anyone who may feel led to harbor them, I almost chuckle. Those in leadership genuinely believe they are searching for a group of rebellious adults. Traitors, weary from the oppression of living underground. Dissenters, bored with the lack of stimulation that relentless gray walls and mundane schedules of Terra Convex. They have no idea that the Agitators they seek are just a few teenagers, armed only with proof of a better option for their lives.

Darcy is looking at each of us with excitement in her eyes. I don't even have the strength anymore to pretend that I am interested in her new idea. Usually, sitting under the window calms my nerves and gives me peace. Lately, though, my mood has become sour and, quite frankly, Darcy's ideas have been pointless. Everyone's ideas have been ridiculous when all options are considered. I can't imagine that this one is any better. She doesn't seem phased that I am not excited to hear this newest idea. I merely look at her with raised eyebrows.

"The next time they send Axel above ground, we can all just leave with him. Run away. Nobody would dare come searching for us. Not above ground. We would be safe." Darcy is excited about the plan that has been unfolding in her mind.

I glance at Axel, waiting for him to point out the holes in her plan. I know there are plenty because he and I have already discussed the idea of simply walking out.

"That won't work. My supervisor has to put the code in for the hatch to open, and he closes the door behind me. He would never allow anyone other than me to walk through that door." Axel explains with gloom in his voice.

"Oh," is all that Darcy can say as she grasps what Axel is saying.

Sensing that he may have hurt her feelings, Axel adds, "It is a good idea though. If I were prone to violence, I guess I could knock him in the head and then we could make a run for it." He chuckles nervously. My face must betray me because he quickly adds, "No, Lia. I'm not going to hurt somebody that is just doing his job."

I shrug and look back down at the floor. As I am about to get lost in my thoughts again, the door to our secret room opens, and Mac enters. As one, we all stare up at him from the cold hard floor. His face reveals that the deed has been done. His union with Abigail is complete. Tonight, Mac will have to sleep in the same bed with one of the most despicable people in Terra Convex. Within two years, he will have to father a child with her. The thought makes me sick.

There are no words of comfort we can give to our friend. His fate has been set by Leadership. All we can do is support him and listen when he needs an ear. I can't imagine the turmoil he is going through right now. I know that I will suffer heartache from the loss of my mother for the rest of my life. The torment that Mac will endure in the presence of his government-issued wife, however, will be relentless and torturous, I'm sure.

Mac joins us on the floor. We sit in silence for some time. Each of us lost in our thoughts. I look at our little group and wonder if I have made the right decision in bringing them into my dream of living above ground. It doesn't seem like it was that long ago when I was coming into this room alone, staring up into a world I had only imagined. I found peace, laying on the floor alone, looking up. When Axel joined me, though, I found much more - I found contentment. Then came the difficult task of trying to convince Darcy and Mac to see this place for themselves. To witness the sun on their face and watch the birds swoop through the air. Now, they sit with me in the dark, waiting to hear what I think we should do next. I hate to tell them that I am out of ideas - other than storming the Leadership wing, and I don't want to mention that. I know if I do, these three will follow and most likely get hurt - or worse - in the process. No, that is something I will need to do alone.

Axel's voice breaks the silence that has settled heavily in the room. "I think I have an idea."

None of us respond. We have been coming up with "ideas" for days. None of which have led to any action. All of which would most likely end terribly for one or all of us. Axel must be pretty confident with his idea though because now he is standing over us, excitement on his face.

"I can leave a note!"

"We've left notes," I reply with an edge of defeat in my voice

He is shaking his head, slightly frustrated, but still smiling. "No, not right here. Up there." Axel says this slowly and with emphasis. He points a finger up at the window.

Darcy, Mac, and I glance around at each other, cautiously. I imagine Axel leaving a note on the window, above where we are seated right now; Lukan finding the note and...

And what?

The world above is locked out. We are locked in.

There is no hope.

Axel must sense my wandering mind. He reaches for my hands, and I give them without hesitation. Pulling me up gently so that I am standing with him, Axel surprises me with a tender kiss on the forehead. He must feel pretty certain about his plan. I can't help but smile.

"Because the leaves are falling, I go above ground once every other week to clean the solar windows. The next time I go out, I can leave a note," Axel points above us, "telling Lukan to come back in exactly two weeks." His voice rises with excitement as he explains.

"When do you go back out?" Mac asks, beginning to grasp his plan.

"Tomorrow. That's what made me think of it." Axel answers with wide eyes. "I was sitting there thinking about how it would be great if I could just talk to Lukan while I am out there. Then I remembered that I actually could if we could arrange a day and time."

"So, you leave the note. Lukan reads it. We wait two weeks and then when he comes back, you can tell him how bad it is and that we have to leave. Hopefully, he has people that can help." Now my voice is rising with the thought of being free of this place in a couple of weeks.

"Exactly!"

"Axel, that is a great idea!" Darcy exclaims with glee.

While Darcy, Axel, and I celebrate an actual plan, I glance down at Mac. He still sits on the cold floor, brooding. Before I can ask him to join us, he says with an audible sadness, and without looking up from the floor, "The only problem is... What if Lukan doesn't want to help us after he hears how bad it is in here? Why would he want to let the evil of Terra Convex out into his world?"

Lukan

The morning light, peeking through the curtains, coaxes me awake. I roll over to face the wall, attempting to rid myself of the sounds of early morning. Along with the crowing roosters and the children playing outside, there are other early morning noises that grate on my nerves. I should be accustomed to these noises. They have filtered through the thin walls of my bedroom nearly every morning for the past two weeks.

The whispers of my family.

Although I can't always make out their hushed words, I'm sure their muttered conversations are about me. They worry about me. Worry about what I might be planning against the Howlers. Against Gallner. They needn't worry. I have no plans. If Merritt's murder taught me anything, it is that we are prisoners in the Howler's world. Nothing can change it. We must accept it.

The whispers get louder. My family is coming to my room. I can hear them quietly arguing about who is going to be the one to convince me to leave the house today. None of them will, of course. I cover my head with my pillow, trying to block out the sound of their approach.

They must know that I can hear them. My hearing is much keener than anyone else in Grayson. I attribute this to only having half of my sense of sight. My brain has found a way to compensate for my shortcomings of only having one useful eye by giving me extraordinary hearing.

Another voice teases through the pillow. I remove the fluffy barrier so I can hear better. A deep male voice is assuring my mother that he can bring her boy out of his despair. His voice is low and accompanied by an occasional groan that almost makes me smile.

Helix.

My blind friend has returned. When he left Grayson nearly two weeks ago, immediately after the Lamentation for Merritt, I assumed he would stay gone until spring. His presence surprises me. It also brings me a faint sense of comfort.

Sitting up quickly, I place my pillow behind my back. Grabbing my eye patch from the small table next to my bed, I hastily cover the scar where my right eye is supposed to be. By the time my mother opens my bedroom door and enters the room with Helix, I am sitting against my headboard with my arms crossed. She can tell immediately that I am aware that I have been the topic of their conversations.

My mom stammers out a "good morning" before needlessly announcing that Helix is here for a visit. In the past, I would have muttered something snarky like, "Really, mom? Helix is here? I couldn't see him standing right here in the middle of my room." Her spirit is as close to broken as mine, though, and I wouldn't dare want to hurt her with a sarcastic comeback. Besides, it is good to see the smile that Helix has brought to her face. It's apparent that she is happy to see the Wanderer.

To be honest, so am I.

Before I can say anything, Helix walks towards me. He uses a long stick to help guide him. When he reaches the bed, he surprises me by sitting on the edge. Tucking my feet underneath me, I sit up straighter.

"Helix, I hadn't expected you until after the thaw," I comment with a slight grin that he cannot see.

A groan starts deep in his belly as a smile spreads across his face. "I was missing you," Helix says.

I stifle a chuckle. It doesn't seem right to find joy after so much loss.

"I invited you to stay. We all did," I answer, nodding towards my mother even though Helix cannot see it.

"You did." Helix acknowledges with a nod. "I just needed to be alone for a bit, and I needed to leave you alone for a bit."

I glance up at my mother who gives me a slight smile.

"So, why are you here now? Do you think my time of mourning should be over?" I say with more bite than I had intended.

Quietly, Helix replies, "No, Lukan. Only you can decide when your time of mourning is over. Maybe it never will be. Maybe the loss you feel will always be part of you. I hope not. I hope that you replace the sadness with something...healthier."

"Healthier?" I am slightly annoyed that everyone thinks they know how I am supposed to be handling everything that I have had to endure.

"Where do you hide your memories of Merritt?" Helix asks.

The sound of her name startles me, and I feel myself flinch. His question is confusing. I look at my mother once more, but she is looking out the window, seemingly lost in her own thoughts.

"I – I don't understand," I finally concede.

"You have fantastic memories of Merritt, do you not?"

"Of course."

"Where are they? Have you been replaying them in your mind as you have laid in this bed for the past couple of weeks?" His voice doesn't sound malicious as he asks, but still, I feel hurt by his questioning.

"I keep replaying that day," I answer honestly, beginning to feel that tears might betray me. "I just keep thinking about how much I hate the Howlers and how much it hurts without her. I think about the pain she must have felt and how I wish I could have taken her place."

My mother, who has moved to the window, sniffles.

"So, if you are so consumed with hate and hurt, where do the good memories of Merritt fit?"

I understand his point now. I have no words. Only shame for becoming so absorbed in emotions that do nothing for the memory of the love I felt, still feel, for Merritt.

"This will always hurt, Lukan. It just doesn't have to hurt as much. Merritt can help you overcome your grief. Just let her memory replace the despair. When you begin to feel that familiar foe of sadness begin to creep over you – and you will for some time – just take a deep breath and remember Merritt. Think about the first time you met her; remember the thing about her that you loved the most; remember her last words to you..."

"She said she loved me," I whisper, with one tear escaping. I allow it to fall without attempting to wipe it away.

"Oh, and I believe she did, Lukan. What a beautiful thing to know that you are loved for all eternity by a beautiful young woman." A warm smile spreads across Helix's face.

Somehow, my blind, wandering friend has lifted my sour mood. I can't help but smile back.

"Yes, it is," I reply quietly.

"I'm going to go fix breakfast. Helix, I am insisting that you stay and eat with us," my mother announces, apparently satisfied that her son is at least beginning to come out of his depression.

"Yes, ma'am," Helix groans happily.

When my mother leaves my bedroom, Helix says, "Lukan, I have an idea. Let's go camping."

"Camping? Now?" The idea is preposterous to me.

"Why not?"

"Um, well, winter will be here soon. I've heard talks of snow flurries already. Besides, the Howlers could come back."

Helix nods and then says, "Then we better hurry."

The idea of being in the forest gives me a feeling of excitement that I haven't felt in weeks. A feeling that I hadn't expected ever to experience again. "I think camping is just what I need."

"I think so too, my friend," Helix replies with a moan from his belly and a warm smile. "I also think that we should invite your cousin, Domenic."

I hadn't expected this. Helix and Dom have never spent any time together. His sudden interest in my cousin confuses me. I start to object, but Helix explains.

"Your cousin is also in a great deal of pain, Lukan. Getting outside the walls of Grayson for a couple of days would be quite healing for him. I imagine that he feels a tremendous sense of guilt."

"Guilt for what?"

"Think about it. If he hadn't followed you to the window, he would not have gotten caught by the Howlers." Helix explains, sending yet another dagger into my already shattered soul.

He doesn't have to continue. I know the rest. "And if he hadn't gotten caught by the Howlers, then Merritt would still be alive," I say quietly.

A groan of agreement from Helix.

"Alright, Helix. Let's bring Dom with us. Once again, you're right. Being in the woods has a way of healing." I concede. "Where are we going?"

Even before he answers, I know what he is going to say.

Helix whispers mischievously, "The window."

I smile broadly. For the first time in weeks, I feel lighter. Although the sadness is still there, I no longer feel weighed down by it.

"I haven't given up on our friend below ground," Helix adds. "I believe she is trying to formulate a plan even now and I don't want us to miss out."

"I would like to think that," I muse.

Leaning in close, Helix whispers with a sly smile, "I guarantee it. They are scheming, and we need to be there for it."

"How do you know?"

"The whispers."

Chapter 4

Lia

"She isn't as bad as you think, Lia," Mac says with a tone of pleading. He has been trying for several minutes to convince Darcy and me that we should allow his newly acquired government-issued bride to sit with us during mealtime.

I cannot believe what I am hearing. "Mac, she hates us. Especially me. She hates you. It's bad enough that you have to live with her. Why do you want to bring her into our circle? Seems like you would be happy to be rid of her for a few hours." I return my attention to my food, taking a bite of a bland piece of toast.

Mac takes a few seconds before he replies. "You don't know her like I do." His voice is quiet, almost defeated.

Nearly choking on my food, I retort, "You've been married to her for a day! You don't even know her." My voice rises into almost a high-pitch frenzy. Looking around, I realize that I have gained the attention of a few of the citizens that are seated near us in the Dining Hall.

I notice Mac close his eyes briefly and take a deep breath. "Abigail and I have been spending time together for the past few weeks."

Stunned at this revelation, I glare at Mac for several seconds before asking, "How long?"

Another pause and a deep breath from Mac, "Ever since I found out who I was betrothed to. I felt like I should try to get to know her. I thought it would make things easier for...us. It did."

"How long?" I ask quietly, attempting to keep my anger at bay. "How long have you been 'spending time together'?"

Mac glances at Darcy before answering, "I don't know...a couple of weeks, maybe."

I stare at Mac with an intensity that he must be able to feel because he refuses to meet my gaze. "Two weeks?" I ask with a hiss. "So, let me get this straight. While I have been mourning the death of my mother at the hands of the government – the government that your wife's dad is part of - you have been making nice with the girl that has made my life absolutely miserable. You're a traitor."

"That's not fair, Lia," Darcy scolds, finally inserting herself into the conversation.

"What?" My exasperation is obvious, and the tone of my voice is beginning to attract more attention from those around us. "You're taking his side?"

"There are no sides to be taken here. We are all friends. Mac didn't choose to marry Abigail; it was forced on him. He is trying to make the most of a bad situation. If he wants to bring Abigail into the group, then we bring Abigail into the group." Darcy turns to face Mac now. "How much does she know about our plan?"

I hadn't thought about this. My blood feels like it is turning cold in my skin. If Abigail knows of our plans, then we are doomed. Hopefully, Mac has had enough self-control in his conversations to keep our secrets.

"She doesn't know anything. We haven't talked much about the Defiance or Agitators."

The Defiance. That is the what Leadership is calling our act of rebellion. All those that have been arrested, tried, and put to death – including my mother, who had no clue as to what was going on – is done so in order to annihilate the Defiance and rid Terra Convex of Agitators. It has become almost an everyday occurrence for Leadership to make another announcement stating that if anyone has information about the Defiance, then please step forward. Of course, nobody has. It hasn't proven to be in the best interest of any citizen to give information to the government. Leadership is wary of all citizens, and if you come forward with information, then you are either part of the Defiance or are simply trying to cause conflict with another citizen. Such was the case when my father handed over my innocent mother to the Enforcers.

My father remains imprisoned. After he turned my mother in as part of the Defiance, Leadership realized that it would be very easy for husbands, who have grown tired of being married to women they never loved, to simply turn their wives in, accusing them of crimes against the government. They are now much more careful about how they deal with the reports they receive that point an accusing finger.

"Speaking of the plan," Darcy says quietly, interrupting my thoughts. "I wonder how it's going with Axel."

Although frustrated with Mac, my thoughts haven't been too far from Axel. Today is the day that he gets to walk out of Terra Convex, and hopefully, leave a note for Lukan. The thought of the man that I love walking through the grass, under the clouds, puts an ache in my belly. Now that he knows the air above us is clean and no longer contaminated with the deadly virus, Axel will be able to remove his government-issued protective mask and be able to hear the birds and feel the wind on his face.

Where is he right now? I can't help wonder and worry.

With shaky hands, I had written the words,

"Lukan, Meet here in two weeks. We are trapped inside. Leadership will not allow us to leave. I am sending this message to you through a friend. He is the only one allowed in or out of Terra Convex as it is his job to clean debris from the solar windows. Please come back so he can explain further. We must talk. - Lia"

Hopefully, the parchment and the plea will be found by Lukan. Hopefully, he can help us get out of here. I'm still not opposed to forcing our way out of here, but I have promised the rest of my little rebellious group that I will be on my best behavior.

I guess that means I should make an effort with Abigail, too.

With a lump of disgust in my throat, I say to Mac, "Okay, I promise to be nice to Abigail."

A smile spreads across Mac's face.

"Let me rephrase that. I promise to be as nice to her as she is to me. That means you need to make sure she understands the rules of our group before she makes the decision to be in it."

Mac's smile fades. "Rules?"

Nodding, I answer, "Yes, rules. She is to sit quietly and have the understanding that she is a guest. Only a guest." Mac obviously doesn't approve, but he remains silent. "Plus, I don't think you should be part of anymore planning."

Mac begins to argue, but Darcy intervenes, "Lia is right. Having Abigail be such a big part of your life makes the Defiance much more dangerous for you. This will keep you safe."

Mac, although obviously downhearted by our decision, seems to understand the reasoning. He gives us a conceding nod.

"I was hoping you would still be in here," I hear Axel say from behind me. "I wanted to be able to eat at least one meal with you today." After he places his tray of food on the table, he sits beside me and places a tender kiss on my cheek. A familiar warmth begins to grow in my belly. His presence, his smile, and especially his tender affection has that effect on me. Always.

I push the feelings aside and focus on Axel. He begins to eat and doesn't seem too concerned that we are all staring at him, waiting for him to tell us about how his trip above ground went.

As if he hadn't just left Terra Convex to go above ground and leave a note for Lukan, Axel casually asks, "Have I missed out on anything today? Everything good?"

With a mischevious grin, I answer, "Mac wants to bring Abigail into the group. We decided it might be alright."

Axel pauses his eating and looks up at Mac. "Is she going to behave?"

I look at Mac in time to see him roll his eyes. Axel glances over at me and gives me a wink. A tiny giggle escapes from Darcy.

"I'm just kidding, Mac," Axel says with a sly smile. "It would do Abigail good to be in our group. I don't think she has ever known what it feels like to be included. I imagine it's difficult to make friends when your dad is a councilman."

"Thanks, Axel. It took a little bit more convincing with these two," Mac replies, gesturing towards Darcy and me.

"I have no doubt," Axel says with a chuckle.

"We agreed to let her join our group, but we decided that Mac shouldn't be part of anymore planning," I explain.

Axel pauses his eating once again and glances up at Mac. "You good with that decision?"

Mac considers his question before answering. "I hate that you guys will be having all the fun without me, but I understand the reasoning."

"It's just safer if he doesn't know what's going on," I add.

Axel nods while he eats but doesn't say anything. He eats as if he is starved, but the anticipation becomes too much for me. I lean into him and quietly ask, " So? How did it go outside?"

He looks at me with a warm smile. "It went well. It was a beautiful day. I left the note and will go back in a couple of weeks. Hopefully, our friend will see it."

We all glance at each other. The air around us is a thick combination of nervousness and excitement as each of us ponders the possibilities of what comes next.

Darcy, breaking the awkward silence, mutters, "Now, we wait."

Lukan

"This was a great idea, Helix," I acknowledge, sitting on the edge of the cliff, looking down at the blue-green water that I long to dive into. I have pleasant memories of diving off this cliff into the water below. Sitting here, reflecting on happier days, gives me a faint sense of contentment. The season for cliff-diving has passed, though. I have no doubt the water below us has turned frigid.

Helix moans in agreement, a blissful smile spread across his face. Dom remains quiet, lost in his thoughts.

As expected, my family was concerned that Dom and I would want to leave the walls of Grayson. They should know by now that the short walls that surround our little community will never do anything to protect the people that reside inside. Helix, with his soothing deep voice and ancient way of speaking wisdom, did his best to alleviate my mother's fears. Nevertheless, as we walked away from my home, my mom could be heard sniffling.

Grayson was quiet this morning. It's citizens spend more time indoors now that the air is beginning to carry a distinct chill. I'm sure, locked safely behind their doors, mothers are coming up with creative ways to keep their children occupied during the cold months. Fathers are stacking firewood close to their home so that when the first bitter night arrives, they can easily grab the wood they need to keep their family warm.

Dom, Helix, and I had walked quietly toward the pillars that stand at the entrance of Grayson. The same pillars that the first inhabitants of this area built back in 1968. Long before the destruction of earth. When the Langston Virus began its deadly sweep across America, Grayson was just a neighborhood with a few homes. The people that lived here, soft and weak from a life of relying on others to provide for them, were quickly sent running away from their lush lifestyles. Those that weren't killed by the virus had to endure a far worse fate at the hands of those that preferred coping with the death of their own loved ones by inflicting savage acts onto others. After months of trying to outrun the virus and the maniacs, a few survivors happened upon the severely damaged neighborhood of Grayson.

Years later, the mostly destroyed neighborhood began to resemble a community. It had become a safe haven for those that were weary from running. For several years, Grayson was safe. The citizens elected governing officials. There were strides being made to repair the electrical grid. It seemed as though the Langston Virus was becoming just another story to be placed in the history books. Grayson and the surrounding communities were well on their way to reemerging from another Dark Ages.

Just like so many other times in the history of the planet, the citizens of Grayson were taught the painful lesson that it does not pay to get comfortable. Shortly after the first election, Grayson and the surrounding communities were abruptly introduced to the Howlers. A group of about a dozen came storming into town, howling, brandishing guns and knives, wearing the stinking skins of animals they had killed but had not tanned properly. The madmen didn't stay long. Just long enough to ensure that the people of Grayson had a clear understanding – the Howlers were in control.

When the Howlers left, Grayson was left, once again, in shambles. Several homes were wrecked, windows busted out, gardens ripped up. Most devastating of all, though, were those that the Howlers murdered and the women that they took with them when they left. The newly elected governing officials were all hanged from trees at the entrance to town. When the Howlers found out that the electric grid was nearly operational again, they destroyed it as well.

This morning, as Dom, Helix and I walked towards the pillars, and the same trees that were used for hanging our first and only governing body, my thoughts reflected back on what I had been taught about our history. I am reminded of the hours that Merritt and I spent reading the history of when the Howlers thrust Grayson back into the Dark Ages.

My memories were interrupted when I realized that we were near Merritt's home. I managed to keep my eye on the ground in front of me as I took each step carefully. It was difficult for me to walk past Merritt's home without the sadness of her death flooding over me. The soothing words that Helix spoke to me the morning before snuck their way back into my mind.

'Merritt can help you overcome your grief. Just let her memory replace the despair. When you begin to feel that familiar foe of sadness begin to creep over you – and you will for some time – just take a deep breath and remember Merritt.'

Helix had said the words to me as an attempt to lift me from my despair. His words found their mark through the pain, but the next thing he said to me is what seems to have begun the healing process. When I confided in Helix, Merritt's last words to me were of her love for me, his warm smile broadened, and his deep voice spoke quietly, 'What a beautiful thing to know that you are loved for all eternity by a beautiful young woman.'

His words swirled inside my head and found their way into the pain in my heart. It seemed to be exactly what I needed to hear. I had just begun to realize my feelings for Merritt when she was murdered by Gallner. I will always live with the regret that I hadn't told Merritt how I feel about her. She might have always been fearful of climbing trees, but at least she was brave enough to tell me her true feelings.

After Helix once again spoke comforting words of wisdom to me, I had the strength to get out of bed and join my family for breakfast. It was the first time in two weeks that I had sat at the table and ate a meal with my family. Afterward, I was able to walk through my neighborhood and give assistance to some of the older citizens that were still trying to prepare their homes for the coming winter. Everyone that I came in contact with gave me awkward hugs of sympathy and stated their affection for me. The gestures were genuine and welcomed. From them, I gained a fresh sense of determination to free my community of torment.

I was grateful to be busy again. While I stayed busy outdoors with my neighbors, Dom and Helix worked to get our bags packed for camping in possibly cold weather.

Sitting on the cliffs now. The cliffs that I managed to share with my cousin not long ago. I can't help worry about the thick tension that remains between Dom and me since Merritt's death. I would like to be able to talk to my cousin. Not necessarily about that horrible day. It would be nice for things to get back to the way they used to be for us.

Thanks to Helix's gift – a handmade bow and quiver of arrows – Dom and I were able to bond during the course of a hunting trip. I had killed my first deer on that trip. Even though Dom was happy for my success, he was a little disappointed that the buck I shot was one that he had been stalking for quite some time. Still, the experience brought us closer.

The day that I killed the buck was the day I found the window in the grass. Thinking about going back to the window now, gives me a sense of nervous excitement. The last time I was at the window was the same day Merritt was killed. It was the same day I had seen Lia and tried - and failed - to get inside her world.

"Domenic, have you ever participated in cliff-diving?" Helix asks, interrupting my thoughts. "Lukan assures me it is quite enjoyable." It's obvious that Helix is trying to bring Dom out of his stupor.

"No, I don't think I have the nerve," Dom responds with a light chuckle. "Lukan has always been the brave one."

His comment surprises me. I have never considered myself as brave. For years, I hid behind my eyepatch; ashamed and guilt-ridden for allowing myself to become maimed. I had spent most of my life telling myself that I was a liability to the community because of my disability. It wasn't until I received my bow from Helix that I realized that I have skills that are quite valuable to my family and to Grayson.

I glance over at my cousin. His eyes are distant as he stares across the vast space above the lake below. The turmoil that is causing his suffering is etched on his face. There is much that I want to say to my cousin, but none of it seems right at this moment.

Dom and I haven't talked much since the day he was drug back into town - beaten and battered - by the Howlers. Helix informed me that Dom feels tremendous guilt for Merritt's death. If he hadn't followed me to the window, and then subsequently gotten caught by the Howlers, then Merritt would still be alive. In the time since her death, I had never considered this. As I ponder this though, I can understand why Dom feels burdened. I am hoping that this time together, away from Grayson and the scene of Merritt's death, Dom will be able to begin his own healing process. I have no doubt that Helix will find the restorative words that Dom needs to hear.

After a while of sitting in silence on the cliff, the excitement of returning to the window becomes too much for me. I suggest we continue on and the others agree. The anticipation is too much to bear. We decide that we will go to the window before making camp. It seems that we are all eager to return to the place that could provide safety for our loved ones.

As we hike through the forest, I recount the story of seeing Lia and trying to communicate with her. Dom and Helix are intrigued by the notion that there are indeed people living their lives right underneath our feet. Intrigued, but slightly unnerved. I told them that Lia had been crying when I saw her lying on the floor. The fact that she was distressed is only slightly more worrisome now as the odor from the chimney of death begins to filter its way through the forest we are trekking through. Dom and I exchange a worried look but keep hiking towards the window.

"That is unpleasant," Helix says quite frankly, referring to the putrid smoke.

"It is," I respond, trying not to gag. "We are almost to the window. Hopefully, the air will be cleaner out in the meadow."

"Do you ever think we will know what exactly is going on with that smell?" Dom asks.

Horrified, he stares at me as I explain the tall metal pipe that is sticking out of the ground in a nearby meadow. "It's a chimney," I say, after telling Dom about how Helix and I found it.

"Does it belong to Lia's people?" Dom asks with a tremble in his voice.

"We believe it does," Helix replies with a troubled groan.

"What are they burning down there?" As if he fears the people living below our feet can hear him, Dom's voice has become nothing more than a whisper.

We reach the edge of the forest and pause. Although I have never seen anyone – not even a Howler – in the meadow, the putrid odor emanating from the distant chimney has given me an unsettled feeling. I'm sure Dom and Helix feel the same.

The meadow is empty once again, and I walk out of the woods and towards the window. Looking over my shoulder, I see that Dom is leading Helix into the meadow. I can't help but smile at the instant friendship that has been formed with my cousin and my blind wandering friend.

When I turn my attention back to the window that lies just ahead, I am stunned. Lying there on the thick glass is a piece of paper with writing on it. Before I even pick it up and read it, I know that it is from my underground friend. Dom immediately notices and is at my side.

"What is it, Lukan?" Helix asks with just a hint of trepidation in his voice.

Before I can answer, Dom explains, "It's a note, Helix. A note from the girl." His voice is full of excitement.

I read the note to my self silently before I read it to Dom and Helix. The words intrigue me. I must have pondered them for too long, though.

With a gentleness in his voice, Helix breaks my trance. "Lukan, please."

My voice shakes with excitement as I read the words written by our underground friend.

"'Lukan, Meet here in two weeks. We are trapped inside. Leadership will not allow us to leave. I am sending this message to you through a friend. He cleans the windows and is the only one that is allowed in or out of Terra Convex. Please come back so he can explain further. We must talk.' It's signed by Lia."

I look up from the paper to see Dom staring at me with wide eyes. A nervous smile is just starting to tease at the edges of his mouth. I can't help but smile too.

"This is a real message from the underground," I say with excitement.

Dom nods and chuckles with eagerness. We are close to celebrating when I glance over at Helix. His face shows no emotion. He seems somber. Distant.

"Helix, what is it?" I ask, pausing our celebration. "What's wrong?"

"Two weeks," Helix comments calmly. "Much can happen in two weeks. To them...and to us."

Chapter 5

Lia

Terra Convex seems colder than usual. As I walk through the dark corridors of this underground world, trailing my hands over the walls, a shiver snakes its way up my spine. Even though the manufactured air feels colder, I know that it isn't really the temperature that has plummeted. No, the chill that is causing discomfort emanates from the people that pass by me. From the people that hand me my meals in the line of receiving. Or sit near me in the Dining Hall. Everyone in Terra Convex is feeling the burden of the Defiance.

My defiance.

I know that the bitter chill isn't really emanating from those around me. The source of their discomfort is me. My curiosity, imagination, and wandering mind is the cause for many to be sent to the Isolation Chamber and ultimately to their death. The thought of so many lives lost is a weight I feel too weak to bear.

This feeling is strange to me. Unfamiliar, yet desired. For decades, the citizens of Terra Convex have had the Proclamation of Existence hammered into them. From early ages, we are taught that the only way this underground community will thrive is to enforce the Marital Responsibility Act – the government chooses who we are to marry; as well as the Population Expansion Mandate – you will provide the community with two children.

The laws that the government has placed on its citizens have done nothing for tangible relationships. According to the laws, the sole purpose of marriage is to produce more product - children. Children born into this bleak underground world with no purpose other than to repopulate what the virus killed out nearly a century ago. Because of this, the idea of relationships has disintegrated into nothing more than duties to be performed for the sake of the survival of Terra Convex.

My mother was raised with these same rules; yet, somehow, she managed to find love for my sister and me. I hadn't realized it at the time, but she was doing her best to show her daughters how to properly use their imagination. She would sit in her chair in the evenings, her favorite book in hand, speaking to us in tones of comfort and affirmation. Bellamira and I were oblivious to the love our mother had for us. Bellamira was caught up in her own musings. I was too absorbed in my own unhappiness. I realized too late the incredible bond that a mother and daughter can have if allowed to love without restraint.

A fresh wave of sadness rushes over me as I realize that Bellamira was still blinded by the rules of our world at the time of our mother's torturous death. Of course, she mourned the loss and was horrified when Matlok recounted the details of what our mother endured at the hands of the Interrogators and ultimately in the Isolation Chamber. Still, Bellamira will never understand the true depth of our mother's love for us. Even now, as I walk the dimly lit corridors of Terra Convex, on my way to a home that I now share with my sister and her husband, I long to speak to my mother. I decide that my sister would be able to get a better understanding of our mother if I let her read the journal.

My mother's last spoken words to me were actually a cryptic message that led me to her hidden journal. A journal that she kept hidden inside a book that was actually in her lap every evening but none of us ever paid attention to. This thought also gives me sadness. How could I have been so self-absorbed that I had never realized what she was doing right in front of me? The guilt is still fresh. In an effort to do better for Bellamira - and all the others that I love - I choose to embrace the guilt. To learn from it. To grow from it. I am determined to become a better sister, friend, and hopefully someday wife because of the guilt I am feeling today.

"There you are," I hear Darcy say with excitement from behind me.

Smiling, I turn to face her as she makes her way toward me in the dimly lit corridor.

I'm not completely surprised to see her in this area of Terra Convex. She visits me in my new home quite often. Since Mac is now married to Abigail, Darcy splits her time between the Hall of Reading and spending time with me. Usually, we are either at Bellamira's or staring up through the secret window. It's been nice having Darcy around more. Axel has been so busy with his work as a Roughneck, that our time together has been limited.

Axel.

I had gotten so absorbed in my thoughts that I hadn't given much thought to Axel and what he is doing today. Today is the day that he...

"Is he back?" I say. My voice sounds like a mix of panic and excitement.

Darcy nods slowly with a grin spreading across her face. "Oh yes. He's back, and he says that he has quite a story to tell."

"Then, let's not keep him waiting any longer," I reply with glee as Darcy and I rush toward the secret window.

*****

With shaky hands, I listen as Axel recounts his meeting with Lukan in the world above. I cannot seem to find any moisture in my mouth. The anxiety of the day seems to have dehydrated me and left my tongue incredibly dry and sticking to the roof of my mouth. I glance at Darcy and wonder if Axel's story is having the same effect on her. Her eyes are wide, intrigued yet nervous as Axel speaks. I can't help but be saddened slightly by the fact that Mac is not with us. He would want to hear this story. It doesn't feel right to keep such things from him. He should be here for this.

Axel explained to Darcy and me everything he could about our friend from the outside world - Lukan, the one-eyed boy from a tiny community called Grayson. He told us that not only is there a town called Grayson, but there are other communities scattered all across the land above us. It was a true test of my willpower to not interrupt with exclamations of

"Communities? There's more than one community?" Not only are there people living above us, but they are thriving.

Marcus DePriest brought our ancestors underground so that humanity might be saved. Instead of repopulating the earth, however, we have remained hidden inside of it. All this time, we could have been enjoying the sunshine on our faces; the wind in our hair. So many lives ended too early because Leadership deemed it necessary to make room for the next generation. I am both elated and furious at the same time.

Once again, I imagine Mac hanging on every detail of Axel's account of the day. He would have too many questions and would interrupt too many times. Especially when Axel explained to us the negatives regarding Lukan and his community.

The Howlers.

This group of madmen seems truly terrifying. A shiver crawls up my spine as I listen to Axel and imagine the torment the Howlers have unleashed against Grayson and the surrounding communities. I am saddened for this friend that I have never actually met. Dismayed at what he is enduring. Selfishly, I am also downhearted as I realize that life above ground is not as serene as I had imagined.

"He's a Wanderer," I hear Axel say, interrupting my thoughts.

Returning my attention to him, I ask, "Who is a Wanderer?" I am ashamed that I had not been listening.

"Helix. He's a friend of Lukan." With a knowing look, Axel tilts his head slightly. "I could call you a Wanderer as well since that is what your mind does so often." He gives me a little wink as I playfully roll my eyes at him.

Darcy, steadfastly focused on Axel's story, asks what a Wanderer is. Axel considers how to answer and then finally says, "I'm not sure because it doesn't really make sense to me, but apparently this man doesn't have a home. He just...wanders around."

Axel describes Helix as a strange combination of brutish yet calming. The strange man's head covered with complex markings that appear to be permanently inscribed. Dressed in thick furs that used to be animals.

"The most bizarre thing of all, though," Axel comments, with Darcy and I staring at him with great expectation, "is that Helix is completely blind."

Beside me, I hear Darcy take in a sharp breath.

"He wanders around alone? Blind?" I am dumbfounded at the idea.

As I child, I remember a young mother had a child that was blind. Apparently, the child was born with this affliction, but it wasn't discovered until he was three years old. Leadership informed the parents that the child would need to go a special care center they had set up just for disabilities such as blindness, lameness, and other calamities. Believing that their child would receive the best possible care in Terra Convex, the parents willingly handed their son to the Enforcers. He was never seen again and was quickly forgotten. Or at least never spoken of again. Now that I know the truth of Terra Convex and the fate of those with disabilities, I shudder to think of what happened to that little boy at the hands of the government.

Once again, I return my attention back to Axel. He nods and acknowledges, "I know it sounds crazy, but Helix seems quite capable."

The three of us sit quietly in the tiny room below the window. Each of us lost in our thoughts. I can't help but wonder if Axel and Darcy feel the weight of the situation weighing on them as heavily as I do. All of my efforts for freedom had been focused on joining Lukan in his world. Now that I know there are madmen that terrorize him and his people, I feel as if all hope is lost.

The memory of my mother sneaks its way into the turbulence of my thoughts. Usually, it is the memory of her final moments that tend to return and haunt me. At this moment, however, it is a slightly less disturbing memory. I close my eyes and allow the memory to replay in my mind. A smile spreads across my face as I realize that Axel also plays a role in this recollection.

When I open my eyes, I am not surprised to see that Axel is gazing at me thoughtfully. His dark eyes are warm as they study my face. I take in his features, spending too much time on the deep dimple on his right cheek. Looking at him now, my hope and determination are renewed.

"Where are your thoughts now, Lia?" Axel asks quietly but with obvious affection. His hands reach for mine. I gladly concede.

"I was just thinking of the time you and I got into trouble for writing the essay about the DePriest's," I explain. Axel's eyes narrow but his smile remains. "They separated us. Put me in Solitary. They strapped me to a chair in a small room and forced me to listen to the Terra Convex Proclamation of Existence. For three days, I didn't move from that chair. No food. No water. The straps dug into my arms and legs. I couldn't move at all. After three days of sitting in the same position - in my own filth, sores on my body, muscles stiff from lack of movement - I was released."

Axel's face has changed. He has become angry as I recount my time in Solitary. I rub his hands softly with my thumbs in an attempt to calm his anger.

"My mother was waiting for me on the other side of the door. She was angry. So angry, and I felt like I was going to endure more punishment from her. As we walked away from that horrible room - and away from the Enforcers that had placed me there - my mother surprised me by placing her arm around my waist. She didn't speak to me until we got to our living quarters. There was a glass of water and a bowl of strawberries waiting for me. As I ate and drank, my mother tended to the wounds left by the straps."

"I'm so sorry, Lia," Axel manages through gritted teeth.

"Perfer et obdura, dolor hic tibi," I say carefully, struggling to pronounce the foreign words correctly.

Axel and Darcy are obviously confused.

With raised eyebrows, Axel asks, "What is that?"

I smile at them broadly. "That's what my mother said to me. You see, she wasn't mad at me for what I said in that essay. Not at all. She was angry at Leadership for punishing me for speaking out against them." I can feel tears begin to threaten. Determined not to shed any more tears until the time is right, I add, "I didn't realize it at the time, but my mother knew what you and I had started. She knew that the essay was just the beginning of the end of Terra Convex. That's why the government punished us. That's why they separated us. They knew...they know their time is coming to an end."

My two friends are smiling. They can sense a new determination in me, and it has renewed theirs. I'm sure, like me, they wish Mac was here with us.

"Say it again," Axel implores.

I do, and his smile widens to reveal the dimple that I adore so much. "Beautiful," Axel says softly.

"But what do those words mean?" Darcy asks.

Closing my eyes, I can hear my mother's sweet voice speaking the words to me. When I needed to hear words of encouragement, she spoke these words to me. I hadn't realized how important that moment was. Now, I speak the same words to my friends in hopes that it brings them the encouragement and determination they need. What comes next will be difficult, painful, and possibly fatal. Nevertheless, we must move forward and find our way out of this living tomb.

Opening my eyes once again, I recite the words. "Be patient and tough; someday this pain will be useful to you."

Lukan

The anticipation of meeting somebody from the underground world invigorates me as I hurriedly make my way through the forest and towards the window. The air is brisk, informing me that winter is nearly upon the land. I slow to a walk as I near the window, and hopefully a place of safety for my family.

The forest is quiet. It seems as if the squirrels are already tucked safely into their warm nests, presumably with many months worth of acorns to sustain them. Most birds have flown off toward areas with warmer weather. Mostly, only the dark red birds remain. They seem to thrive in the cold. Merritt and I read about these crimson feathered creatures. They are called cardinals, and they were her favorite. Every winter, we would watch as the cardinals began to arrive. They were easy to spot against the white snow. Now, alone, I watch several of the beauties flutter around playfully with each other.

There is an empty space in my heart that was completely Merritt's. It aches for her now.

I am halted by the sudden memory of Merritt's smile. The twinkle in her eyes. The hidden red in her brown hair. The past couple of weeks have been hectic, and the chaos of it all has given me little time to think of Merritt and what could have been. I am ashamed that I have not given Merritt's memory more of my time. The pain and shame that I feel now nearly knocks me to the ground. Placing my hands on my knees, I bend over, allowing myself to take just a moment to embrace the emotions before I continue on. I can imagine Merritt looking at me with a look of disapproval. She would not be happy that I am wallowing.

A twig snaps behind me causing me to flinch. Turning quickly, I am surprised to see a young man. I am not alarmed by his presence. He is obviously not a Howler. There is no doubt that he is from the underground. His clothes, although stained dark in spots and somewhat tattered, are the same bland color as Lia was wearing. Even though his dark hair is greasy, it is obvious that there are curls that are just waiting for a shower to give them back their bounce. He looks at me with wide eyes. I imagine my face mirrors his.

"Lukan?" The young man utters, bringing me out of my stupor.

I nod. "Are you Lia's friend? The one that cleans the window?" I know that he is, but I don't know what else to say. We both stare at each other awkwardly.

The cleaner of the window simply nods. He takes a step towards me and replies, "My name is Axelrod. My friends call me Axel."

We continue to stare at each other in silence for several uncomfortable seconds. Neither of us knows what to say. I can't help but wish that Helix was here with me. He is much better with words.

Finally, Axel asks rather sheepishly, "Is everything okay? You seemed a little...upset when I approached." Quickly, he adds, "I'm sorry. I don't mean to be nosey." He looks away, embarrassed at the awkwardness of it.

Slightly embarrassed that Axel saw me in my vulnerable moment, I look away when I answer honestly, "I...lost somebody recently. The pain is still fresh."

I'm surprised when Axel takes a few more tentative steps towards me. "I understand. We are also feeling the sting of loss. Lia especially."

His voice is smooth, but his statement is unnerving. Without any further explanation, the truth of the matter comes crashing down on me. I now know that my fears of Lia's underground world have been accurate. It is no sanctuary. My mood takes a drastic turn, and my gloom becomes impatience.

"I can't stay out long," Axel says abruptly. He must sense my disposition changing.

"Why did you come out at all? What did you hope to see or do out here?" I'm not sure why I am angry all of a sudden. Perhaps it is the hopelessness of the situation that is weighing too heavily. I turn and take a step away from Axel, trying to collect my thoughts. Trying to come up with a solution.

"I came out to see you. You are the one thing that has given Lia hope. She believes that you hold the key to our future." Axel's voice is almost pleading.

Turning back towards him, I reply, "The key? I don't have the key to anything. I have no idea what's going on down there, but please believe me when I say that life is less than ideal up here." My voice trembles with emotion that I am trying to keep at bay.

"I'd like to hear about your life, Lukan." His words are filled with kindness. His voice is desperate.

"You've already said that you can't stay out long and this story is not short." The tenderness in his voice and the look of compassion in his eyes has quieted my anger a bit.

Axel looks down at his feet and then behind him. It's obvious that he is contemplating the amount of time he has already spent above ground and how much more he can spare. He runs his left hand through his thick hair, nervously. "What should I tell Lia?"

I contemplate his question for a few seconds. So many things Lia needs to know about life above ground. So many things I want to say to her.

"How often do you come out? Will you be back out again soon?" If I can give her the information in bits, maybe eventually we can figure out a way to help each other out.

Axel looks around at the trees that are closest to us. "I'm pretty sure my time for cleaning windows is coming to an end soon. At least for awhile. The trees have nearly lost all their leaves. Without the leaves on the windows, I have no reason to leave Terra Convex. Until it snows, that is."

"Terra Convex?" I ask.

"It's the name of our world," Axel explains simply.

I had been so excited to meet somebody from the world below my feet. Now, I feel dejected as I think of all that I will not be able to say to or learn from Lia. Words fail me as I consider the message to send back with Axel.

"It's our government," I hear Axel say, pulling me from the despair that was beginning to pull at me. Looking up at Axel once more, I give him my attention. "The laws they have over us are...oppressive. We have been taught that life above ground is impossible. Lia figured it out, though. She figured out that it was all a lie. Some have been tortured and killed. Lia's mother..." Axel's voice, thick with hopelessness, trails off.

My heart hurts for what they are enduring underground. I imagine that there is much more that needs to be said but at the same time, really doesn't. A thought occurs to me, and before I can stop myself, I ask, "The smoke. The foul odor that comes from the ground. What is that?"

A vacant look crosses Axel's face as he answers, "That is our fate."

His words send a chill up my spine. I want to ask more about this, but I know our time is short.

Axel asks once again,"What should I tell Lia?"

Lia. Everything seems to go back to the plain girl on the tattered blanket. Lia sent this man above ground to speak to me. Lia discovered that there is life above ground. Lia lost her mother. Through it all, though, Lia seems to be relentless when it comes to finding a way out of her underground prison.

"It's Lia," I say with an air of realization. "Lia's the key."

Axel releases a forced chuckle. "She believes you are the key." He shakes his head in defeat and begins to turn away. It's clear that he is done with our meeting.

"What do you believe?" I ask, desperate to stop him from leaving.

Axel turns around and stares at me for several seconds. "Lia believes that we can have a life outside of Terra Convex. A real life where the government doesn't choose our job, our lifemate, the names of our children, or when our life is over. She believes that your world is our only hope. Lia believes that you are the key."

With sadness, I comment, "My world holds no hope. My world is filled with murder and destruction and heartache. We are fighting a losing battle against a group of madmen that we call Howlers. I am not the key. To be honest, I was hoping we could find safety in your underground world."

Another chuckle that holds no humor comes from Axel. "Sounds like we need to join our communities together. Maybe then, we could find a way to defeat your Howlers and overturn our government."

I smile and nod, but I'm sure he can sense that there is no hope in our situation.

Once more, Axel asks, "What should I tell Lia?"

I consider the message that I want the girl from the underground to have from the outside world. It should be something meaningful since she has held so much hope. I hate that I can't give her what she needs.

"Tell her not to give up hope," a familiar throaty voice says from the forest.

I feel a smile spread across my face as I turn and watch Helix make his way through the thick treeline. I hear Axel take several steps in retreat.

"It's okay," I say quickly. "He looks menacing, but he isn't. He's a friend."

Helix treks out of the forest with tremendous grace considering his blindness. He wears his customary fur coat made with several different types of animal furs. A cloth covers the scars where his eyes used to be. The sunlight shines off his hairless, tattooed head. I imagine, to somebody that has lived his entire life under the dirt, this large man approaching us seems rather intimidating. I glance over at Axel. He peers suspiciously at Helix with wide eyes.

Taking a step towards Axel, I say, "I assure you, Helix is a friend."

"I am," Helix comments with a warm smile and deep belly groan. "It took me some time, but I finally caught up with you, Lukan." Helix is at my side now and leans toward me slightly. "Keeping your mother distracted so that you could meet our new friend proved more difficult than I anticipated." His chuckle calms me. I can't help but smile.

"You're blind," I hear Axel say with obvious confusion.

I turn my attention back towards him as I remember the first time I met Helix and had the exact same reaction. Nobody ever expects to meet a blind man wandering through the wilderness. Looking at Axel now, I wonder if I had stared at Helix with the same wide-eyed amazement the first time I saw him. I'm sure that I did.

"Indeed. I am blind," Helix replies, still smiling. "So, what is the plan?"

"There is no plan, Helix." I feel tremendous disappointment to have to tell my friend that there is no safety underground.

"Perhaps, not yet, but there will be soon. Do you feel the change in the air?" Helix asks with a sly smile.

Axel and I exchange a curious look. Axel's eyes are still wide with wonder.

"Our worlds, both above ground and below, are about to become much bigger. I believe that together we can come up with a plan to be free of the misery placed upon us by others. Until then, we need young Lia to hang on to hope. She knows what must be done. She knows that the path is treacherous. Do not give up hope."

Chapter 6

Lia

I have intentions of giving my mother's journal to Bellamira. She needs to know the love of her mother. In time, I will. When it is safe for her to have it. For now, though, I keep my mother's journal tucked safely inside the waistband of my pants. I carry it with me. Always. When I begin to feel the weight of the oppression of this underground world, I read her words. When I learn of yet another citizen of Terra Convex being drug away from their home or workplace because they are "ungrateful for the generosity of President DePriest," I read her words.

I read her journal often.

At first, I felt tremendous guilt. Her words seemed so personal. So private. I felt like I had no right to them. The more I read, however, the more I realize that the words were meant for me all along.

When my mother was a young girl, she found the window I lay below now. She asked questions. She believed there was life above ground. She was punished because she was right. She was punished because she learned the secrets of the government. I'm so thankful that she had the foresight to write down her thoughts. When I was a young girl, my mother could see the same burning curiosity in me that Leadership thought they had quelched from her when they branded her hand.

As I lay on my tattered blanket, looking up at the gray sky above me, I hold the journal on my chest. There are no more leaves on the few trees that I can see from this position. They have all been released and blown away by the wind from that sad gray sky above. Even though the landscape above me seems to also be going through its own mourning process, I still relish my time gazing through the window.

I'm not surprised to hear the door beside me open. Axel or Darcy often find time to sneak away from their duties to lay under the window. I am surprised, however, when I see that neither Axel nor Darcy are the ones that opened the door. The sight of my dear friend, Maclin, is welcome and refreshing. Since his union with Abigail, I have missed his presence under the window while we discuss our plans and our possible future above ground. In true Mac form, he smiles down at me as he shuts the door and then lays down next to me. For several minutes, Mac and I watch the world above in silence, as red birds flutter around, sometimes even landing on the window.

"I hate this, you know?" Mac finally states.

I know that he isn't referring to laying on the cold, hard floor staring up into the sky, watching beautiful red birds fly above us. No, he hates the fact that he is no longer part of our Defiance. He hates that he has been left out of so many conversations and plans. So do I.

"I know," I answer quietly. "I hate it too. We all do. You have to understand that it is for your own safety, though. You know that, right?"

Out of the corner of my eye, I see him nod his head. Of course, he understands. The consequences of Abigail discovering that her mate's closest friends are the Defiance would be disastrous and deadly. Even if Mac doesn't get caught distributing the damning parchments, he would be punished just the same for knowing and not turning the rest of us in.

"I feel like I'm being punished for being in a union with Abigail." His voice is solemn, and I can hear the pain in it.

"You aren't. You know that you aren't."

"I can help. With whatever you three are working on, I can help." Now Mac's voice is pleading.

The sadness in his voice saddens me. I can understand his pain. I would be miserable if I couldn't be part of this little rebellion. More than anything, I want to tell him everything that he has missed out on. For several minutes, I remain quiet. He doesn't interrupt my silence. I'm sure he knows I am contemplating telling him.

My contemplation is interrupted though as once again the door beside us opens and shuts. I am surprised to see Darcy and Axel standing inside the little room. Darcy's eyes widen as she realizes that I am not alone on the floor. Mac and I sit up as a smile spreads across Darcy's face. She rushes to Mac and the two embrace each other.

Axel sits next to me on the floor and greets me with a tender brush of his lips on my forehead. With the ones I love the most surrounding me, I find peace. My heart leaps into my chest warmly. Not only because of Axel's affection towards me but the sense of wholeness I feel having all my friends together again under the window.

Even though Mac and Abigail join us quite regularly during meal times, the conversations seem forced and without substance. In this room, we can talk freely without her disapproving comments or sneers. Its obvious by Darcy and Axel's reaction, they feel the same.

"I'm glad you're here, Mac," Axel starts. "There is a new development, and I believe you should know about it too."

"What is it?" Mac asks with a hint of trepidation in his voice. "What's happened?"

Axel opens his mouth to explain, but I stop him short. "Wait. We agreed it is best if Mac doesn't know what is going on. We all agreed." I'm not sure I am ready for Mac to know that we have communicated with the outside world.

"Lia, I came here to tell you something," Mac says as he nervously looks at me. "I don't think Abigail is as bad as you think."

I respond by rolling my eyes. "I know you and Abigail have gotten close. You're trying to make the most of a bad situation. I respect that..."

"No, Lia," Mac interrupts. "I'm saying that I think she believes in the Defiance. She believes in life above ground. Or, at least, I think she wants to believe."

My mind immediately goes to a dark place. I quickly imagine that Abigail knows that my friends and I are the Defiance and she is making her way to Leadership to turn us in. My heart, which was blissful just minutes ago, feels as if it is being wrenched from my chest as I consider the implications of Abigail, daughter of a councilman, knowing the true identity of the Defiance.

Before I can say anything, Axel says with a quiet sternness, "Explain please, Mac." He obviously is feeling the same consternation.

"She brought one of the flyers to our living quarters a few days ago," Mac starts slowly.

My friends and I have been leaving notes all over Terra Convex for weeks now. It started out with just a few words on each parchment that we scattered throughout the community – THERE IS LIFE OUTSIDE; THIS WORLD IS A LIE; DEMAND ANSWERS; DON'T TRUST THE GOVERNMENT. The unassuming parchments - with simple text - received an immediate reaction, both from the citizens and the government. The government answered immediately by arresting anyone in possession of a flyer. The citizens began to murmur their displeasure over the government's reaction to the parchments. Just a murmur. We had hoped for more. We had hoped for a rebellion. We increased the number of flyers we distributed, as well as the wording we used - FREEDOM SHOULD NOT FEEL LIKE OPPRESSION; HUMANITY HAS NO FUTURE UNDERGROUND; IT'S TIME TO BE REBORN; THERE IS A WAY OUT; YOU ARE NOT POWERLESS; TIME IS RUNNING OUT.

Leadership would not sit idly by with this new round of condemning parchments circulating through Terra Convex. They immediately began broadcasting threats for those who had decided to defy them and promises for those who turn them in. More arrests were made. Many, including my mother, were tortured and left to die in the Isolation Chamber. The thought of Abigail bringing one of our flyers into the home that she shares with one of my best friends gives me a sick feeling in my belly.

"I tried not to react to it. I simply asked her why she had it." Mac continues. With a sound of amusement in his voice, he adds, "I tried to act like I was scolding her for having brought it home." Mac looks at each of us, but he can tell that none of us see the humor in what he is saying. "Abigail couldn't really answer why she had the parchment. She could only say that the words intrigued her. I cautioned her that she could get into trouble for having it and then I dropped the subject completely."

As I listen to Mac recount the story, I can't help but wonder if Axel and Darcy are as dry-mouthed as I am at this moment. Axel's hand has found mine. I can't tell if the gesture is for my benefit or his own. Whatever the reason, I am grateful for it. I glance up at his face, but his stoic features do not betray him.

"A few days later," Mac continues. "she brought up the subject again."

"Do you believe she is trying to trap you? Trick you into revealing the Defiance?" Axel asks in a calm voice.

Mac shakes his head. "I don't think so. I really don't. She seems...interested. She has said things like, 'What if it's true?' 'I wonder what it really is like above us.' Abigail wants to know about life above ground. She is curious about how we would live if life is possible outside of Terra Convex."

The room is silent as each of us consider what Mac is telling us. Of course, the purpose of the secret writings was to cause the people of Terra Convex to rethink their life underground. We want to reintroduce curiosity and imagination into this bland world of routine and uniformity. None of us had considered, however, that Abigail would find the parchments intriguing. The thought of it is both worrisome and appealing.

I feel Axel and Darcy's eyes on me. They are waiting for my reaction to Mac's story. Waiting to see how we are to proceed with this information. I look at them and shrug my shoulders. I am at a loss. Diverting my eyes from their expectations, I glance down into my lap. My mother's journal rests there comfortably. So comfortably, in fact, that I had forgotten that it was even there. It is like the loosely bound parchments, with her elegant handwriting, has become a part of me.

Looking at the journal now, I am reminded of something that my mother wrote...

Your determination is the fuel that gives you the strength you don't seem to realize you have. When you doubt yourself, remember that I love you (I should have been telling you that all along, I love you). When you doubt others, remember your mission. When you doubt your mission, look up. Look up! That is where your hope lies.

Much of what my mother wrote was written when she was a young girl. These words were written to me, though. I cherish them greatly. She felt strongly that I would be the one to free the people of Terra Convex.

"'When you doubt others, remember your mission. When you doubt your mission, look up.'" I quote without having to open the journal. These words are part of me now. Not just memorized but seared into my very soul.

I look at each of my friends. They look at me with a strange combination of confusion and respect. Smiling, I hold up the journal. "My mother's words to me. Before there ever was a rebellion. Before the government gave us the title of Agitators or Defiance, my mother knew my role." I pause briefly to ensure that my emotions stay below the surface a little longer. Looking directly at Mac, I continue, "She knew that I would doubt those around me. She knew that the government would try to drive a wedge between us. We can't let that happen. We must remember the mission – to free this community and show them the world above."

Axel, Darcy, and Mac are smiling now. A renewed sense of determination twinkling in their eyes.

"'When you doubt your mission, look up.'" Axel recites proudly.

Smiling broadly, I say the next memorized line from my mother's journal, "'That is where your hope lies.'"

Lukan

Life at Grayson seems to be getting back to normal. After everything our little town has been through recently, it is almost refreshing to see families and friends enjoying each other's company. I enjoy hearing the laughter of the children and the playful arguing of couples. My mind, though, is constantly aware that the Howlers could return at any moment and destroy our serenity.

It is nice to have Helix in town. It feels right having him here. He, Dom, and I have been able to spend quite a bit of time together. Mostly while giving our assistance where needed to those who are preparing for the upcoming winter months. The people in town have embraced Helix. Even while wearing his thick Howler-like furs, with his intricate tattooed head and neck, and his blindness, Grayson has accepted him as their own.

When we can, the three of us discuss and try to formulate a plan to ensure the Howlers cannot control us any longer. Helix hasn't given up hope on our friends that remain captive in their underground prison. Although I feel great compassion for them and their predicament, it is imperative that we find a solution for Grayson before we can focus on Terra Convex.

A couple of days after we returned from our meeting with Axel at the window, we found time to speak with Dom and fill him in on how it went. After listening intently, Dom sat in silence for several minutes; his face took on the appearance of a young man conceding to his fate.

"Well, that's it, then," Dom said with great sadness. "We are doomed to a life of torment."

"I still believe that there is a way to be rid of the Howlers," Helix groaned with as much enthusiasm as he could muster.

"There has to be a way to win against them," I added, trying to sound confident.

"How were wars won before the Langston Virus?" Dom asked nobody in particular as he ran a shaky hand through his hair.

I was ashamed to admit that I hadn't paid much attention to any of the pre-virus histories that Merritt had read to me before her death. We had spent a lot of time reading the geography books and dreaming of traveling to far off places, but not much time learning the history of those places.

"I think there are books in the Community Building that talk about war," I advised.

"I can't read very well, but I may know somebody that can help," Dom commented without looking up. It's obvious he was grasping for an answer and felt no confidence in what he had just said. "Nyssa."

A rattled laugh escaped me as I considered Dom's solution to our problem. At the age of 112, Nyssa is the oldest living resident of Grayson. She was 22 years old when the Langston Virus began sweeping across the world with an unquenchable fury.

There are not many that survived the virus. Those that did not contract the deadly virus were faced with even more misery at the hands of looters, rapists, and murderers. The Langston Virus, like so many other disasters and catastrophes in our world's history, revealed the true nature of people.

Nyssa is a survivor, though. Not only did she survive the virus, and the chaos that ensued, but she has also been able to withstand the Howlers. For some reason, when the madmen visit and plague our town with their hysteria, Nyssa has always been left alone. They never approach her or her home. Perhaps, because she is the oldest living person in all of this region. Perhaps, the Howlers actually have a sort of respect for this dear old woman.

Dom looked somewhat offended that I would laugh at his idea for a solution to our problem.

"I'm sorry, Dom, but I don't see how an old woman at the edge of town can help us," I explained.

Dom rolled his eyes and shook his head in annoyance.

"Tell me about Nyssa," Helix said quietly.

Dom and I exchanged a look, and I gestured my hand for him to go ahead and explain.

"Nyssa is an elderly woman that lives at the edge of town," Dom began, repeating what Helix had already heard me say.

"Yes. That much I understand," Helix said with a relaxed groan. "How can she help us?"

"She was alive at the time of the virus. she may know things about our ancient armies that could help us." Dom explained.

Helix considered Dom's explanation for several seconds, giving me time to also ponder the possibility of her knowledge.

"Actually, I like it, Dom." I acknowledged. Dom looked at me with surprised eyes.

"As do I," Helix agreed, flashing his teeth in a broad smile. "Let's give Nyssa a visit."

Now, as we walk toward the edge of town to give Nyssa a visit, I walk behind my friend and my cousin. I watch them with great respect, marveling at their instant friendship. Dom and Helix are talking comfortably with each other just ahead of me. I hadn't realized that I was lagging behind so far. I am startled when I hear my name. Turning, my heart drops into my belly when I see Merritt's mother standing on the porch of her house looking at me with sorrowful eyes. She is clinging to a book that I recognize as one of Merritt's favorites. We had sat and read this book together many times.

It's obvious that Merritt's mother wants to speak with me. A quick glance over my shoulder reveals that Dom and Helix have stopped. They wait patiently for me, but Dom does not make eye contact.

Merritt's mom does not wait for me to join her on the porch. She must see that the pain is still heavy enough that it has me seemingly cemented to the path. She approaches me with a smile that does not reach her eyes.

"Elyn," I acknowledge quietly, avoiding eye contact but trying not to be rude.

"Lukan, it's good to see you. I've been worried about you." I can hear Merritt in her mother's voice and a lump forms in my throat. It seems to have closed off my ability to speak. "I wanted to come see you, but I thought you probably needed time." Elyn glances over my shoulder, at Dom and Helix, and then continues, "Where are you guys off to today? Causing mischief, I hope." Merritt's mom flashes a sad but playful smile. Her words are exactly like something Merritt would say.

I am struck with the idea that Merritt will continue to live on through her mother, as well as the memories of her that I cherish. I still haven't found my voice, but Elyn doesn't seem phased by my silence. She holds the book out for me to take. With trembling hands, I take it from her carefully.

"You and Merritt spent quite a lot of time reading this Geography book. She would want you to have it. I want you to have it."

The book feels heavy in my hands. I am haunted by the weight of Merritt's bloodied body lying in my arms. Attempting to rid myself of the horrid memory, I dip deep into my Merritt memory bank. Looking at the book, I am reminded of the countless hours we would spend thumbing through the pages of the thick book, dreaming of life in other parts of the world.

Suddenly, Elyn's arms are embracing me. I was lost in my thoughts, not expecting the sudden show of affection. The one-sided embrace is awkward, but I finally find my way out of my stupor and return her kindness. Releasing me, Elyn steps back, wiping tears from her eyes.

"You better get to your mischief," Elyn says with a sly smile.

With a weak chuckle, I glance over at Dom and Helix. They are waiting patiently, smiling warmly at me.

"We are going to visit Ms. Nyssa," I explain to Elyn. "No mischief."

Her smile remains. "Well,sometimes mischief has a way of finding its way to young men. Be safe."

"Yes, ma'am," I reply with a shy smile.

Grasping the book, I turn away and walk towards Dom and Helix. Even though the pain of Merritt's death remains fresh and tormenting, I feel as if I just may be strong enough to endure the loss. The book doesn't seem quite as heavy as it did when Elyn first handed it to me.

*****

"What do you have there, Lukan?" Nyssa asks with a genuine interest.

The oldest resident of Grayson, although surprised, was genuinely pleased to have visitors. It took her several minutes of shuffling to make it to the door and open it. Her immediate reaction was to eye us warily as we stood awkwardly on her front porch. It didn't take Helix long to convince her that we were there simply to talk. Conceding to his request to allow us to enter, Nyssa quickly welcomed us into her home. Now, as Helix, Dom, and I sit on her surprisingly clean couch, Nyssa eyes the book that rests in my lap.

I look down at the large book that I had just received from Merritt's mother, Elyn."It's a Geography book," I answer, giving the book a tender pat. Memories of Merritt attempt to distract me, but I keep them at bay. I am perfectly willing to give the memories my attention. Now, is simply not the time.

"Ah, dreaming of far off places, I imagine," Nyssa replies in almost a sing-song voice.

Still feeling quite uncomfortable, crowded onto a couch that is over a hundred years old, an awkward chuckle escapes me. I quickly stifle it.

Thank goodness for Helix. Apparently, with his inability to see, he has become attuned to the art of easy conversation. His deep, calming voice, along with the melody in Nyssa's voice, instantly puts the room at ease. Helix asks the dear old lady about her life here in Grayson. He seems truly interested in her hobbies and what she does to pass the time. She is obviously pleased to speak of her knitting and her gardening. We all listen with genuine interest, amazed at how much this shriveled up woman is capable of doing by herself.

Eventually, Helix gets to the reason Nyssa is being visited by a blind man, a half-blind teenager, and the town's great hunter. I was nervous that she would become agitated with us once she realized that our knock on the door was more than just a neighborly visit.

"Ms. Nyssa," Helix begins with a groan from his belly. "Do you remember much from the time before the virus?"

Nyssa releases a raspy chuckle and leans forward, slapping her knee. She seems to have just heard a funny joke that the rest of us missed out on. Rocking back and forth, laughter erupting from deep in her belly, Nyssa answers, "Oh yes. I remember it all very well. You act as if age has stolen my mind from me." Her laughing subsides as she attempts to catch her breath.

Dom and I exchange a perplexed glance. His face conveys that he also doubts the sanity of the oldest person in Grayson. With a subtle shake of his head, Dom rubs a shaky hand over the back of his neck.

"I remember it all very well," Nyssa repeats. Her gray eyes that were alert just a moment ago have become distant as if she is seeing the past play out once more in front of her. "My mother was the first in my family to be taken by the virus. She was already at the hospital. She was a nurse there, so when the afflicted began pouring in..." Nyssa's melodic voice trails off as the memory takes hold.

An awkward silence takes over the room as Nyssa becomes lost in her memories of grief. I notice a slight tremble in her worn and wrinkled hands. There is wetness around her eyes that wasn't there just a moment ago. The sight becomes too much for me, and I finally find my voice.

"Ms. Nyssa, we certainly didn't come here to reopen the wounds that the Langston Virus left when it claimed your loved ones," I say with sincerity. "What we are really wondering about..."

"My infant son was taken from me next," Nyssa continues, interrupting me. "Followed by my husband and father. They were preparing the van for us to flee town. Thugs murdered them and took the van." My heart hurts as the anguish in her voice paints a picture of death and mayhem. "Alone. Frightened. All my belongings gone with the van and the thugs. I was forced to flee on foot."

Nyssa pauses. She seems to notice the three of us bunched up on the couch for the first time. I attempt a consoling smile but am aware that it holds no potency. "I'm so sorry," I squeak out nervously. Hopefully, she can sense the sincerity in my words.

"No, I am the one that is sorry, Lukan. You, three fine young gentlemen, didn't come visit this old lady to hear about her sorrow. So, tell me. Why are you here?" A warm smile has spread across Nyssa's face, replacing the grief that was there just a second before. I sense beauty beneath the wrinkles that time has placed upon her.

"Before the Langston Virus, how did the ancient world win wars? How did they defeat their enemies?" Dom asks abruptly? Apparently, the brief glimpse into the past that Nyssa shared with us was a bit too much for my cousin. I imagine that the thought of madmen and murder brought up memories of the time, not too long ago, that he was held captive by the Howlers.

Nyssa sits back comfortably in her rocking chair as she considers Dom's questions. With a weathered hand, covered in nearly translucent skin, she rubs her left knee in a way that indicates she may be enduring some aches and pains in her old age.

Finally, she answers, "I was a young woman at the time of the outbreak. Caught up in my life as a wife and new mother. To be honest, the wars that ravaged parts of the world never had an impact on my little world. Like many, I lived in my own bubble without any regard to the struggles felt by others. I am ashamed to say." Nyssa seems truly ashamed. Her head rests on her chest as if the shame has suddenly become too much to bear.

Sensing the old lady's remorse, Helix quickly interjects. "Oh, sweet Nyssa. I, of all people, understand clearly the guilt you feel over living life in a bubble. Since I was blinded by the Howlers, I have spent my life in the sanctuary of solitude that I created. I justified it by calling myself a Wanderer, but the truth is, it was much more comfortable for me if I didn't have to worry myself with the problems of others. That is how I survived. Clearly, that is how you survived as well." Helix smiles warmly and continues on with his customary throaty voice. "There was something about meeting Lukan that made me want out of my bubble. Made me want to be rid of it completely. Now, I will do whatever is in my power to help him keep Grayson safe." Helix lowers his head as if eyeing her, even though his eyes are nonexistent and a cloth covers his scars. He adds,"One hundred and twelve is not too old to exit your bubble. I believe you have much to share with us that will help this community."

The old lady ponders the words of the blind man. I, once again, am in awe of his ease of saying exactly what is on his mind, no matter the situation. Dom's face reveals that he is also envious of Helix's manner of speech. Slowly, another toothless grin spreads across her face.

"You are seeking a way to destroy the Howlers," Nyssa says with a tilt of her head and coy grin.

Dom and I exchange another glance. "Yes, ma'am," he acknowledges.

"You expect that the old ways of war are the key to your victory?" Her words and her sing-song voice almost sound like a riddle she is trying to answer.

"That is our hope," Helix answers with a groan.

The air in the room seems to have changed somehow. I feel myself becoming slightly claustrophobic on this crowded couch, in this dimly lit cottage. For reasons I cannot explain, I am forced to resist the urge to flee this place.

Nyssa begins to rock in her chair. she strokes her chin thoughtfully. With closed eyes, a hum, barely discernible at first, begins to emit from her throat. As time passes, the hum becomes louder, and it seems as if it is indeed a melody. I glance at Dom who appears as if he is ready to be gone from here as well.

Nyssa's humming stops abruptly, but the rocking continues. "I believe you know what must be done. There is nothing from the past that can help you. Stop looking there."

Helix, Dom, and I sit in silence. I wonder if my cousin and my friend feel the same dejection that I feel.

Helix tenses as if ready to stand. "That seems like sage advice, Nyssa. Thank you for your time," he says pleasantly.

As if Nyssa didn't hear Helix, she asks, "What do you have with you, Lukan?"

I am confused by her question. We have already discussed the book. I can't imagine why she would want to revisit the subject. Still, I answer her. "Geography book."

The rocking ceases, and the old lady leans forward slightly. Her graying eyes seem to pierce right through me. "What else?" Two simple words but the way she says them sends a chill up my spine.

I consider her question by doing a quick mental inventory of everything I have with me. Suddenly, I realize what else I have that would be of any interest to her or hold any meaning to our visit. "My bow," I reply with a faint amount of confidence in my voice.

Since Helix first gifted me with this hand-crafted bow and quiver full of arrows, I have not left my home without it draped over my back. Except for the times that the Howlers have visited, it is always on me. It has become a part of me. Like my eyepatch that hides my disability, I carry my bow to reveal my strength. Dom carries his as well. Even though our season for hunting has ended, as we prepare for winter, our bows and quivers are never away from us.

Looking at Dom now, Nyssa asks, "When hunting, how are you able to outsmart the animals that seemingly have the advantage over you?"

Dom glances at me nervously as if he needs reassurance to answer the old ladies question. I nod slightly, and he answers her. "I stalk them."

Nyssa nods. "How do you know where they are, to be able to stalk them?"

Dom thinks about it and answers, "We look for signs that there are animals in the area. Tracks, usually. We follow the tracks. Quietly." Dom looks at me again. "They never know we are there."

"I believe you know what must be done," Nyssa says melodically, repeating herself from earlier. "The answers to your questions are right here."

The room is silent as we all become lost in our thoughts. Like Helix and Dom are surely doing right now, I ponder the ancient woman's words. As the air in the cottage becomes heavy, I hear a familiar groan begin to grow from Helix, and I know that he is in deep thought.

Helix is the largest of the three of us crowded onto the couch. Sitting between Dom and me, Helix tilts his head toward me. Through his groaning, I hear a soft word emitted, "Lukan."

Narrowing my eyes at my blind friend, I feel the eyes of Dom and Nyssa on me. I expect Helix to say something to me since he just said my name but he remains silent.

"Helix?" With tremendous curiosity, I prompt him to continue.

Helix seems lost in his thoughts. Dom looks at me questioningly. Nyssa has begun rocking again. She seems content to be in our company, whether we are speaking or sitting silently.

"Lukan is the key to how we defeat the Howlers," Helix finally says quietly.

"Me? How can that be?" I ask with a nervous chuckle.

"Let's leave Ms. Nyssa to her slumber," Helix replies, avoiding my question.

Glancing at the old lady, I am surprised to see that Helix has somehow surmised that our hostess has fallen asleep. It appears that she has rocked herself into a slumber. She seems quite peaceful in her rocking chair, with her head tilted to the side and a soft purr coming from her throat as she snores. Of course, he is aware that our hostess has fallen asleep. Even in his blindness, his sense of hearing is acute.

Dom rises from the couch and stokes the fire in the fireplace, ensuring that when Nyssa wakes from her nap, she will wake to a warm house. I approach her quietly and lay a quilt over her. As we walk to the door, I turn to get one more look at the oldest lady in Grayson. I can't help but want to stay here and listen to stories of the world before the Langston Virus. I imagine she has much to tell, and much that this community can benefit from.

"Thank you, Nyssa," I say quietly before I shut the door to her cottage, leaving her sleeping peacefully in her rocking chair.

Chapter 7

Lia

The Dining Hall is full. It seems like every table is occupied and the line of people that wait to receive their meal snakes around the room. Without looking up from my tray of bland food, I can hear whispered conversations and murmuring taking place all around. The citizens, content with their life of oppression, remain unaware of the true nature of the beast that rules over them. Still, the newly distributed parchments seem to have awakened something inside this underground world.

With a newfound sense of determination, we – the Defiance – have begun placing fresh parchments around the Terra Convex. The wording, more damning to Leadership, would most certainly send us to our deaths if we are ever caught.

LEADERSHIP KILLS BY SENDING OUR ELDERLY TO THE ISOLATION CHAMBER

NAKED, HUNGRY, AND ALONE – PEOPLE ARE DYING IN THE ISOLATION CHAMBER AT THIS VERY MOMENT

END THE NIGHTMARE IN THE ISOLATION CHAMBER

The flyers seem to have caught everyone's attention. The threatening announcements have increased to two, sometimes three times a day. There is a tension, thick and heavy, that hangs in the air that I am sure is due to the increased presence of Enforcers. There is an Enforcer in every corner of this expansive room. Walking in the corridors, Axel and I saw several of the brutish security guards standing along the walls. Their job is to watch and wait for those obviously bent on revolt, to come strolling by them.

They have no idea that they are waiting for us - my friends and me. Just a few unassuming teenagers with a common goal of revolution. When we walk past those that have strict orders to capture us, they remain clueless.

Of course, none of the goons are aware of who is spreading the rumors about life on the outside. The government felt certain that they had shut the revolt down when they tortured and killed my mother. Imagine their surprise when the warnings began again shortly after her death. Imagine their surprise when they realized they had murdered the wrong person.

I hadn't heard any news about my father's well-being in the past few weeks. All I know is that he remains in the custody of Interrogators. Matlok informed me that my father is still living but is being tortured. Apparently, his torture is a sort of punishment for giving them false information by turning in my mother. More than anything, I wish I could be there to witness the torture that he is experiencing. I imagine him whimpering as he tries to explain his error. The thought of it makes me smile slightly.

My smile diminishes at the sound of Abigail's voice. I can't help but roll my eyes and purse my lips when she begins to talk. Since Mac was forced into a union with her, he has tried to bring her into our little group. Any other girl in the Convex would be welcomed as Mac's wife. Not Abigail. It would be like inviting Bermingham the Beast to sit and eat with us. The thought of it creates a knot in my belly that begins to crawl up my throat.

Mac seems convinced that Abigail has a genuine interest in leaving Terra Convex. Darcy, Axel, and I can only trust him and hope that he is correct. Still, we remain guarded around her, and I remain annoyed by her presence.

Mac clears his throat. When I look at him, it's obvious that he noticed my reaction to his wife's voice, and is slightly annoyed with me. I flash him a sheepish grin.

"I need to help Mrs. Bermingham grade some tests," Abigail is explaining. I suppose she is talking to Mac; nobody else at the table seems to be listening. "I also need to create some new assignments. It seems like the class is becoming bored."

I hate that she speaks of the class as if a member of that class isn't sitting at the same table as her.

"It is a conundrum," I say with snarkiness and a smirk.

With a harsh sigh, Abigail retorts, "That's why people don't like you." Her face is contorted in exasperation that pleases me.

"I like her," Axel comments with a smile. "A lot, actually." He seems quite proud that he is able to declare that to Abigail. I return his warm smile, and he gifts me with a wink that makes my heart flutter.

Obviously annoyed with the subtle affection between Axel and me, Abigail continues her ridicule of me, "Why do you even talk like that?"

"Mostly, just to annoy you," Now that my smirk has turned into a smile and my mood has improved greatly, Abigail's mood begins to plummet. Not that she has ever been in a good mood.

"Okay. Okay." Mac interjects, attempting to be a peacekeeper.

I can feel Abigail's eyes on me. Without looking up, I know that she is scowling at me. In an attempt to appease Mac, and accept the imp into our group, I remain focused on the tray of food in front of me. Axel's hand comes to rest on my knee. His way of reassuring me that I can handle Abigail. I welcome the gesture.

"Axelrod," It's a voice I do not recognize coming from the end of the table. Startled, and a little troubled, I look up to see a Roughneck standing next to where Axel sits.

Like Axel, the man's hair is long and unruly. His clothes are similar to the rest of the Terra Convex population, except much dirtier. His face, thin and pale, has spots of grease that is characteristic of the men that work in our world's underbelly.

"Dalen," Axel addresses the man, obviously as surprised as the rest of us at the table. "Is everything alright?"

The man, Dalen, looks at each of us. I detect a bit of nervousness as his eyes flinch around the table. He shifts his weight from one foot to the other. His eyes seem to linger on me a little longer than they did the rest of those at the table. I try to push aside the feeling of paranoia that being part of the Defiance has given me. He doesn't answer right away.

"Dalen?" Axel presses calmly.

Seeming to come out of his odd stupor, Dalen turns his attention back to Axel. "It has started snowing. When you finish your meal, the windows need to be cleared off."

"Of course," Axel replies. He starts to stand, but Dalen cuts him off.

"Stay. Finish your meal. No hurry." Dalen smiles, but it does not match the look in his eyes.

Axel pauses briefly and then replies, "Yes, sir."

We all continue to stare at the man, waiting for him to say more or leave. He stands at the end of our table, looking as if there is something else he needs to say but can't find the words to do so.

Finally, Axel comments, "You're welcome to join us, Dalen." Axel motions to the seat across from him.

Dalen looks as if he is considering the offer. With another glance around him, he replies. "Thank you, but I have to get back to work." A slight pause before he adds, "You know, I'm not sure I would come back in if I ever walked out." A nervous chuckle chokes out of his throat before he turns and leaves the Dining Hall in a hurry.

We all watch Dalen leave. The exchange leaves a heaviness hanging over our group. I imagine that we are all – except for Abigail – feeling the same anxiety over Dalen's peculiar behavior. I hope that Axel has an explanation for this man. Perhaps, he is just odd.

Axel had been watching Dalen walk away. Now, he turns back towards me. His eyes tell me that he too is perplexed by the man's behavior. Axel's eyes are wide as they search mine. I consider the exchange between the two Roughnecks, trying to decide if Dalen is friend or foe. Although he chuckled as he said the ominous words, his eyes were conveying much more than humor. They seem to pierce through and say something that words could not.

It could be that he, like so many others, has tired of this life and the thought of going out is both alluring and unnerving to him. I also have to consider that he is among those that will do anything to ensure their own safety by turning the Agitators over to the government.

"What was that about?" Abigail demands shrilly, interrupting my thoughts.

Of course, not wanting to say as much to Abigail, Axel simply explains, "When it snows, the windows become covered. If the windows are covered, we lose power. I need to go outside and clear them off, so that doesn't happen."

"Outside?" her voice grates on my nerves. This is the first time she is learning the work it takes so that she can live comfortably under the surface of the earth.

Ignoring her, Axel leans into me, "I guess I have to go to work." Sensing my anxiety, he gives me a quick but soft kiss on the cheek. "Dalen is my supervisor. Nothing to worry about." Before Axel stands to leave, his dimple-revealing smile returns and my nerves are somewhat settled. "I'll find you later."

Without taking my eyes off of his, I nod. I didn't realize that I had taken his hand in mine. Now that I know I have it, I don't want to let it go. Reluctantly, I do, and he walks away. Across from me, I am only slightly aware of Darcy explaining to Abigail the role and importance of Roughnecks to the Terra Convex. For once, she is quiet and without snarkiness.

Meanwhile, my heart is in my throat as I consider the dangerous path we are all taking with the Defiance. I can't help but wonder if the government suspects my friends and me of being Agitators. Watching my friends as they attempt to finish their meal, I am aware that they feel the same heavy burden.

My eyes land on Abigail and I am startled to find that she is staring at me thoughtfully. I sense uncertainty behind her stare. Normally, when she is looking my way, there is a keen and apparent look of disapproval on her face. Now, however, like Dalen, her eyes are trying to say something that her mouth cannot. She gives me a faint smile. After years of ruthless criticism and bullying from her, I can only narrow my eyes as I contemplate what her role might be in the Defiance.

*****

After Axel walked away from the Dining Hall, I went to class with a heavy heart and a mind filled with a thousand thoughts. None of which pertained to learning. The afternoon passed by slowly. More than anything, I wanted to go to my secret window. I wanted to see if Dalen was being truthful. Was it truly snowing or had a trap had been laid for the man that I love? When Axel left me in the dining hall, he seemed confident that Dalen was simply summoning him to do his duty. His confident smile and the warm squeeze he gave my hand did little to rid me of my fears. Sitting in Mrs. Bermingham's class, though, my imagination began to run wild with possibilities of Axel's capture and torture.

After class, I hurried to the window.

Standing here now, in the middle of the room, I am horrified to find that snow still covers the window. Not a thick layer of snow. I can still see the gray sky above, but it's obvious that Axel hasn't cleared it off yet. My heart begins to stutter a bit as I attempt to calm myself.

"It's okay. It's okay" I announce to the empty room. "There are more windows than just this one. It's just taking him time to get to this one. It's okay."

For several minutes, I pace around the tiny room, wringing my hands. From time to time, I find myself glancing back up at the window, hoping to see Axel just on the other side. I imagine him above me, wiping the snow away, smiling that smile that showcases the deep dimple in his right cheek. This goes on for some time. Each time I look up, disappointment gnaws at me.

When the door opens suddenly, I feel like a heavy weight has been lifted off my chest. Axel stands before me with a curious look on his face. He is neither smiling nor frowning. Mostly, he looks perplexed. Like he is trying to solve a riddle, and the answer is just barely out of reach.

"What is it? What's happened?" I ask, nearly in a panic. Usually, his rich smile would be covering his face. As he leans against the closed door, though, his eyes are narrow, and his hand rubs nervously at the stubble on his chin.

"Nothing," Axel replies, realizing my alarm. He places reassuring hands on my shoulders. "It's just that..." His voice trails off, apparently chasing his thoughts. "It's nothing." Axel flashes a smile that does not meet his eyes. "What are you doing in here? Is everything all right?"

Aware that Axel is trying to change the subject, I answer truthfully, "I was worried. The whole conversation with Dalen was....odd. You have never been approached in the Dining Hall to perform a task that could clearly wait until after mealtime." I motion to the snowy window above us.

Axel nods, and I can see that there is something on his mind. I don't want to press him, but yet I do. "Axel? Whats bothering you?"

"It's just... strange," Axel starts. "Dalen opened the hatch door for me to come back in, just like he always does. This time, though, after he shut it, and I was taking off my protective suit, he said something to me."

My mind once again goes to a dark place. I imagine that this is the end for us.

"What? What did he say?" the pitch of my voice is much more shrill than I intend for it to be.

"He repeated what he had said in the Dining Hall – 'I'm not sure I would ever come back in if I ever walked out.'" Axel stares into my face, trying to judge my reaction.

When Dalen had said those words in the Dining Hall, a slight shiver had crawled up my spine. The look on Dalen's face seemed like he was trying to say something then. Now, hearing from Axel that Dalen had actually repeated those same words to him again, sends an ominous quiver through my arms. I can understand why Axel seems so perplexed.

"How did you react to that?" I ask quietly.

"It caught me off guard. At first, I didn't know what to say. He rarely speaks to me." Axel explains.

"So, what did you say?" I press.

"It was so strange. I just told him that he wouldn't want to go out there right now. It's too cold," Axel explains the encounter. "That's when he said...." Axel trails off, remembering the encounter with his supervisor. I wait patiently for him to continue. "That's when he said that it seemed like the perfect time for enemies to get what they deserve."

I narrow my eyes, trying to understand what Dalen was attempting to say to Axel. "Enemies?"

Axel nods. "His exact words were, 'Exiled into a cold, unknown world seems like an ideal punishment for somebody that lies and kills. This could be the perfect time for enemies to get what they deserve.'"

Silently, Axel and I ponder over his supervisor's words. What exactly was Dalen trying to say? Enemies? Punishments? None of it makes sense to me. Who does Dalen have as enemies? Is it the Defiance? My nerves are nearly shot as my over-active imagination begins to run wild with possibilities.

"There's one more thing, Lia," Axel begins. Looking up into his face, I can sense that he is contemplating my reaction to what he is about to tell me. "Before I walked away, Dalen asked, 'How are Amelia and Bellamira handling the death of their mother?'"

I feel my hand involuntarily go to my throat as I try to swallow down the fear that threatens to rise from my belly. Since my mother, Marcella, died in my arms in the Isolation Chamber because of my father's lies and false accusations, some of the citizens of Terra Convex have quietly and inconspicuously given me their condolences. Mostly with sad looks in my direction, light consoling taps on the shoulder. Nothing verbal. Although Leadership is now fully aware that our mother was not the leader of the Defiance, as my father had accused her, it remains unwise for anyone to publicly console us for our loss. If the government heard that the daughters of an alleged Defiance member were receiving empathy, there would be harsh punishments handed out.

Axel continues, "I told him that you were doing as well as could be expected. That you both continued to be productive members of Terra Convex, serving our community in the roles that leadership has set upon you."

Smart. That is exactly what the government would want from its citizens, grieving or not. I can't help but smile at Axel's quick thinking.

"Dalen replied with, 'Marcella was an amazing and gracious woman. This world was made better by having her in it.'"

These words strike me to my core, erasing my smile. Many people in Terra Convex had a great appreciation for my mother. She was kind and spoke gently. She also worked hard as a seamstress. Her talent for mending even the worst rips and tears in uniforms, making them look new again, had been second to none. However, as well-liked as she was, nobody had ever said that she was amazing or gracious. Citizens of Terra Convex just didn't speak that way about others. They certainly didn't speak that way about a woman whose youngest daughter was known for being outspoken, imaginative, and perhaps even somewhat rebellious.

"What was he saying?" I try to make sense of the bizarre conversation.

"I'm not sure," Axel replies. "What does your sister know?"

I am shocked by his question. "Bellamira? I don't know. What do you mean?"

"Does she know of this place? Of the window? Does she know your part in the Defiance? Or why your mother is dead?"

With every question, I can feel my throat tighten up.

I think about my mother's journal. I can feel it as it rests against my back. Several times, I have contemplated giving it to Bellamira. Several times, I have decided it would be best if I kept it in my possession.

"She knows nothing. I have to protect her. She is the only family I have left." My voice sounds thick in my ears.

Axel can sense my distress. He sighs heavily. "Where do you want to take this Defiance, Lia?"

His question startles me. Not sure what he is asking, I struggle to find my words.

"We can continue to scatter flyers all over Terra Convex, but what is that doing for the Defiance? We can sit down here and make plans for our lives once we overthrow the government but where is that getting us? Nowhere." Axel is pacing now.

Something about Axel's trip to the outside world has invigorated him. Perhaps it was the cold wind in his face or the beauty of the snow covering the world above us. Regardless, he has come back with a renewed passion for ending our captivity in the underground.

"We just keep talking. Dreaming. We keep getting others worked up and frustrated, but they don't even know what they are upset about." His voice is raising slightly. Not out of anger – but passion."We need to do something. We need to get others involved. I don't mean with flyers that damn the government. I mean, we need to actually talk to people. Get in their face. I don't know Dalen very well, but I believe he is sympathetic to you because of your mother. His eyes were telling me that he wants to get involved. He wants to do something." Axel's brown locks bounce around his face as he paces the tiny room, imploring me to action.

His words pound into my head. Of course, I am in agreement with what Axel says. Still, when I imagine a true revolt against the government, I feel the weight of my mother's body in my arms.

"What can we do, Axel? The Enforcers are looking for us. We will be killed before we can actually incite a riot or anything." My voice comes out small and timid.

Axel has to know that I'm right. That's why we have been silent for so long, letting the flyers do the work for us.

"I believe there are Enforcers that want to be part of the Defiance. They are tired of having to arrest innocent people. They do not relish the task of discarding the dead bodies of those in the Isolation Chamber. They are tired of smelling the rotten flesh of their loved ones as they burn for asking questions. They want change as much as we do. I believe there are Enforcers that are looking for the members of the Defiance for the sole purpose of joining them."

My heart thuds heavily in my chest. I can't help but smile at Axel's passion. The fierceness in his eyes seems to give me the strength I need. His words are empowering, but they are also frightening. There is so much at stake, yet so much to be gained by moving forward with a plan against the government.

"What do you want to do, Axel?" I ask quietly, only slightly afraid of what his answer will be.

Pulling me into an embrace, he speaks softly, "To start with, I think it's time you and your sister get to know each other better."

Lukan

Helix, Dom, and I sit on the short rock wall that surrounds Grayson. We are bundled up in our thickest clothes, watching the snow fall from the sky. The citizens of Grayson are inside their homes, avoiding the cold. The three of us cannot seem to stay idle for too long, though. As the snow falls, a sense of urgency falls over us.

"Do you remember the story I told you of the young warrior?" A smile has spread across the blind man's face.

Since our meeting with Nyssa, Dom and I have been trying to understand why Helix believes I am the key to the final victory over the Howlers. I am just a boy with one eye. When Helix asks this question, though, I begin to understand. He wasn't speaking of me, after all. Indeed, the tale of the young archer remains fresh in my memory. I think of that story often.

"Yes," I answer. "His name was Lukan Augustus."

Sensing the confusion that has now edged its way over Dom, Helix gives a quick recount of the young warrior, Lukan Augustus.

Helix begins the story the same way he did when he told it to me the first time. He explains that when Lukan was young, the enemy of his village somehow heard of his skill as an archer. They captured him, forcing him to hunt for them. Provide for them. Years went by. The clan that had stolen Lukan from his family forgot that there could possibly be animosity. Lukan provided for them without complaint. They trusted the archer. They had no idea that even though he had provided for them all those years, he was also training his home village how to be archers. Lukan had secretly been creating an army. When the time was right, Lukan's army struck. They surrounded their enemy, and when Lukan gave the signal, the arrows were relentlessly fired into the camp.

"Not one survivor left," Helix concludes the story.

Dom's eyes are wide with intrigue. I imagine that I had the same look on my face when Helix first told me the story. In Grayson, boys do not often hear stories of young men becoming heroes. We are not told tales of strength or bravery. Parents teach their sons to hide from the Howlers. I have no doubt that hearing the story of the archer has sparked something inside of Dom. Something liken to curious bravery. The story had the same effect on me when Helix first told it to me that day on the cliffs.

"Wow, Lukan. I didn't know you were named after somebody so famous," Dom says with a coy smile.

With a chuckle, I reply, "Neither did I. How does this help us, though?"

"'Lukan is the key.'" Helix repeats the sweet old ladies words. "So are you, Domenic."

"How is that?" Dom asks, surprised that he would be included.

"The Howlers have no fear of Grayson. They underestimate the power that is held by those that wield the bow. That is you, Dom." Helix explains. Turning his head in my direction, he adds, "That is you, Lukan."

Dom and I look at each other. Dom's face tells me that he is as perplexed by Helix's words as I am. Still, the idea of what I think Helix is suggesting sends a chill up my spine, while also enticing me.

"I'm afraid Grayson will have to find another 'key' to victory over the Howlers," Dom comments, looking away with dejection. "There are more of them than just two archers can dispatch." He looks at me with a frown and shrugs his shoulders in defeat.

I nod in agreement. My cousin makes a good point that Helix cannot argue. The amount of Howlers seems to grow with every visit to Grayson. I'm positive that we haven't even seen their full numbers yet. They travel all over this area wreaking havoc, pillaging towns. In order to maintain control of Grayson and the surrounding communities, I would venture to guess their numbers to be in the thousands. Another chill causes me a shiver.

Looking up at the darkening sky, I allow the ever-thickening snowflakes to land on my face. I welcome the cold that this early winter snowshower brings. Most people dread winter, and the white and gray it brings with it. I embrace it, flourishing in the darkness and harshness that it brings. The frigid air seems to clear my head and rejuvenate me. While others stay hidden inside their homes until warm weather returns, I can be found traipsing around in my homemade snowshoes. During the harshest weeks, which are brief but sometimes brutal, the citizens of Grayson are thankful that I don't mind the cold. I bring them firewood for their fireplaces and stoves. Or I walk through town with heavy bags full of smoked meats, delivering food to the citizens of Grayson.

Merritt enjoyed the cold also. She would often accompany me on my deliveries or walks around town. After we finished taking care of Grayson, we would sit together on the same short rock wall that I rest on now. We would gaze out across the snow-covered landscape. Huddled together in the cold, we would daydream about the far off places we wanted to go. Places we had read about in the geography book that now sits on the antique table in my room. Never to be opened again.

"All of Grayson must be willing to help," I hear Helix moan, interrupting my thoughts of Merritt.

I consider this for a moment. The citizens of Grayson, although weary from the relentless abuse received from the Howlers, seem quite content inside these walls. Even though the visits by the madmen are torturous, they are few and far between. This gives the people of this community stretches in time of peace and order. I can't imagine the conflict that would arise within these walls at the very mention of battling the Howlers for our freedom.

"You would have to convince them," Helix continues. "You would have to train them in archery."

Dom and I exchange an incredulous glance. What Helix is suggesting is preposterous and obviously not well thought out. This conversation seems like a waste of our time. We need to be coming up with real solutions. Unfortunately, at this point, there doesn't seem to be any.

"Helix, Dom and I are the only ones in Grayson that have bows," I explain, attempting to keep the irritation from my voice.

"Besides, you haven't been in Grayson long enough to understand the mindset of these people," Dom adds. "They are content with hiding their boys in the woods and waiting for the Howlers to carry out their destruction and then leave. They won't fight."

Next to me, I can hear Helix take a long deep breath. I glance at him. Even though I have known him for awhile now, and am fully aware that he would never cause me any harm or allow any harm to come to me, his size is quite intimidating. Not only is he tall, but he is broad and muscular. His voice is deep and thick, demanding attention when he speaks. He lets his breath out slowly and stands with a groan and a grunt.

"There is only one person in Grayson that must be persuaded," Helix announces as if he hadn't heard Dom. "Once he has been convinced, Grayson will follow." He is smiling now.

Dom and I stand up also. "Who?" I ask, curious now, but still reluctant.

With his guiding stick in hand, tapping along the rock wall, Helix steps over and begins walking towards town. He doesn't wait for Dom and I. It's obvious that he is confident with the plan that is formulating in his mind. We hurry to join him.

"Who, Helix?" I ask once more.

His smile is broad. "Your father."

Chapter 8

Lia

I hadn't considered how the truth of my life would affect Bellamira. She sits in her chair, face buried in her knees which she hugs against her chest. She sobs quietly. I hadn't considered that revealing that I am the true reason our mother is dead, would seemingly destroy my sister. Along with the guilt and sorrow that I have been carrying with me since the death of my mother, now I also have just a tinge of anger that Axel would have suggested that telling Bellamira everything would be a good idea.

Wanting to speak with my sister alone, I waited until her husband, Matlok, left for his job as an Enforcer. Bellamira and I have spent many evenings alone. We have had many conversations. Mostly about the mundane activities of our day or who has been recently betrothed or the terrible blandness of the food recently. Never about subjects such as this. She has always known about my relentless curiosity and imagination. She knows that our father had our mother arrested, and ultimately killed, because of the flyers that I had created. Still, I have never opened up to her about the window, the outside world, Lukan, or my role in the Defiance. Understandably, she is shaken to her core. Like most in Terra Convex, it is much more convenient for her to bury her head and pretend that what she is hearing simply isn't true.

It is true, though. All of it. Not so long ago, I wasn't much different than Bellamira. After being put in Solitary for upsetting Leadership with my essay on our government, burying my head – essentially, stifling my own thoughts and ideas – was much easier, safer really, than rising above the oppression. Thankfully, I had my friends – Darcy and Mac – and I had the window. My friends have made life in Terra Convex tolerable. The window has given me a chance to imagine more than cold dark walls and bland food. When I realized that there truly is life above ground and that the government has been lying, my life took a whole new meaning. I knew then that every daydream I have ever had has been leading up to the day when I finally get to step outside and feel the sun on my face.

As I sit quietly and watch Bellamira cry, I am struck by a thought. Something that Axel had said comes back to me. I close my eyes so I can concentrate on the conversation we had when he returned from clearing snow off the windows.

'Marcella was an amazing and gracious woman. This world was made better by having her in it.'

Words that Dalen had said to Axel. Words that, at the time, struck something inside of me. It had seemed odd for Axel's supervisor to say something like that. It is almost as if he knew my mother personally. I begin to consider that perhaps they had been classmates. They did seem to be about the same age.

Another thought begins to tickle at the back of my mind. I am barely aware that Bellamira has quit crying and is now wiping at her eyes and nose. The thought lingers. My mother's journal rests on Bellamira's table between us. It beckons me, and I am reminded of something that I had read in it. Something that, at the time, wasn't important to me because it didn't seem to give any clues to how I can change our current situation. Now, the words scream at me from the closed book, and I snatch it up quickly.

Thumbing quickly, I find the page I am looking for and delve once more into the secret life of my mother.

The day I have feared is upon me. I knew it was coming. Today, I was given to Harrison. He made it clear that he wouldn't have chosen me to be his wife. This is no revelation to me. He and I have never gotten along in class. His arrogance and ego are more than the walls of Terra Convex can contain. I imagine that burning and disfiguring my hand was not enough; the government decided to add the union to this treacherous man as my life-long punishment.

I don't know which is more painful – knowing that I have to live the rest of my life with a man that I do not love... or knowing that D will live the rest of his life as a Roughneck, never to find love again.

As the Enforcers were escorting me to the Hall of Union, or Execution Room as I refer to it, my heart broke into a thousand pieces. Not because of what was about to transpire but because of what I was losing. D stood in the corridor. With a look of anguish that only I could recognize, he watched as I walked past him towards the man I must commit my life to. We locked eyes. I wanted to run to him. Wanted him to fight his way past the Enforcers and save me from the wretchedness of the situation. All we could do, though, was stare into each other's eyes. Before I rounded the corner, I saw the single tear escape and roll down his dirty cheek. I closed my eyes and let the Enforcers lead me.

Lead me to my fate. My life sentence for asking too many questions.

My mother's words, from so long ago, seem to speak to what is nagging at my thoughts.

D

I feel my breaths come in quick gasps as I realize that Axel's supervisor, Dalen, is the man my mother spoke of in her journal. He is the man she loved. At the time of my parent's union, D was a Roughneck. This revelation explains his response to Axel. Of course, if the love of his life – even after all these years – had died because of Harrison, then he would want to exact revenge. What better way to do that than to send him out of Terra Convex. The idea is intriguing to me. It is something that I will need to discuss with Axel. Suddenly, I feel an urgency to leave this room and find him.

Looking up, I am surprised to see Bellamira staring at me from her chair. Her face is wet with tears, but her weeping has subsided. She glares at the journal in my lap, her eyes twitching between the book and my face. I consider telling her what I just learned about our mother and the man, Dalen. Bellamira's emotional state indicates that now is not the time. She seems unable to absorb any further revelations right now.

I am struck, suddenly, with the thought that perhaps Bellamira will turn me in to the Enforcers. Her face is difficult to read. She seems angry, confused, and completely heartbroken. I struggle to find the words to bring comfort to her.

Finally, after some time, she speaks. "Why did it have to be you?" She spits the words out as she would something bitter.

Assuming that she is referring to my role in the Defiance, I answer truthfully, "Because I have always believed that there is more to this world than what we have been given. Because I've never trusted the government. I always felt like there was the possibility of life above ground. I was right."

Bellamira rolls her eyes and shakes her head. "Not that. Why did mother pick you to give her journal to?" She looks away, obviously on the verge of more tears. "She always favored you."

It finally occurs to me that Bellamira's response isn't what she has been told but who is telling her. She isn't angry that our mother is dead because of a rebellion that I started. She's angry because our mother chose to deliver her most sacred secrets to me in the form of the journal. This idea offends me briefly, but I push my irritation aside.

"She didn't 'favor' me, Bellamira. I think she just... I think when she looked at me, she could see some of herself from when she was a child. Before the government punished her for asking too many questions; for having a unique thought." I counter.

"Why didn't she tell me?" Bellamira's lip quivers slightly.

"Because it was too dangerous," I answer truthfully.

"But not too dangerous for you," there is a bite to her words.

My irritation with her self-pity is growing. I am trying to be patient and let her work through all of her emotions, but I feel like her jealousy is clouding her judgment.

"No. It's dangerous for me too. I live every day in fear that I will be found out by Leadership. If I am, then I will meet the same fate as our mother." I retort, attempting to keep the annoyance out of my voice.

"How do you do it? How do you live every day with fear and distrust? I mean, you couldn't even trust your own sister."

There it is. The real reason Bellamira is upset. She feels like she has been left out. Excluded from a secret.

"It isn't because I didn't trust you. I was doing everything I could to protect you. Your husband is an Enforcer. Yes, he was kind enough to allow me into the Isolation Chamber to see our mother, but still, anyone that works for the government cannot be trusted." I explain with truthfulness.

Bellamira looks down and begins to fidget with a loose string on her uniform. "Matlok can be trusted." She looks up to meet my eyes. "He believes in the Defiance. Believes in their cause. Your cause."

I am not surprised by this. Matlok has risked a lot for me before. Not only did he take me to the Isolation Chamber to see my mother, but he has kept me informed about the state of my father's well being. Both of those actions would be considered punishable offenses in Terra Convex. Still, neither of those actions mean that Matlok has any interest in joining the Defiance.

Bellamira must sense my apprehension. She continues, "Matlok also believes there is life above ground."

She pauses, obviously contemplating if she should say more. Her sudden nervousness has seized my attention, and I lean forward in my seat.

"He has heard...grumblings from some of the councilmen." Her eyes are on me once again.

"Grumblings?" I begin to feel a tightness in my chest. "What has he heard, Bellamira?"

With a loud sigh, my sister concedes to the fact that she must tell me everything she knows. "There are several in Leadership who believe that President DePriest is lying – has been lying – about life above ground. That is why there is so much pressure to find the Defiance. Leadership believes the Defiance is actually their own councilmen."

This information is almost too much. I had expected her to tell me that my friends and I were about to be caught. Instead, she is telling me that we aren't even suspects. The thoughts running through my head become cluttered as I contemplate what this means for the Defiance.

Standing, I begin to pace back and forth in the small space. I feel an incredible urge to run from this room and find Axel, Darcy, and Mac. They need to know this right away.

"Wait. Where are you going?" Bellamira jumps from her seat as I grab up the journal and rush to the door.

Realizing my error, I walk to her. I embrace her briefly. This is rare for us, but she graciously returns my affection.

"Thank you, sister," I say into her ear. "You have no idea how much you mean to me, but I have to go tell my friends what I have just learned. This changes everything." I release her and go to the door to leave.

"I want to go with you," Bellamira declares suddenly.

I turn toward her slowly, taking in her face. Her eyes are wide, and her breath is quick.

"I want to go with you," she repeats, swallowing hard. She closes her mouth and attempts to look as if she isn't afraid of what she has just uttered.

I consider this. Consider what it would mean for her to be part of this rebellion. I begin to shake my head slightly as I imagine my sister being punished for my transgressions.

Before I can argue, though, Bellamira approaches the door, placing her hand on the knob. She looks me in the eyes and states with a sly smirk, "I can't let my little sister have all the fun."

I appreciate that she is trying to bring humor to this situation. "Bellamira, it's dangerous. I don't want you to get hurt. I couldn't live with myself," I counter.

"Amelia, I believe in what you are doing with the Defiance. *I believe*. Let me be part of it. Please." Her eyes are pleading, and I can see the sincerity in them.

With a heavy heart, I nod. "Ok, but in the Defiance, we don't go by our government issued names."

"I don't understand."

"Well, Maclin is Mac. Darcius is Darcy. Axelrod is Axel. Of course, we don't use those names when we are around others." I explain.

"What's your name?" She quizzes.

"Lia," I say proudly, even though I'm sure she has heard it used before.

"I like it. What will mine be?"

"What do you want it to be?" I ask with a grin.

Without any hesitation, she answers with excitement, "Mira."

With a smile and a nod, I reply, "Okay, Mira. Welcome to the Defiance. Now let's try not to get ourselves killed."

Lukan

My father's face is set in stone with narrowed eyes, pursed lips, and creases above his nose. I've seen this look before. It is the look of a man at a loss for words, attempting to process what his one-eyed son has just told him. He stares out the window, lost in thoughts that I can only assume are filled with questions he doesn't yet know how to form into words.

The look on my mother's face is quite different. She displays sheer terror. She has effectively processed my statements and now sits, pale-faced and wringing her hands. Her breath is coming in quick gasps as she considers the ramifications of what has just been told to her and my father.

I have dreaded this conversation with my parents. Since finding the mysterious window in the tall grass, I have imagined all the different ways this conversation could go. When I have imagined it, the scene has been similar to the way it is at this moment. Me, sitting comfortably on the couch in front of the big window that looks out onto the street. My parents each in their own cushioned armchairs. Our living room isn't large, but it is big enough for this family of four to sit comfortably and not feel cramped. Of course, with Helix sharing the couch with Dom and me, along with the reason for the conversation, the room seems to close in on me somehow, making me feel claustrophobic.

"Lia and the window have become very important parts of who you are, Lukan. Your parents may not understand it. They will most certainly be frightened of it. They are your parents, though, and will be glad that you have confided in them." Helix explained as we neared my home. I still wasn't convinced even as we walked into the warm house.

I look over at Dom. His head is down, and he picks at a small tear in the knee of his pants. It's obvious that he cannot meet the eyes of his aunt and uncle. Obvious that he wishes to be elsewhere.

Looking at my parents now, it seems that my mother is frightened and my father just doesn't understand. That is to be expected. My mother's thoughts always tend to immediately go to the worse possible scenario. My father thinks things through and comes up with solutions.

Helix wanted me to do the talking. He said they needed to hear it from me, not him. As I explained the window and how I found it, I garnered strength just by having Helix next to me. My father interrupted me just a couple of times. He had legitimate questions. Questions that any attentive parent with an inclination to worry would ask. Questions that I had no problem answering. When I reached the part of the story where I saw Lia for the first time, my parents were obviously shocked. When I told them that I had actually met Axel, my mother gasped. I felt it wise to take a pause and let them process. the idea that there is actually a world beneath our feet may prove to be too much for my parents to bear.

The five of us sit silently. Each lost in our own thoughts. The room is silent except for the crackling of the fire in the fireplace and the clock that ticks the seconds away. The hands of the clock on the mantel tick by much too loudly. I begin to imagine the ticking to be footsteps. Not just footsteps, but the stomping of Howlers as they march toward our home. The thought sends a shiver up my spine, and I realize that time is of the essence. My parents will have to accept what is below us and help defend Grayson.

I begin to fidget where I am seated on the couch. My father must sense my agitation.

"What do you want us to do with this information, son?" my father asks. "Why are you telling us all of this? I'm sure it would have been easier to keep it a secret."

That's a good question. I carefully consider how I should answer him. I look to Helix for guidance. He sits between Dom and me, groaning softly with each breath. The room is warm, and I begin to think that the blind wanderer has taken advantage of the comfortable couch and fallen asleep.

Finally, I decide to simply tell my parents what needs to be done. "We would like to arm the citizens of Grayson with bows and arrows. Train them in archery. When the time is right, attack the Howlers camp."

Another sharp gasp from my mother. She is clutching her throat as if it has closed up on her.

My father sits forward in his seat. He reaches a hand out to my mother. She gladly takes it. I wonder if the act is to give her strength or if he is hoping to receive strength from her. For a brief moment, I reflect on the relationship between my parents. Theirs is the marriage that all other relationships in town should envy. A wave of sadness washes over me as

I realize that I will never know love the way my parents love each other. With the loss of Merritt, I lost much more than my best friend. I lost the one person that I feel completed me and made me feel whole.

The thought of Merritt, and what the Howlers took from me, ignites the fire I need to continue on with my plea to my parents.

"I know it seems like a crazy idea, Dad," I begin. I try to think of how I can explain myself without sounding like a lunatic. Then, a thought occurs to me. "It's been done before. Helix, tell them about Lukan."

"Lukan?" My mother asks, confused.

"Yes, he was an archer a long, long time ago." I look to Helix in hopes that he will explain. He sits next to me nodding but giving no indication that he is willing to share the story again. I give him a nudge with my elbow. "Go ahead, Helix. Tell them."

After much stammering and groaning, Helix recounts the story of Lukan the Archer to my parents. I am confused by the way Helix acts while telling the story, though. He acts as if the story is unimportant. His rushes through the story and shows no enthusiasm whatsoever in telling it. I tell myself that his odd behavior is just because I had interrupted his slumber on the couch and he simply was not prepared to tell the story yet again.

"I'm surprised you haven't heard of Lukan the Archer," I add when Helix is finished. "I figured that you named me after him," I add with a chuckle, trying to add a lighter note to the intense conversation.

My mother shakes her head slightly. Her mouth is open as if she is trying to think of the right words to say. We sit in silence once again. I give my father time to think about what should be done.

Finally, he says, "The element of surprise is intriguing." I can't help but let a small smile creep across my face.

"Avis! Surely, you are not considering this." My mother scolds my father.

"Think about it, Lue," my father explains. "The Howlers consider us weak. They feel like they can come here anytime they want and do whatever they want to us."

"Because they can, and they do!" My mother's voice is shrill as she realizes that her husband is actually considering a devious plan against the Howlers.

"That is what is so great about Lukan's plan. The Howlers are convinced that we are going to hole up here in Grayson for the winter. They won't even consider that we are training to rise up against them. Think of their surprise when the arrows begin falling from the sky." My father's voice rises, and his hands move through the air portraying flying arrows.

"Will you help us, Avis?" Helix asks. His voice sounds hopeful.

Helix can't see it, but my father sucks his bottom lip in , holding it there between his teeth and nods his head thoughtfully. Finally, he answers, "What do you need me to do? I will gladly help. As long as you know that I am no archer. I will have to be trained also." He chuckles, and it helps to lighten the mood in the room.

Except for my mom. Staring at the floor, she hugs a throw pillow up to her chest. Clearly, she is pouting, feeling the sting of being outnumbered by the men in her life.

"You are well respected in the community. Whether you have been given the official title or not, you are the leader of Grayson." Helix is leaning forward slightly, appealing to my dad's ego.

"You speak too highly of me, Helix. I am just a regular citizen. There is no reason to think that the people will listen to me," my father replies with a slight redness to his cheeks.

"And yet they will, all the same," Helix assures my father.

I can't help but smile because I know Helix is right. This town respects my father and sets his opinion above all others. He is the one they come to when there are problems and when they are looking for answers. I can only hope that when he brings this plan to them, they will remember all of the reputable counsel he has given them in the past.

"Please don't do this, Avis." My mom is nearly in tears.

Before my dad can reply to her, Dom breaks his silence. "He must, Auntie."

We all look at Dom as if we are just realizing that he is sitting here with us. He has been so quiet during this exchange that I had almost forgotten that he was here.

"Domenic, surely after what you went through at the hands of the Howlers, you are not in agreement with this plan?" My mother seems baffled at the idea.

Dom nods slowly as he answers, "It is because of what the Howlers did to me that I am in complete agreement with this plan. We must make this work. We must take action."

A small sob escapes my mother. Although strong in so many ways, the fear that harm may come to her men – my father, Dom, and me – is her weakness. My dad reaches out and takes his wife's petite hand once again. Gently, he pulls her from her chair and into his lap. He whispers into her ear as he holds her tight.

After several minutes of consoling her, my father looks at me and says, "I will call a meeting. I will explain everything that you have told us. I'm afraid that the people of Grayson will not react well when they learn that there is a whole other world that lives just under our feet. I also fear they will revolt when they learn that you are planning an attack on the Howlers. You must be ready for hard questions and stern lectures. You must be ready to lay the plan out point by point."

My father's words shock me. "I-I thought you would be the one doing the talking. You will explain it much better than I can. The people of Grayson don't have the same respect for me as they do for you."

"They respect you more than you realize. Besides, you are the one that has actually spoken to somebody from the underground. You are the one with the plan of attack. It has to be you," my father explains. "I will be the one to appeal to their emotions."

"What does that mean?" Dom asks.

"I will remind them of what they have lost because of the Howlers. I will remind them of the death and destruction that the Howlers have brought upon this community." There is sadness in my dad's voice.

I know that my father doesn't relish the idea of bringing back painful memories to the people. He will not enjoy using their emotions against them. So many have lost so much. He knows that the wounds that remain with me because of Merritt's death are still fresh and painful. I understand why this approach is important, though.

My mom remains in my father's lap. She gets her strength from him. I wonder if their show of affection is making Helix feel uncomfortable. Even though he cannot see them, I'm sure he feels the change in the room as the mood lightens because of their deep love and understanding of each other. This display is nothing new for Dom and me. Of course, my mom isn't always wiping away tears when she sits in a tight embrace on my father's lap. Usually, they are laughing as they tell each other about their day.

With a sniffle, my mom looks back to us on the couch. "I don't imagine I will have much to do with shooting a bow." She attempts a smile. "I'm not sure what I can do to help."

"Just support your men," Helix replies with a pleasant groan in his throat.

"I will. Of course, I will. Lukan, I would like to hear more about the girl. Lia?" My mom's voice is quiet and timid.

I think for a moment, trying to determine how to answer. I don't know Lia. I have only seen her a couple of times. Everything I know about her has come from Axel. He seems to know her very well. The way he spoke of her, I would venture to say that there is affection between Lia and Axel.

"She reminds me of you, mom," I start. "She is strong and brave. Everything that the world has thrown at her, she keeps standing. Keeps enduring. When she is given more than she can handle, she leans on the people that she loves and her strength is renewed. Because of the strength and determination that is deep inside of her, she will always rise above whatever trials she has to endure." Standing, I walk over to my mother and give her a gentle kiss on the cheek. Then I add with a whisper, "Just like you."

Chapter 9

Lia

Mira, the newest member of our little rebellion, stares with wide eyes up into a sky that she thought she would never see. Watches beautiful red birds and squirrels that she thought didn't exist. Even though the sky is gray, and the heads of the trees are bare, the world above is beautiful and teeming with life.

She does not take her eyes from the sight above her. I watch as the tears that had been pooling up in her eyes finally make their escape and begin creeping across her temple and into her unwashed hair. Smiling at her reaction, and the fact that there are no more secrets between my sister and me, I sit on the floor and lean against the wall. I quietly allow Mira to observe the world above her and accept everything she has been told today. Sitting here, watching her, I see our mother in Mira's profile and a lump forms in my throat.

The door opens quietly. Even though I am not alarmed, the gasp that escapes Mira causes me to jump up. I am grateful to see my friends. While their expressions are somewhat guarded at the sight my sister in our secret place, Axel, Darcy, and Mac all smile when they see me. They greet her warmly.

"She wants to join us," I explain. "I've told her everything. She even believes that her husband, Matlok, wants to help."

"He's an Enforcer," Mac states with a sharp tone and a look of doubt.

"And your wife is the daughter of a council member. Yet, you believe she should be part of the Defiance," I counter quickly, with an obvious edge to my voice.

Realizing that this exchange could get heated, Axel steps up to Mira and welcomes her. "We are grateful to have you, Bellamira. I know that your sister is thrilled."

With a shy nod, my sister acknowledges Axel and the others. "Thank you. I don't know what use I will be to you, but I really want to help." Looking directly at Mac, she says, "I promise you that Matlok is on your side. He has seen and heard too much to be loyal to the government."

Mac nods his head and runs a hand through his hair. He seems embarrassed by his words.

Darcy approaches Mira and gives her a hug. "Welcome, Bellamira."

"Actually, she has dropped her government-issued name. She wants to be called Mira," I explain with a proud smile. "It was her idea."

"Very nice," Axel comments with a smile and a nod. "You really are diving right into the Defiance, aren't you?"

With a sharp nod of her head, Mira asserts, "I want to make sure the government, and even my father, receive punishment for what happened to our mother." Her voice wavers slightly, and I realize that she is trying her hardest to be strong in front of the Defiance.

Placing my arm across her shoulders, I say, "They will pay. I promise."

Everyone nods in agreement. Darcy reaches out and pats Mira's hand reassuringly. The group feels whole with my sister here with me.

"Axel told us about his odd conversation with Dalen. Lia, what do you make of it?" Mac asks, leaning against one of the walls and sliding down until he is sitting with his knees up.

We all take our cue and begin to find our places on the floor. It appears that the meeting of the Defiance has come to order. I lead Mira over to where Axel is now sitting on the floor. As I join him, he leans in and kisses my forehead tenderly. I close my eyes briefly and relish the affection that I cherish.

Suddenly, I remember what I had read in my mother's journal about the boy she called, "D." Excitedly, I explain, "I read something very interesting in the journal today. I think it will explain Dalen's behavior and strange wording."

Pulling the journal from my waistband, I read the passage to my friends. I am aware of their eyes on me. I am aware of the hope they hold in every new revelation. They listen with eagerness. When I finish, we sit in silence. Each of us contemplating Dalen and his role in our rebellion.

When nobody says anything, after some time, I finally break the silence. "Dalen and my mother were in love. She asked too many questions and was punished with the searing of her hand. Dalen was sentenced to work as a Roughneck, never to marry."

I pause and look at Axel. He stares intently into my face. Without saying a word, I know that Axel is reminded of when I was put in Solitary and he was forced into the life of a Roughneck. Both of us enduring punishments for writing an essay that spoke poorly of the president.

As if reading my thoughts, Axel presses his lips against my ear and whispers, "Worth it." His words and the warmth of his breath on my ear, causes heat to spread across my face and down my neck. I'm sure the others can see my reddened cheeks but there is much to be done, and my embarrassment should not be the cause of any delays.

"So, does that mean that Dalen wants Harrison punished for what happened to your mother?" Mac asks, attempting to bring Axel and me back into the conversation.

"That sure is what it seems like to me," Axel answers.

"Me too," I concur, glancing at Mira to gauge her reaction.

She is quiet for a moment. Out of respect, we all allow her the time she needs to process. Mira has been a true Terra Convexian for her entire life. Always believing that the government and everything she was taught was true and for her own good. I'm afraid that too much of the actual truth could prove to be more than she can bear in one day.

Finally, Mira responds. "If Dalen thinks that sending somebody outside is punishment, and Harrison deserves punished, then let's do it. Let's send him out. It will still be a better death than what our mother endured."

"I want to punish Harrison just as much as anyone here," Darcy begins. "Still, I feel like we could be setting ourselves up for disaster. We don't know that we can trust Dalen. Just because we are almost certain that he and your mother had a relationship twenty years ago doesn't mean that he isn't fully committed to the government. What if this is all a trap because Leadership knew that they had a relationship?"

Darcy makes valid points, and the room becomes silent once again as we each contemplate her words.

"I think we all realize the risk," Axel starts. "When we started this, we knew the risks. There have been times that it really did seem easier to just not come back in after walking around up there. Down here, it's just gray and stale. The air stinks. *We* stink." This gets a chuckle out of us. "Up there, the wind blows, and you can smell the grass. You can feel the sun on your face." Axel turns to me, "Lia, I think that is what you are going to love the most – warmth. Listen, what we are doing is scary. It's dangerous." Axel looks up and points to the window. We all follow his eyes. "There *is* life up there. Life that can be ours. *That* is worth the risk."

After several moments of silence as we all stare into the sky above us, I break the silence. "I think we should do this. I think we should speak to Dalen. See what his true motivations are. Axel's right. It's worth the risk. Besides, they can only take our lives, and if we aren't using them for the Defiance, we aren't really living." I look at my little group of friends. My eyes settle on my sister. "Mira, do you think you can talk to Matlok? Or would you rather I do it?"

Mira thinks for a moment. "I want to do it. I want him to know that I really want this. If we go in together, he may think that I was coerced. He needs to know that I am serious. I'll speak with him tonight."

"Okay, then I will speak with Dalen. Mira will speak with Matlok. Hopefully, in a few days, we will know where their loyalties lie, and Harrison will be exiled. Punishment for his part in the death of your mother, Marcella," Axel explains rather formally, making eye contact with each of us to ensure that we are all in agreement.

We all nod our agreement.

"I guess the only other thing to consider is the possibility that our friend, Lukan, may find Harrison and take pity on him," Darcy mutters.

"That thought crossed my mind too," Axel replies. I'm glad he had thought about it because that thought never entered my mind. "Harrison won't get far, and I don't believe Lukan will be away from his settlement."

"Why not?" Mac asks.

Axel looks up through the window once again. We follow his gaze. Without looking down, he answers, "That sky. Those gray clouds are menacing. Harrison will not leave here equipped to survive the snowstorm that I believe is coming. His fate will be sealed as soon as that hatch door closes behind him."

Lukan

"This is lunacy!"

An irate man in the crowd yells out. I'm not exactly sure who the angry voice belongs to, but it sounded a little like Mr. Prescott. Usually, the plump-cheeked fellow is cordial. Never have I seen him without him greeting me with a friendly salute and a smile that makes his eyes disappear beneath his cheeks. It is unlike him to be cross. Even more out of character for him to raise his voice.

Mr. Prescott isn't the only man of Grayson that is expressing disdain. There are others in the crowded Community Building that are bellowing their annoyance with the idea I have presented to them.

Of course, it is lunacy. I know that it is. Who am I, a 16-year-old boy with only one eye, to believe that a small community like Grayson could stand against the Howlers? I agree that the idea is preposterous. Dangerous. Lunacy.

The people of Grayson can't know that though. I can't reveal to them the intense fear and dread that I have. Just the the thought of carrying out such an impractical strategy has formed a knot in my belly. No, I must convince them that the plan will work. Not only will we be rid of the Howlers who have terrorized us for so long, but we will be well on our way to rebuilding this world.

The people of Grayson filled the auditorium of the Community Building this morning, eager and curious as to why a town meeting had been called at such a time as this. Winter seemed to be coming earlier this year. The temperature had plummeted overnight. With no source of heat, the Community Building was frigid. Mostly, it was the men of town that showed up for the meeting, leaving their wives and children in their warm homes. There were a few women, my mother included, here to support their men. Helix and Dom sat on both sides of her.

When I first began to speak to the crowd, I could see my breath. My voice was shaky. I hoped that those listening would attribute to the cold, and not to the intense anxiety I felt at speaking to such a large crowd.

A lot of the men grumbled as I spoke. Some listened with wide eyes and mouths agape. I bore my soul to these men, revealing all my secrets. The window. Lia. Axel. Everything I knew about the world below our feet. Of course, this revelation elicited more murmurings and grumblings. Rightly so. Grayson has become so accustomed to their simple life inside the short walls, with only the Howlers to think about, that the idea of another civilization living just inches below where they are sitting is difficult to comprehend.

"Yes, Mr. Prescott. It does seem like lunacy," I hear my father say. "Throughout history, the greatest plans seemed like lunacy. However, with careful planning, and cooperation from all, the most insane strategies have ended with triumph. I believe what Lukan is presenting..."

"He's your son! Of course, you will go along with what he says," Another bitter voice bellows from the crowd.

My father is quiet as he contemplates how to answer. I glance over at him, saddened by the fact that he has to endure the hatefulness of these men because of me.

"Indeed, Lukan is my son." My father climbs down from the stage and leans against it casually. "Just like all of you, he is also a member of this community. If any of you were to approach me with an idea of how to free Grayson from the ever-tightening grip of the Howlers, I would be happy to listen."

My father pauses, looking across the room, apparently waiting for ideas to begin spewing from the mouths of these men. All he receives is looks of anger and disgust. He begins to slowly walk into the crowd, approaching one of the crotchety old men.

"Ned, do you have a plan?" He asks with a kind smile, placing his hand on the man's shoulder.

"Yes, Avis. I plan on staying warm in my home during the cold months. When the Howlers come back in the spring, I plan to give them whatever they ask for," Ned replies with a smugness.

My father's smile does not diminish. He gently pats the man on the shoulder and walks on through the crowd. A few steps away, he stops again.

With the same patient smile as before, my father asks, "Ezra, do you have a plan?"

The man stares up at my father for several seconds before answering with a bite in his voice, "Same as Ned. Same as everyone else in here, Avis. Try to survive through the winter, and then pick up where we left off with the Howlers before winter."

Looking around the room once more, my father asks, "Is that the consensus then? Everyone just try to stay warm and cozy in your homes until spring, and then hope that your family isn't murdered when the flowers bloom again?" He is walking back up to the stage now with his arms crossed over his chest. "Just keep hiding your boys. Keep giving the Howlers everything we work so hard for? Hope for the best?" Although his patient smile remains, I sense just a tad bit of irritation in my father's voice.

"It's worked for us this long, Avis," I hear Mr. Jameson say.

Before my father or I can counter, a woman's voice from the back surprises us both. "No, it hasn't. It hasn't worked for us." Elyn, Merritt's mother, stands by the doors, wrapped in a thick blanket. Her husband rushes to her, obviously surprised by her sudden appearance. Her eyes are sad, but she stands with her head high, seemingly ready to rebuke anyone that disagrees with her.

"How many women have been taken? How many boys have been forced to join the Howlers? How many of our resources have they pillaged from us? Do I need to remind you that my daughter's blood still stains the steps outside this building? You had to walk over them just to enter." Elyn's voice is beginning to gain strength. "The men who believe that everything we are doing for the Howlers is working, are men who have not lost a loved one to those horrid beasts. How much more do we have to endure?"

The room is silent. Eerily silent as we all consider Elyn's words. Her eyes lock on me, and she gives me a sad smile.

"Whatever you have planned, Lukan, I want to be part of it," Elyn states with an intensity in her eyes that reminds me of Merritt. With a smile, I nod in agreement.

I am surprised when some of the men in the crowd begin to stand.

"So do I," Mr. Cragston agrees loudly.

"Me too. I have a little practice with a bow. Maybe I can help," Mr. Carmichel states.

"I've always wanted to learn how to use a bow, Lukan."

"Count me in."

"I'm with you."

One-by-one, several of the men of Grayson stand and declare their willingness to train and attempt to defeat the Howlers. I am surprised by the intensity and eagerness in their eyes. Suddenly, I am struck with a swell of pride for my fellow citizens.

All of this because of Elyn. I look toward the doors and am surprised to see that she has gone. Obviously, she said what she felt needed to be said, and then slipped out the door. I make a mental note to stop in and speak with her soon.

"You are all idiots. You're going to get us killed," an elderly man yells before hobbling out of the room. Several other naysayers join him in his exit.

Looking around the room, I realize that there are more people leaving than there are staying. My confidence level begins to shrink as I look at the faces of the men that have remained. All stare at me with eagerness, and I suddenly feel the weight of the responsibility for their lives.

Sensing my sudden trepidation, my father leans in close and whispers in my ear, "These are good people. As are the ones who left. They will not let you down."

"I believe in them. I only doubt myself," I reply quietly. "I could be leading them to their death."

My father nods. "Perhaps. Or you could possibly be leading them to find their true potential in this world. There are warriors among us. They just have to be shown."

Chapter 10

Lia

The days passed by at an eerily slow pace. Moods inside Terra Convex were a strange mixture of anxiety and confusion. Enforcers were arresting fewer citizens now than when the Defiance first began.

In the past few weeks, several of those that had been arrested were released. They rejoined life in our underground world with permanent reminders of the torture they endured. The scars left behind, both mentally and physically, were meant to serve as a warning to the bearer and the observer. They were clear, painful messages from the government – "There is no limit to the pain we will inflict on the Defiance." The message echoed through the walls of Terra Convex silently.

The days after Harrison disappeared into the world above left me with guilty feelings of contentment. Although my very existence would not be possible without him, Harrison was never a father to me. Not once in my childhood, or Bellamira's, did he show love, compassion, or kindness. A lot of this is because of the ridiculous laws the government has placed over its citizens. Harrison was never shown love by his parents; therefore, he never knew how to show love to others.

The day that Harrison was exiled, I said those very words to Axel. He recounted with, "If that logic were true, then you would be unable to love. None of us would have the capacity to love."

I considered Axel's words. It did cause me to wonder how my mother, sister, and I were ever able to feel or show affection for others.

"I believe there is evil in some, and goodness in others. A place such as this, buried beneath the earth with no way of survival - other than what others allow you to have - is a natural breeding ground for those with the capacity to exhibit evil behavior." Axel explained when I didn't respond immediately. "You, on the other hand, are pure goodness."

I scoffed, "Ha. Pure goodness? I'm rebellious and nosey. I have no respect for authority." My voice cracked slightly as I added, "I've gotten people killed."

"Those people are not your responsibility, Lia. The weight of their deaths belongs on the shoulders of the government. Leadership ordered their punishment, and soon they will pay for their actions." Axel's eyes were narrowed. Clearly, he was going weary of this world.

Axel didn't have much to say about the actual moments of Harrison's exile. There wasn't much to say. The whole ordeal took less than half an hour. The most unnerving part of the exile was actually Matlok's role.

Since the Interrogators realized that Harrison had wrongly accused my mother of treason against the government, they had kept him in Solitary. That was his punishment for making Leadership look incompetent in the eyes of the citizens of Terra Convex. My mother was the first of many to be interrogated, beaten, and sentenced to a long drawn out death in the Isolation Chamber. The difference between my mother and the others that met the same fate as her is that there was never any evidence proving that she was a Defiance sympathizer. The rest were all either caught with Defiance propaganda, or they asked too many questions.

In order to exile Harrison, Matlok had to convince the Solitary Guards that he was being taken to the Isolation Chamber. This proved to be an easy task. The real risk came when Matlok had to escort Harrison from Solitary to the hatch door. These two places were at opposite ends of Terra Convex. They literally could not be further away from each other.

Luckily, the trek from Solitary to where Axel and Dalen waited at the hatch door went smoothly. Although it wasn't explained to Harrison along the long walk through Terra Convex, Axel said that it seemed that he had accepted his fate, whatever that may be. Matlok described the sneers Harrison received along the way. The citizens of Terra Convex were well aware of what he had done to end his government-issued marriage. As he passed by them, head down, eyes on the floor, he was forced to listen to the murmuring of his neighbors and co-workers. The revulsion that

Harrison felt as he made that long walk just added to the punishment he was marching towards.

Once at the hatch, Dalen placed a cloth over Harrison's eyes. Without any explanation, the hatch door was opened. Both Dalen and Axel stepped out of Terra Convex, with Harrison between them. Dalen led Harrison up the short concrete staircase and several yards into the surrounding forest. Harrison repeatedly asked their intent. Neither Dalen or Axel said a word or gave an explanation. Not until they led him to a spot they felt was far enough away from the hatch. They turned him in circles several times and then sat him on the ground.

Before they walked away, Dalen whispered in Harrison's ear to count to 100 before removing the cloth. Axel told me that Dalen had said more, but he hadn't heard what it was. I thought about asking Dalen but was struck with the thought that maybe he would not want anyone to know. Given Dalen's past relationship with my mother, I could respect his desire to make sure Harrison knew exactly what was about to transpire, and why.

When Axel and I had approached Dalen with the plan for exiling Harrison, he wept. For too many years, he had kept his love for my mother hidden. He had watched her grow from the young girl that he adored to the mother of two daughters. His love for her never fading.

Dalen made it clear that he wanted to become part of the Defiance. We gladly welcomed him into our group. I had feared that he could harbor some ill feelings towards me – daughter of Harrison. Instead, Dalen consoled me at the loss of both of my parents. He seemed to find a way to be near me, constantly ensuring that I was not regretting my decision. After spending a few days with Dalen, I began to get the sense that he was trying to be the father that Harrison had never been. The father that Dalen wished he could have been with my mother as his wife.

That first night, after Harrison's exile, my sister and I found time to be alone under the window. We clung to each other, sobbing. The tears that wet our faces were not for Harrison. They were for our mother.

This act felt like a productive step closer to finally being able to get some closure for the void that her loss left in our lives. Walking out of Terra Convex surrounded by my friends - my new family - will be the final stage.

Every girl needs her mother. I just wish I had realized that when I was younger. Thankfully, I have her journal. It was as if she knew that I would need her words even when she wasn't around to speak them to me. Equally valuable to me now is the strengthened bond I have with my sister.

In the days since the exile, Mira and I have spent more time together under the window. We could have created more damning parchments while sitting in her living quarters but we chose to do it here instead. Under the snow covered window. Axel had given us a lantern due to the darkness the snow caused in the room. It did nothing for the cold that filled the room, so we worked quickly.

It had started snowing heavily right before Harrison was sent out of our underground compound. Axel had relayed this to me with some hesitancy. Apparently, he felt that the snow only sealed Harrison's fate, and Axel was afraid that this information might cause me to feel regret. It did not.

Sitting on the cold floor now, across from my sister, the lantern glows brightly between us. Mira and I work diligently on the parchments that spew the truth regarding our government. We work quietly, lost in our thoughts, regrets, and fears.

"Why hasn't Axel cleared the windows since it started snowing?" Mira asks, breaking the silence that had engulfed us. "Won't that affect the power?"

I smile, pleased that my sister remembers the importance of Axel's responsibilities. "He will go out tomorrow, I believe. Dalen wants to wait until the storm passes. He doesn't want Axel to become disoriented in the whiteout." I explain with a shiver at the thought of Axel becoming lost in the snow.

We return to silence and are startled when the door opens. Relief spreads over me as I watch Darcy and Mac walk into the room. They are both carrying armloads of books. This is curious to me, but I don't have time to consider the purpose of the books because I am struck with fear and anger as I watch Abigail follow them in.

Jumping up, I demand, "What is this?"

As if he doesn't know what I'm asking, Mac sits his load of books onto the cold floor with a smile, and says, "Darcy had a fantastic idea. You want to tell her, Darcy?" Mac helps Darcy set her books on the floor.

"No. Not the books," I say through clenched teeth. Pointing at Abigail with a spiteful finger, I add, "Her. What is she doing here?"

"My husband invited me," Abigail explains with a coy smile. It is easy to see that she is pleased with my obvious disdain for her presence. I glare at her, and then at Mac.

"What have you done?" I hiss at Mac through clenched teeth. "You invited this..."

"Lia, you let me in when nobody wanted to trust me," Mira interrupts, attempting to calm the situation before I say more than can be forgiven.

"This is different," I begin. My finger wags in Abigail's direction. "More than anything, she wants us caught and condemned. She has always hated me."

"That's not true," Abigail retorts. "Well, I have always hated you...but I don't want the Defiance caught or condemned."

Mac, clearly exasperated with his wife, runs his hand over his face. "Abigail, please," he mutters. "Lia, listen. I invited Abigail because she does believe in what we are doing. She wants out, and she believes that the government is keeping us here. Abigail has every right to be part of the Defiance." Mac's voice is pleading. "Isn't that the reason for the Defiance? The reason we have been leaving parchments all over Terra

Convex? To get support from the community so that we can revolt against the government properly?"

I try to remain angry with him, but the words Mac uses causes me to snicker a bit. "Revolt against the government properly?" I repeat, trying to stifle my amusement. With a slight shake of my head and an obvious eye roll for Mac, I reply, "Yes, Mac. That is the goal. We need people to believe." Glancing over at Abigail, who still wears a snarky smile that makes my blood boil, I take a step towards her and add, "Don't mistake this gesture as anything other than respect for Mac. My desire to get my friends to the freedom that the land above us promises is much greater than my hatred for you."

Abigail's eyes narrow, but do not leave mine. It's obvious that she is considering a snarky retort. For whatever reason, she simply replies, "All I want is to get out of this tomb. If I have to endure your presence to make that happen, then that is exactly what I will do."

Even though I know that she is trying to provoke me, I can't help but admire the fire I see in her eyes.

With a nod of approval, I acknowledge, "Sounds like we want the same thing. Hopefully, we can do this without killing each other."

Lukan

"Bad weather coming," Mr. Jarvis says to me as I place firewood onto his hearth.

Every day, I stop by to see the old man. Dom and I do our best to check in on all the elderly people that live in town. Especially now that winter is upon us. We make sure they have enough food to eat, and wood to keep their fireplaces burning.

Usually, our town's fiddle player is pleasant. With his old age, comes failing eyesight. Making it difficult for him to string and tune his fiddles. I often visit him in order to help with those tasks. When I do, he shows his appreciation by playing some of his favorite tunes.

Today, however, Mr. Jarvis' mood is contrary. He sits in his ancient rocking chair with a scowl as his gray eyes watch me stack the firewood, and stoke the fire.

"Bad weather coming," he repeats grumpily as he shifts his position in the chair trying to get comfortable. "I can feel it. Bad weather."

"I can send Mrs. Klifton to see you. She can give you something for your pain." I reply.

"Won't help. These old bones don't do good when the weather turns sour." Mr. Jarvis pats his knees tenderly.

It's true the sky is beginning to darken. The clouds are filling with moisture, causing them to lower closer to the earth. Soon, they will begin to dump fluffy snow onto the land. Our first snowstorm of the season. Earlier than years past. I'm thankful that Dom and I were able to help get Grayson ready for winter. Even more thankful that we were able to help Helix gather the materials he needs to prepare the bows and arrows so that training can start when the storm passes.

My mind can't help but wander. I replay the strategy over again, trying to imagine the day that we surround the Howlers camp quietly. I imagine our small group of hastily trained men and women surrounding the camp as the Howlers sleep. On cue, arrows will be nocked, and bows will be pulled back to their maximum draw with two fingers. At the signal – which has yet to be determined – release. Each arrow will fly, and another hastily put in its place. Nock. Draw. Release.

Mr. Jarvis groans again, bringing my thoughts back to the task at hand. I glance over at the old man, and I feel pity.

"I hope, when you are an old man, there will be a nice young man to help you do the things your bones and joints won't let you do anymore," Mr. Jarvis comments.

"You're not that old, Mr. Jarvis. It's just the cold affecting your arthritis. I'll go get Mrs. Klifton. I'm sure she has something to help you."

Standing, I walk to his chair and help him get to the couch where he lays down with a groan.

As I cover Mr. Jarvis with a blanket, he says, "I'm 124. That is pretty old. I imagine I may be the oldest person alive."

I'm shocked at what he has just said. I thought Nyssa was the oldest person in Grayson. Now I'm learning that isn't the case. Mr. Jarvis, even with his graying eyes, arthritis, and withered skin, has always seemed much younger than 124 years old. He is always walking the streets, talking with his neighbors. I would have guessed his age to be closer to ninety.

"So, you were what? Early thirties when the Langston Virus hit?" I ask, attempting to hide my surprise.

"I had just turned 34." He answers matter-of-factly.

I am stunned. With so many questions coursing through my mind, I find it difficult to decide what to ask Mr. Jarvis first. I long to know all about the world before the Langston Virus. Before the death and devastation. Before the riots, looting, and mayhem that turned men into Howlers.

Mr. Jarvis grumbles something under his breath, and I realize that now is not the time for questions. Now, the old man needs to rest. Standing to leave, and give Mr. Jarvis peace and quiet, he stops me with a strange comment.

"When I was a young man, folks had a lifespan of about 80 years. I have outlived that by nearly 45 years." His eyes are closed as if he is trying to fall asleep. "Why do you think that is, Lukan? Why do you think people live longer now than they did when there was medicine to heal them and luxuries to please them?"

I had never thought about this. There have been many elderly people in Grayson die well after their one-hundredth birthday. As a community, we have tremendous respect for the elderly, celebrating their lives with feasts and gifts. During the brutal months of winter, it is the elderly that we worry about the most. We visit them often to ensure that they have everything they need to live comfortably.

"I have a theory," Mr. Jarvis says when I do not answer. Looking back at him, I see that his gray eyes are staring into mine. "I have a theory that the world reset itself with the virus."

"Reset itself?" I ask, trying to understand.

"Before the virus, we were a people filled with greed and contempt. We raped, stole, murdered. We had grown lazy and ignorant – relying only on computers to link us with other humans. Our water and land had become poisoned by our own hands. We had lost all respect for the earth, for others, and for ourselves." His voice wavered slightly as his aging mind seemed to replay a memory from his past.

I couldn't help but see the similarities to the Howlers. The raping, stealing, murdering. Laziness. Ignorance. All attributes of the madmen that terrorize us. The parallels sent a chill up my spine.

"Sounds familiar, doesn't it?" Mr. Jarvis asks, sensing my thoughts.

I can only nod.

"Before the Langston Virus, people heavily on medicines. Not medicine like what Mrs. Klifton gives us. No. These were created with harsh chemicals in sterile rooms called laboratories. It was almost as if we couldn't live without them. We used these medicines for everything. From baldness to cancer. From sleep aids to sleep deterrents. Not just in our medicines, but in everything that we consumed there were man-made chemicals. Nothing was natural anymore. None of the things that our bodies needed for survival were created by the land. Why? Because even the land was poisoned with the chemicals created by man. What had been created to give us quality of life, actually took life from us."

I had never heard Mr. Jarvis say so much. Never had he spoken of life before the virus. My mind is swirling with the new information. I have so many questions, but it's obvious that the pain from his aging joints has taken its toll on him. His eyes are closed again. I stare at him for a long time, replaying what he has told me. Quietly, I go to the rocking chair and sit. I know I should leave the old man to sleep peacefully. Still, for some reason, I just don't want to leave him here alone. Rocking quietly, I watch him sleep.

After a few minutes, Mr. Jarvis opens his eyes groggily and continues, "That's why people live longer today. That's why you will live longer. The earth has finally rid herself of the nastiness that we had created long ago. She is fresh and natural again. Reborn. Her gift to us is longer life." His eyes find mine across the room and beckon me. I walk to him and sit down on the floor once again. "Lukan, don't abuse the gift you have been given by the earth. She is the only one you will get. Take care of her."

Chapter 11

Lia

As it turns out, Darcy's 'fantastic idea' really was quite clever. For days, our restless group of revolutionaries crafted what we considered the perfect weapon against the Leadership. Not only did Darcy come up with the idea for the weapons but after much discussion, we came up with a plan of attack.

The plan was the most terrifying piece of the war against the government. It would take effort on the part of all of us committed to the Defiance. The books would play a critical role in our ultimate freedom or demise.

"Books," Axel had said with an obvious hint of doubt in his voice. He held a book in his hand, turning it over in his hand, trying to make sense of Darcy's explanation.

Darcy's face was bright with excitement as she explained it to Axel. "Think about it. Enforcers are looking for parchments. We have used that method for so long that's all they know. If they see a book, they won't think that laying inside of it, is the propaganda we have created."

Still holding the book, Axel opens the cover dubiously. He glances over at me, trying to understand. "So, we are going to fold up the parchments, place them in the books, and hope that people pick up the book?"

The excitement on Darcy's face falls. "Well, when you say it like that, it sounds a little pointless."

Mac, and I - along with our newest rebels, Mira, Dalen and Abigail – watched the exchange between Axel and Darcy. We could see the disappointment on her face as she realized that there really wasn't much difference between leaving parchments in plain sight or inside of books.

"I just wanted to help," Darcy said with sadness. "I thought it would be neat to hide information inside the books."

Axel turned the book over in his hand again. Opened it. Thumbed through it. I sat on the floor watching him, knowing that his mind was working on a good use of the books. I couldn't help but smile as he took two steps to the pipes, and leaned against them thoughtfully.

"If only we had something a little more...incriminating," Axel muttered, almost to himself.

"Incriminating?" Mac asked, trying to understand.

"It's fine to leave the parchments laying around randomly throughout Terra Convex, but these books should be used for something more." Axel pulled an object out of the back pocket of his uniform.

"What's that?" I asked. I assumed it was a tool of some sort, but it had a sharp tip that was intimidating.

"This is a knife,"Axel explained. "It is very sharp. It helps cut things that cannot be torn with just my hands."

With that, Axel plunged the tip of the knife into the open book. I heard an audible gasp escape Darcy. Axel worked the knife through the pages of the book for several minutes. Paper from the book began to fall to the ground, littering the floor around Axel's feet, and causing Darcy to pace the room. As I watched, I knew exactly what Axel was doing. I wondered if my mother had used the same method when she crafted the book that concealed her journal. Wondered if she had used a knife.

As Guardian of the Histories, Darcy's appreciation for books is much stronger than the rest of our group. It's clear to everyone watching that Axel is hollowing out the book, in turn causing great distress to Darcy. Standing, I approached my friend, and put my arm around her shoulders in an attempt to alleviate her nerves as she watches in horror.

When finished, Axel turned the book for everyone in the room to see. As I suspected, Axel had hollowed out a perfect rectangle in the middle of the book. A perfect hiding spot for anything that needed to be smuggled through the corridors of Terra Convex. The question was, what did Axel plan on smuggling?

Darcy gasped and placed a hand over her mouth. With wide eyes, she stammered, "You destroyed it. That was a classic. Probably the last one on earth."

Axel looked at the damage he had done to the book. "That may be true, Darcy, but look..." Axel closed the book and handed it to Darcy.

Turning the book over in her hands, it looked as if it were intact. I could see her begin to marvel at the possibilities.

"What are you thinking, Axel?" I asked, attempting to steer Darcy's anxiety away from the damaged classic, and back onto a plan of escape.

"We can use these books to sneak information to the people of Terra Convex. The Enforcers will never know. Just like your idea, Darcy." It was obvious that Axel was still formulating a plan. Still, the idea had our mind's spinning with possibilities.

"That's a lot of work for propaganda," Dalen stated. "What we're doing already is working just fine."

"Dalen's right," I agreed. "It would be great for something more dangerous."

"But what?" Darcy inquired, holding the book to her chest.

We all sat in silence as we contemplated what would be more dangerous than the parchments we were already leaving all around Terra Convex.

"If only we could get our hands on the journals," Abigail said to nobody in particular.

As one, we all turned towards Abigail, hoping she would elaborate. Instead, she sat next to Mac picking at a fingernail that was somehow annoying her.

"Journals?" Mac finally asked his wife.

Abigail looked up from her fingernail and realized we were all staring at her. Instantly, a look of discomfort crossed over her face. For somebody that had always wanted to be the center of attention, she certainly didn't seem to want it now.

"Um, yeah, apparently there are secret journals in the President's Quarters. They are the true histories of Terra Convex," Abigail explained with a hint of nervousness in her voice.

My mind began to spin with the possibilities. The true histories of Terra Convex could prove invaluable for the cause. They could reveal the true nature of the government.

I glanced around the room. Everyone was staring at me. Their eyes wide with anticipation and apprehension. I could feel the weight of their expectations on my shoulders. I had found the window; had been the first to communicate with the outside world. Because of that, they looked to me as the leader of their rebellion. It was almost more than I could bear.

"Well, we have to get those journals," I acknowledged with as much confidence as I could muster.

"That's impossible," Abigail coughed out with a shrill chuckle, obviously appalled at the thought. "You could never get anywhere near the President's Quarters. Nobody can. It's guarded day and night."

I looked at Axel, trying to gauge his reaction to this new information. His dark eyes gazed into mine as he shook his head ever so slightly. It was obvious he knew what was going to happen now that I knew there were journals. Journals that could change the whole Defiance.

"Why would you bring up the journals if you knew we couldn't get to them?" Axel asked Abigail with annoyance.

Abigail said nothing. With a huff and a shrug, she crossed her arms over her chest.

"We have to get those journals," I implored the group. "There has to be a way." Turning my attention to Mira, I said, "Could Matlok get on the security team for the President's Quarters?"

Mira was surprised that I would ask. With wide eyes, she shook her head slowly. Her mouth opened and closed as if she were trying to say something. "I-I-I'm not sure," she finally managed.

I looked my sister in the eye and calmly explained, "Everyone has a job to do. Your job could be to convince Matlok to join that security team."

"Don't guilt her into that," Abigail objected.

Abigail opened her mouth to say more, but before she could, I stopped her. "Everyone has a job to do, Abigail, and you just did yours by telling us about the journals. Thank you for your service. You may go now."

"Matlok is tired of all the lies from Leadership. I think he would do what needs to be done," Mira said quickly, trying to diffuse the situation between Abigail and me.

"I've been thinking," Mac said, "we don't need the journals. If we could get into the President's Quarters, we could just steal the code to the hatch door and leave. I don't think the Enforcers would risk going outside to get us. Then, maybe others would leave too."

"Why do you have to steal the code?" Abigail asked. "We could all just be ready the next time he opens the door for Axel to go out, and clean the windows." She pointed at Dalen, and then to Axel, and then added with more snarkiness than I could tolerate, "I mean, since we all have jobs to do."

Every word that Abigail spoke made me want to ram my fist into her nose, and laugh as blood poured down into her mouth. I had envisioned that so many times in my life, and now she was right here in my secret room. Although I didn't want to be the one in charge, I felt like I was the right one to teach Abigail a lesson in manners.

"Actually, the code isn't going to be much use anymore," Dalen commented.

He had our attention, and my ire towards Abigail was set aside for the time being.

"What do you mean?" Axel asked.

"The order came down today – no one will be going outside of Terra Convex until further notice," Dalen explained. "I think that Leadership is feeling nervous about the Defiance."

"They think people are going to try to escape out the hatch," Mac mused. "Do you think they suspect you are part of the rebellion?" he asked Dalen.

"I don't think so," Dalen answered. "I don't think they trust anyone."

"What about the power? If we can't go out to clean the snow and debris off the windows, Terra Convex will lose power." Axel's eyes were wide with worry.

"They would rather risk everyone's death than admit that they have been lying to their people for ninety years," I pondered aloud.

The room was quiet as we all considered what this new information meant for Terra Convex and the Defiance.

"We have no choice," I began calmly. "We have to do this. We have to find those journals."

"And do what with them?" Mac asked. "Even if we find them, without the code, we can't get anyone out of Terra Convex."

"With the journals, we can convince the citizens of Tera Convex to join us," I explained.

"Okay. Then what?" Dalen questioned. His face conveyed that he is willing to take the Defiance to the next level of rebellion.

"Then, we fight. All of us. We destroy the government." Axel answered as if reading my mind.

With that, the war on President DePriest, and the Leadership began. All because of a stack of books.

Of course, I wanted to be the one that snuck into the President's Quarters. I wanted to be the one that revealed their secrets and their lies. I felt like it should be me. If not for me, these people would not be sitting here staring at me, waiting for answers and direction. If not for me, my mother would still be alive.

We all have jobs to do. Breaking into the President's Quarters should be mine.

I began to imagine the moment that I had the journals in my hands. Imagine sneaking past security. Grinning at the thought of outsmarting the brutes that guarded the president.

"Not you," Axel stated bluntly with a look on his face that told me that there would be no arguing with him. His mind was made up.

Although his response angered me – he should know that I have never taken well to being told what I can and cannot do – I managed to plaster a tender and gracious smile on my face. I approached him, placing my hands on his arms, and gazed up into his dark eyes. I made sure not to let my eyes wander to his dimple, and become distracted with Axel's rugged handsomeness.

"It's sweet that you are worried about my safety. I love you for wanting to keep me safe." Standing up on my toes, I tried to reach him for a kiss. Expecting him to lean down, and grant me the kiss I am initiating, I am surprised when he only stares into my eyes. It was obvious my tactic wasn't going to work on him. Stepping away from him, I cross my arms over my chest. "I'm going. That's the end of the discussion."

"I do want you to be safe," Axel replied slowly, without taking his intense eyes from mine. "But this isn't about keeping you safe."

"What is it then?" I asked, confused.

"You're being watched," Mira explained from her seated position on the floor. "We both are. Because of our parents."

"She's right. If either of you gets anywhere near the President, you will be taken straight to the Isolation Chamber." This time, Axel put his hands on my arms. Unlike when I did the same to him, his gesture is genuine. Looking up at him, I can see that his eyes have softened. He may say that it isn't about keeping me safe, but I believe that it is.

"Leadership already knows your feelings about the president. You two made that pretty clear with your essay," Mira explained further, referring to the essay that Axel and I had written the year prior when we were working on a project for class. Our words landed me in Solitary, and Axel sentenced to the lonely life of a Roughneck. "It can't be you, Lia."

Mira was right. I knew she was right. I just didn't want to concede. If it couldn't be me that broke into the presidential quarters, then who? I looked around the tiny room. An uneasiness spread over me as I realized that I would have to ask one of these people to do something that could cost them their life. With big eyes, they all stared back at me, waiting for me to give them some guidance. I could feel the weight of their expectations on me, and it was almost more than I could bear. All I could do was shrink down to the floor, and place my head in my hands, trying to clear my thoughts. I needed to find a way to do this without involving any of these people.

"Let me do it," I hear Mac speak up, followed by a gasp from Abigail.

"No. No, I won't allow it," Abigail interjects.

Mac ignored his mate, and continued, "Abigail can get me the directions to the President's Quarters because her dad is on the council." This brought on even more argument from Abigail. "I can be in and out quickly, and nobody will suspect me. I'm sure all the journals from the past ninety years are together. I will grab as many as possible." As Mac spoke, Abigail realized she was fighting a losing battle and snapped her mouth shut. "We can tear out the most incriminating pages, and hide them in the hollowed out books. Then, we can leave the books lying around Terra Convex for the citizens to find."

The room was filled with silence as we all considered Mac's ideas. So much risk. Mac made it sound like a simple task that he could complete during his mealtime. We all knew that wasn't the case.

"That's too much to ask," I said after awhile. "You have a new wife to think about."

"Don't you put this on me," Abigail snapped at me.

Ignoring her, I continued, "I can't ask anyone to do something so dangerous. I don't expect anyone to want to do this. It has to be me."

"We all have a job to do," Mac repeated my words. "This job should be mine. I don't have a lot to offer the group. Let me do it."

I felt my throat closing up. Mac had been my best friend since we were kids. We had grown up together. Me hiding my curiosity; Mac hiding his art. I couldn't bear to think about what would happen if we were to get caught stealing from the president. I bury my face in my hands again.

I feel Axel's arm wrap around my waist and his face in my hair. In my ear, he said softly, "You can't carry all the risk, Lia. I know you feel like you need to be the one to run into danger. It doesn't have to be you. Not all the time." Axel then placed a tender kiss on the side of my face, and I leaned into him, hoping to garner some of his strength.

With a nod, I relent. "Okay, Mac. Let's go over your plan again. Anybody with anything to add, please jump in," I say calmly even though my gut was in turmoil.

Abigail released an exasperated huff, obviously frustrated that Mac will be risking his life for this group that she has barely become a part of.

"Your disapproval has been noted," I commented without looking at her.

Lukan

The storm came barreling over Grayson with a fury, and refused to relent for six long, dark days. The first storm of the season is always the most difficult, and most dreaded. Although this one is particularly brutal, it is an ideal chance to learn what must be done to prepare for the storms that are yet to come this winter.

Dom and I, along with several of the men in town, trudged through the wind and snow to check in on the elderly and widows. The town calls us the Guardians. It had been decided before the storm who would go to which homes. Each street had somebody that would make rounds, checking on the neighborhood. On our street, I walked east toward the entrance of town; Dom walked west towards the woods. We would bring in firewood and stoke the fires for the elderly, and ensure that everyone had adequate food and water. Probably one of the most important things we would do, though, was simply spending time with them.

The winter months can be brutal in many ways. Not just the cold but also the loneliness and darkness. It has proven to be too much for some. Too many times, a Guardian has walked into a home occupied by the corpse of a citizen that just couldn't handle the dark days of winter. It was difficult to explain to the townspeople that their neighbor had chosen to take their own life because of the loneliness that winter brings. It had been decided that not only will we, as Guardians, ensure the citizens of Grayson have adequate food, water, and heat; but also companionship. After a few winters with this new mindset, less self-inflicted deaths occurred. Sometimes, all any of us would do is simply sit. The lonely didn't necessarily need somebody to talk to; they just needed another heartbeat in the room with them.

This winter already seemed different than ones in the past. Grayson has a different mindset. Although the weather is much too brutal to spend time training for the wrath we hope to unleash on the Howlers, those in agreement with the plan of attack are in their homes with their new bows and quivers of arrows.

Before the storm arrived, Helix and several men gathered the materials needed to build the bows and arrows. With that task complete, he instructed them on how to construct the weapons with their freshly gathered materials.

Word spread through town that the blind Wanderer was in the Community Building constructing weapons from woodland materials. Even those that disagreed with our plan came to see this feat. They didn't voice their displeasure as they did during the attack plan meeting. Rather, they stood in awe of the blind man's ability to create something from nothing.

Once the weapons were crafted, with the storm nearly upon us, everyone that was willing to join the fight against the Howlers was given a bow, and a quiver full of arrows. They were told to spend the time during the storm to get to know their weapons.

"Pull the string back without releasing it. Do this over and over. You will have to build the muscles in your arms to properly shoot your bow repeatedly. By the time the storm passes, you will be ready to begin archery lessons," Helix advises the group as they examined their weapons.

As the storm nears its end, I find myself anxious to begin training for the attack on the Howlers. Find that I am eager to spend time outdoors. The walls of my home seemed to be closing in around me. The ground is still covered with thick snow, but the sky is clear and blue. The past few days have gone by slowly. With every passing minute indoors, I could feel myself begin to go mad.

Standing in my house, staring out through the large window in our family room, I think I see something out of the corner of my eye. Something out in the whiteness of winter. Something that doesn't belong but somehow does. In all the white, I think saw...

Dark hair with wisps of red...blowing in the breeze.

I have only ever known one person to have hair that color...but she is dead.

Squinting, I try to focus my eye, but only see snow. Perhaps, I have been confined to these walls for too long, I consider. I decide to go outside to get some fresh air. Turning towards the sound of my parents laughing, I realize that my mother is setting the table for an early dinner. My father follows her, telling her a story that I'm sure she has heard before but still finds amusing. I smile at their subtle affections toward each other.

"I'm going out," I announce as I begin putting on the thick fur coat that Helix made for me. I still marvel at the craftsmanship of the garment, and the blind man's ability to create without sight.

"Dinner is nearly ready. Don't be gone too long." I hear my mother say in her melodic voice.

"Yes, ma'am," I reply, shutting the door behind me before the cold invades.

Once outside, I stand on the front porch scanning the area that had caught my attention earlier. There is nobody there of course. The streets of Grayson are empty as the evening begins to overtake the day. I watch as the wind picks up, carrying comes. Then, I look in the direction of the caves that I look forward to revisiting. I imagine Mrs. Klifton will need me to scavenge the plants and herbs once the thaw is complete, and the spring flowers begin to emerge. I sit in the spot for some time before I remember that my mom had said dinner was almost ready. My empty belly reminds me that I need to eat. Standing, I turn and step back over the wall.

"Lukan."

The voice halts me. Still distant, it sounds almost as if it is back in town. I begin running towards the Community Building, certain that I am losing my mind. I wouldn't be the first to have found madness while trying to survive winter.

As I run, I see Helix ahead. He seems to be out for a casual pre-dusk stroll. Even in his blindness, he knows that I am approaching. He stops. Alert. Slightly alarmed.

"Did you hear her?" I ask breathlessly. Helix's sense of hearing is much keener than even mine. Living most of his life without sight, his other senses have become much more acute.

"Who?" Helix asks with obvious confusion.

I shake my head. Agitated by the whole ordeal. "I don't know. I thought I heard...." My voice trails off. A thought occurs to me. I remember now who the voice belongs to.

It can't be, though. Merritt's dead. Murdered by Gallner.

"Heard what, Lukan?" Helix asks with compassion.

Realizing that my mental state is indeed becoming affected by the snow, I shake my head. The first storm of the season and I am already losing my mind. Too many people are counting on me for that to happen.

"Nothing, Helix," I answer sorrowfully. "I think I just needed to get outside."

Helix tilts his head to the side as if he is trying to decide if I am being truthful. Although I cannot see the worry in his non-existent eyes, his mouth is open slightly as he tries to decide if I am truly okay.

Changing the subject, I add, "My mom made ham and beans for dinner. Come eat with us."

It takes only a second for him to consider this. I can see that he is still concerned. Finally, though, he smiles. "Will there be cornbread?"

I smile at this. Although I know he is worried about me, he knows not to tary on the subject. "Yes. Fresh cornbread."

Helix moans from deep in his belly, and we begin to walk toward my home. As we walk, I glance over my shoulder towards the Community building. In the distance, I think I see it again.

Brown hair with wisps of red flowing in the cold breeze.

Chapter 12

Lia

Across from me, I hear Mac clear his throat. I look up to see him staring at me. His look tells me that he is ready to proceed with the incredibly dangerous plan. I nod and look at Axel. I know he will give me the strength I need for what is to happen next. Axel returns my look with a confident smile. The hand that he has resting comfortably on my knee under the table squeezes slightly. The most surprising thing that Axel does is lean over and kiss me softly on the cheek. I lean into him slightly. His touch comforts me and gives me just enough bravery to move forward with the plan.

"If we're going to do this, I need to be gone before Abigail gets in here," Mac says quietly, interrupting the intimate moment between Axel and me.

The day I have dreaded has arrived. This could be the day that we finally get our hands on the damaging words of our leadership – the words that turn all of Terra Convex into the Defiance. Or, this could also be the day that Mac loses his life *for* the Defiance. I shiver as I consider the possibilities.

We have spent the past two weeks hollowing out books and rehearsing the plan to steal the journals. If it were up to me, I would delay just a little longer. Would spend just a little more time under the window with Mac. that just isn't possible, though. There is no longer time for sitting under the window, daydreaming. Time has become our biggest enemy.

Two days ago, Dalen and Axel explained to us just how dire our situation is. Because Leadership will no longer allow the Roughnecks to exit Terra Convex to clear the debris, crucial systems in the compound would soon begin to shut down. Without the power provided by the sun, the air filtration system, along with the water filtration system, would surely fail.

"How long? How long do we have?" Darcy asked with a hint of panic in her voice.

"We're okay for now. We probably have a month. Maybe two," Dalen answered.

"The air will be fine. What most do not know is that we are actually breathing outside air. It's pure. However, when circulation fans fail, we will begin to breathe in too much of the carbon dioxide that we expel. We will essentially begin to suffocate in here." Axel explained.

A shiver snaked its way up my spine. Without proper air circulation, Terra Convex would literally become a tomb.

"And the water?" I managed to ask through the fear that was rising up into my throat.

"The water comes from two different wells that are underneath the compound," Dalen began. "It goes through filtration that is powered by the solar panels – the windows. Without the power they provide, the water will not go through the filtration process. We will be drinking foul, contaminated water."

Silence engulfed us as we each thought about the ramifications of the debris-cluttered windows.

"Okay, so all this means is that we need to move forward with the plan to break into the president's quarters. Not only will I get the journals but I will get the codes he has assigned to the hatch. We will get out of here with the codes. We'll leave the journals for anyone that wants to follow." Mac's voice was full of confidence. He had fully embraced the dangerous task he had volunteered to do.

"We can't just leave," Dalen sighed.

"Why not?" Mira asked.

"It's freezing outside. We aren't prepared to be outside during winter." Dalen explained kindly.

There was murmuring all around me as I rubbed my hands over my face attempting to clear my thinking enough to gain a course of action against this new problem. I could hear Mira and Abigail complaining to each other. Mac and Darcy were attempting to calm them. Dalen and Axel simply watched and listened. Although I didn't want to rush Mac into harm's way, I knew we must act fast.

"This changes nothing," I announced reluctantly. "We will move forward with the plan. We will just have to do it a little sooner."

"But if we can't leave, why do we need to risk Mac's life?" Abigail asked. Although she still didn't seem like part of our group, I was at least thankful that Mac had another person in his life that seemed to care for him.

"If Mac can get the codes, Axel can get outside to clear off the windows, buying us more time. That will get us through the winter. With the journals, we can persuade the rest of the community to revolt, and overthrow the government. That will give us a winter of peace." I paused, and then added, "I hope."

"You hope?" Abigail's already shrill voice turned to ice. "You hope? You're risking his life on hope?"

I wanted to leap across the small space, and ram my fist through Abigail's too perfect nose. In my mind, I felt like even though the group would be slightly disappointed in my slight lack of self-control, they would find me justified in my actions.

Instead, I took a deep breath, and calmly said, "Yes, Abigail. In spite of all the hurt I have had to endure – in spite of the darkness of this underground world – I have hope. Hope is the only thing stronger than fear."

"Lia, I need to go before Abigail gets in here," Mac says once again, bringing my wandering mind back to him and Axel sitting with me in the Dining Hall.

With the impending doom of Terra Convex, the plan had to be put together quickly. Too quickly for Matlok – who was indeed eager to join the Defiance, as it turns out – to be transferred from civilian Enforcer to

Presidential Security Detail. We still felt like we could put together an effective distraction for Mac to sneak into the President's Quarters.

"I actually know one of the men on the detail," Matlok explained. "Not well, but good enough to approach him."

"Approach him?" I questioned.

"Sure. I will simply walk up to them, and distract them with tons of questions about their job, and the process for me to transfer." Matlok was smiling as he explained his incredibly simple plan.

I could only stare at him. As grateful as I was to have him on our side, willing to aid our rebellion, I just couldn't see how his plan would work. Before I could think of a proper argument, though, Axel spoke up.

"That is actually just crazy enough to work," Axel commended.

"Are you serious?" I asked before I could stop myself. Realizing my rudeness, I continued, "Matlok, I appreciate your effort, but that just seems a bit too obvious."

"Exactly! That's why it's such a great idea. They would never think that an Enforcer would be willing to assist a rebel. Those guys are all ego. They love to talk about themselves. If I get them talking, they won't pay attention to anything going on around them." Matlok was certain that this would work.

Axel agreed with a huge grin, and I could tell that he was envious of Matlok's job in the Defiance. Begrudgingly, I agreed also, and that part of the plan fell into place.

As a group, we felt like we had worked out every detail of the plan. Because Abigail continued to voice her disapproval of Mac's involvement, it was decided that she would be left out of one important detail – the day and time that the plan was to be put into motion.

Today is that day and the time is now. Glancing over at Matlok and Bellamira where they sit quietly, eating their meal, I catch Matlok's eye and give a subtle nod. He returns my nod and leans over to give his wife a kiss on the cheek. After he whispers something in her ear, he stands to leave. Mac, Axel and I pretend like we are focused on our meal and not watching Matlok as he exits the Dining Hall.

The plan is now set into motion. Without any way to contact Matlok, there is no way to undo anything that transpires from this point forward. I feel my throat begin to tighten at the possibilities.

Once he is gone, I glance over at my sister again. She is watching me with wide, anxious eyes. I give her a small smile, hoping that she will see confidence in the gesture and not the true terror that I feel in my chest.

Across from me, I feel Mac's eyes on me. I expect him to look frightened. I expect him to change his mind and decide that he doesn't really want this incredibly dangerous job. Truthfully, I wish he would realize that he shouldn't do this. It should be me.

"Mac, listen," I start. More than anything, I want to keep him at this table with Axel and me.

"I'll see you in a bit. Okay, Lia?" Mac cuts me off with a smile and a wink.

Before I can object, my best friend from childhood stands and walks away from the Dining Hall, leaving me there with a sinking feeling in my belly.

Lukan

Like all storms, the first one of the winter passed. One morning, the sun decided it was its turn once again. It climbed high into the sky, shining down on the land with intense brilliance. The temperature soared, and the snow began to melt.

All of the town's children began to say their goodbyes to the snowmen they had created. Some cried over their loss. As the snow turned to mud, however, their spirits lifted. Soon, they were busy creating mud pies and driving their mother's crazy by tracking mud into their homes.

The men took this time to inspect their homes and outbuildings for any snow-related damage. It appeared that most of Grayson managed to come through the first storm of the season unscathed. This was a relief as it was time to begin training.

Targets had been built and placed outside of town. Near the woods where the car graveyard lies, now stands a line of targets made of straw. We decided to place the training area in this part of Grayson because the Howlers never approach from this direction.

The men seemed eager, excited even, to begin. They had also grown bored while waiting out the storm. Helix, Dom, and I spent the first day just showing them how to hold the bow properly, nock the arrow, and pull it back without allowing it to slip. It was obvious that they had used their time during the storm to become acquainted with their weapon.

As I watched the group of about eighty, I had a strange combination of anxiety and pride. It didn't seem to be enough to conquer the Howlers. Yet, it seemed like the perfect number. There were not only men but also women who were eager to join the fight. The youngest of the outfit was twelve years old. The oldest, ninety-seven – who, surprisingly, had no difficulty pulling the bow back.

Hopefully, those that were adamantly against the plan of attack would see the benefit of at least learning the weapon. Perhaps, then they would see its worth. If anything were to happen to Dom or me, others would have to be able to hunt for the community.

Since there were so many willing to train and fight, we staggered them. We trained twenty at a time. There was still work to be done for Grayson, so while those were training, others were taking their turn at chores around Grayson. Husbands and wives that wanted to fight together, took turns training and staying home with the children.

This went on for some time. Day after day of relentless whooshing and thwacking as the arrows were released and found their mark. The group became quite good in a short amount of time.

"They are calling themselves, Kismet," Dom announced at dinner one evening.

"Kismet? What is a kismet?" I asked after swallowing a bite of food.

"It means fate," Helix explained. He had been joining us for dinner on most evenings. Even though he has proven quite capable of taking care of himself, my mother insists on feeding him every chance she gets. "Apparently, your army believes they are the Howler's fate." With a proud smile, Helix adds, "That is encouraging."

I consider the meaning behind the name. "Kismet," I repeat. "I like it. Who came up with it?"

"Elvin," Dom answers.

Elvin is the oldest in the outfit. At 97, he was only seven when the Langston Virus took his family. He was on the run for many months. Sometimes with a group. Sometimes all alone. Finally ending up in a survivor's camp of some sort. He has said that although it was called a survivor's camp, it was a gruesome place of death. As a child, he was forced into a life of torment and oppression at the hands of the camp guards. His only relief was that there was an extensive library at the camp where he spent his free time, learning and studying – and retreating into other worlds in his imagination. Elvin has endured a lot in his life. It makes sense that he is willing to fight the Howlers.

"Kismet," I say again. "The fate of the Howlers."

Chapter 13

Lia

"Attention citizens of Terra Convex – Your continued support and unfailing loyalty to the Leadership of Terra Convex has not gone unnoticed. Although there have been attempts to tear our community apart, you have stayed true. Even while the Defiance littered our sanctuary with deceit, your allegiance never faltered. Because you have shown integrity while faced with diabolical actions of rebels, I – your president – would like everyone to attend a celebration. I have ordered tomorrow to be a Free Day. No work or classes – only celebrating. So, gather your families together and meet me and the rest of the Leadership in the Grand Hall. There will be Enforcers available in every corridor to ensure you find your way. Once again, thank you for your continued support."

*****

The secret room is tiny, making it difficult to pace out my anxiety and dread. It's been six hours since Mac left Axel and I sitting in the Dining Hall. Two hours since President DePriest announced that tomorrow is Free Day, complete with a celebration.

Never in my life have I heard of any place in Terra Convex called the Grand Hall. Never has there been a celebration of any sort. The announcement by the president seemed too informal. Even though I tried not to read too much into his voice, he sounded almost giddy. I have no doubt that Mac's delay in returning to the window and the announcement are related. Pacing does nothing to ease my nerves.

The door to the room swings open, slamming into the wall. Before I can react, Abigail rushes into me, shoving me into the pipes behind me. Pain from the impact shoots down into my legs nearly causing them to buckle. Distracted by the pain in my back, I don't realize until its too late that Abigail has her hands on my throat. She is screaming something in my face, but I am too stunned to comprehend her words.

Abigail's face is wild with fury. Her hair, greasy from lack of showering, sits heavily on her shoulders. Her breath is putrid and hot as she spews hatefulness at me in the form of words and occasional spittle.

"This is on you," Abigail screams, squeezing my throat with her tiny hands. "You got him killed. You did this."

The pain in my back subsides enough that I realize that Abigail is actually trying to strangle me. I grab onto her hands and begin to wrench them away from my throat. Even though she is tiny, she is much stronger than I ever imagined. Or maybe it is just her anger that fuels her strength.

I'm thankful when I see Dalen rush into the room, closing the door behind him. Apparently, he could hear Abigail's screams. I feel Abigail's hands release my throat as Dalen pulls her off of me. She kicks at me, continuing to cry. With no regard for Abigail's well-being, Dalen tosses her into the corner and turns his attention to me.

"Are you okay, Amelia?" Dalen asks, helping me off of the pipes.

Still trying to catch my breath, I simply nod, rubbing at my throat.

Sobbing, Abigail murmurs, "You sent Maclin to his death. You did this."

Although my fear was that he had been caught, I had hoped that Mac's delay in coming here, to our secret place, meant something else entirely. I tried to imagine that he had simply gone to his living quarters after breaking into the president's quarters. Abigail's emotional state all but confirms my worst fears.

Dalen stands on guard between Abigail and me. Waiting to jump in again if needed.

Slowly, I sink to the cold floor. I do not take my eyes off of Abigail. Hot tears threaten as I consider what Mac is most likely enduring at this moment.

All because of me.

The door opens once again. This time, Axel enters the room. Seeing me on the floor, and Dalen's protective stance, Axel rushes to me.

"Lia?" Axel whispers.

"Of course," Abigail spits out. "I'm the widow but go ahead and comfort her."

Ignoring Abigail, Axel questions, "Mac hasn't returned yet?"

All I can do is shake my head.

"We don't know that he's dead," Axel says, turning towards Abigail. "We don't know that he has even been caught." Returning his attention back to me, he adds, "I'm sure he's just laying low somewhere."

Looking deep into his eyes, I ask, "Are you sure, Axel? I mean, are you really sure?" There is a bite in my voice. I know he is only saying the words he thinks will make me feel better.

His eyes betray him. He cannot hold my gaze. Averting his eyes, he quietly admits, "No, Lia. I'm not really sure. I'm just hopeful."

The door opens once again. Mira and Darcy come through, with Matlok following behind. As soon as I see Matlok, I jump up and rush to him.

"What's happened?" I implore.

Matlok cannot meet my eyes. There are no words necessary. It's obvious by Matlok's downheartedness, Mac has been caught and is now in the custody of the Leadership. His fate has been sealed.

Behind me, I cannot drown out the sounds of Abigail's sobbing. A tremor begins at my fingertips and works its way up through my body into my head. I feel my head shaking. My eyes search the tiny room for Axel, hoping he can give me the strength to endure what I know is coming next. He is next to me in an instant, reaching out to support me as my knees fail and I begin to plummet to the floor. Lowering me down to the cold, hard floor I hear Axel whispering in my ear.

"This is not the end, Lia. This is not the end." Axel's words echo in my head as I sit in a heap with his arms wrapped around me.

Axel's words are meaningless to me. Without knowing exactly what has happened, I am certain that this is the end for Maclin.

Lukan

The morning is brisk, and the sounds of birds singing their happy song of gladness fill the air. It is a beautiful morning to emerge from home early. Before the rest of Grayson begins to stir. I have been so busy training the Kismet, that I have neglected my own target practice. The training field is clear, and I take advantage of the time alone before any others arrive.

I pull an arrow from the quiver that hangs comfortably on my back. My right hand fits squarely in the handhold of the bow, while my left nocks the arrow and holds it there with two callused fingers curled around the string. As I push my right arm out straight, I pull with my left, until the string is just touching my left cheek. Once I have my eye on the target, I straighten my curled fingers. The string releases with a whoosh and the sound of the flying arrow piercing the air is just barely audible. The sound of the impact makes a distinct thwack that seems to echo through the leafless trees.

My right arm remains outstretched, holding the bow. My left hand is still near my face where the string has just been released. I stand like this for several seconds as I look pridefully at the bullseye with my arrow in it. Not bad for a half-blind kid, I think to myself with a smirk.

Beyond the targets, something catches my eye. A petite woman with dark hair is walking through the antique car cemetery. I feel my brow crease as I ponder why a woman would be out walking through the cars on such a cold morning. As I watch her, she turns slightly, and the breeze blows her hair, revealing a dash of red.

My breath catches in my chest. It can't be.

"Merritt!" I yell, throwing my bow down and running towards her. "Merritt!"

As I round the first car, I scan the area. There is nobody here. A sound comes from behind me, and I spin around. There. Beyond the trees, Merritt meanders slowly. I call for her again, but she doesn't respond. I run towards her but somehow when I reach the edge of the trees, she is gone once again. I turn in circles, desperate to find her. I am fully aware that Merritt is dead. Still, she is here with me. More than anything, I want to see her once more. I want to hold her and tell her that I love her. The regret and pain that I have been trying to avoid all this time seem to be trying to take over.

"Lukan?" I hear a voice come from behind me.

Spinning around, I am surprised to see my father standing at the edge of the car cemetery. He waves to me. His face conveys worry and confusion. I'm embarrassed to think that he heard me crying out for a dead girl.

Slowly, I make my way towards my dad. When I reach him, he climbs onto the hood of an old rusted vehicle and sits. He pats the area next to him, inviting me to join him on the hood of the car. The metal is cold and still wet with melting frost, but I accept his invitation and sit next to him.

"I was...I was doing some target practice," I say, hoping that we won't have to talk about the other thing I was doing. The thing that proves that I am probably going mad.

My dad nods but doesn't press me. "You are a gifted archer, Lukan."

"Thanks, dad," I reply with a shy smile.

My dad and I sit in silence for several minutes. The air is warming, and Grayson is beginning to stir.

"Merritt would have loved all of this," I say, sweeping my arm towards the targets. With a chuckle, I add, "She would have been scared, but intrigued. She would want to prove that she could shoot a bow."

My dad chuckles with me, but the sound of it holds sadness. He looks away, and asks rather bluntly," Is that why she visits you now?"

I am surprised by his question. "How do you know she visits me?"

"The ones we love never leave us. She is in your heart. She's part of you. She's part of this town. Perhaps, her fight with the Howlers isn't over yet. She longs to be part of Kismet." My dad smiles at me again. There is no condescendence in his voice. Only affection.

"What do I do when I see her? I can't be running around town calling out her name." I feel my voice begin to catch.

My father considers this with pursed lips for several seconds. "Hm, I'm not sure she wants you to run around town, calling out her name. She was never one to want to bring attention to herself. I would say, when you see her again, smile and let her be. Let Merritt watch over you."

Chapter 14

Lia

The Grand Hall, as it turns out, is the just another name for the Isolation Chamber. In an effort to occupy her mind after learning that Mac had indeed been captured, Darcy found refuge in the only place in Terra Convex able to provide her with a feeling of safety – The Hall of Reading. Locking herself away from the murmurs in the corridors, Darcy found her solace surrounded by the knowledge of ancient days.

As Darcy replayed the events of the day, she realized that not once in her life had she ever heard of the Grand Hall. Before leaving the tiny room with the secret window, there was much discussion about the message from the president. All in the room agreed that they had never heard of the Grand Hall either. At that moment, Darcy took it upon herself to research Terra Convex and find out exactly where the Grand Hall is located.

As soon as she realized the location, she came rushing to inform me. At my sister's living quarters, I answered the door to a very distraught looking Darcy. Immediately, I felt the color drain from my face as I considered what she was here to tell me. Expecting to hear the words, "Mac is dead," I was surprised when instead she said, "The Grand Hall is actually the Isolation Chamber." Closing the door behind her, and settling her on the couch, I began to question where she had learned this information.

"That can't be," I stammered. "That room is full of people – dead and dying." My stomach lurched at the memory of my brief time in the expansive room.

Darcy explained how she came upon the information. She spoke of the hours that she had spent searching for specific histories of Terra Convex. When she finally found what she had been searching for, she immediately came here, to my sister's home.

"It's true," I heard a voice say from behind me.

Turning quickly, in a panic, I realized that it was Matlok. He had come through the door and closed it behind him without any of us hearing.

"It can't be true," I argued. "All those people."

Matlok did not reply. He stared into my eyes for several seconds before letting his gaze fall. Without saying a word, he dropped into a nearby chair. There were no words that needed to be said. His demeanor said much more than words could. I don't think that I could bear to listen to what had been done to all the people that the government had kept in that room anyway.

I was reminded of the day, not long ago, that Matlok told me that Leadership had ordered a cleansing of the Isolation Chamber. At the time, nobody knew why such an order would be given. We had thought it was because of us, the Agitators. That thought still lingers in the back of my mind.

Standing here now, in what was called the Isolation Chamber just 24 hours ago, I don't dare look around. Although the room is quite large, plenty big enough for all the citizens of our underground community to fit into, I begin to feel as though I am being compressed to the point of passing out. The air in this room is ripe with the putrefaction of those that had been removed. The living that now fill this space breathe in the air of death and breathe out in hot rapid bursts. I don't have to survey the area to know that I am just inches from the very spot where I held my mother as she breathed her last breath.

There is nothing in the Grand Hall to convey that there will be a celebration of any sort. At the front of the large room, there is a platform. It is obvious from its appearance that it was hastily built, with piping and metal, for this very occasion.

Axel stands to my left. I glance up at him. His height makes it possible for him to see over most that stand between us and the platform. His gaze is distant and brooding. Usually, Axel makes a strong attempt at balancing my distress with his optimism. That is not the case today.

The room is filled with murmuring as the people speak in hushed tones to those around them. Everyone is trying to figure out exactly what is happening. It would appear that nobody is expecting the celebration we were promised.

At once, the room quiets as everyone's attention is focused towards the entrance of the room. My height makes it impossible for me to see what has captured their attention. It feels as if there is no point in even trying. I drop my head and wait for our time in this room to end.

"Several men have just entered. They are wearing fancy clothing," Axel explains quietly, knowing that I cannot see.

"Leadership," I acknowledge with no desire to look up.

The murmurs return with a quiet fervor. I look up at Axel to gauge his reaction. He looks down at me with wide eyes.

"President DePriest," is all that Axel can say.

President DePriest has never made a public appearance in my lifetime. As far as I know, the president before him never made a public appearance. The DePriest's have successfully maintained a secret life within this compound for ninety years. If my emotions weren't spent on Maclin's well-being, the presence of the president would be impressive to me.

"Good citizens of Terra Convex," I hear President DePriest's voice boom out over the crowd, hushing them in an instant. "For many decades, your ancestors - and now you - have enjoyed the liberties provided to you by your Leadership. Because of the graciousness of my grandfather, Marcus DePriest, who had the foresight to invite your ancestors into Terra Convex at the beginning of the great outbreak, you are now the only living creatures on earth." He pauses and begins to clap. Those on the council soon join in. It takes a few seconds of President DePreist's nonstop applause before the rest of the crowd understands that they also need to join in.

Axel and I look at each other. Neither of us clapping. His face is covered with confusion and dread that I'm sure matches my own.

The president ceases clapping, and the room follows suit. Continuing, he says, "Despite the graciousness that has been bestowed, however, there are few among you with a complete lack of appreciation."

President DePreist's voice has changed from that of exuberance to one of disappointment. My heart begins to stutter a bit.

"Perhaps, these few – the Defiance - wish that their grandparents had been left out in the rot of the world above." It is at this moment that those in the Grand Hall realize what I have known all along – this day is not for celebrating. "Perhaps, they wish death on us all."

At once, there is a collective gasp in the large room. Without being able to see the stage, I look to Axel for indication of what is transpiring. His face has gone white, and his eyes are wide. Axel must feel my eyes on him. He turns to me slowly and takes my hand in his tenderly.

Axel doesn't have to speak a word. I know, without seeing, what has just happened. Leadership has just presented the crowd with the reason for the gathering today.

"Maclin," I hear myself say.

With a look of terror and regret, Axel nods. Pulling my hand from his, I begin to shove my way through the crowd. I'm confident that I will not be able to save Mac from whatever Leadership has in store for him. Still, I must get to him. I must see his face and let him see mine.

The crowd complains as I clumsily make my way towards the platform. Once I make it to the front of the crowd, I am immediately halted by two large Enforcers. With tremendous force, they latch onto me. I do not resist. Mostly because I am stunned by what I see.

Maclin. His thick blonde hair, matted with blood. His eyes, clear blue and sparkling just yesterday are now swollen shut with large purple bruising. His uniform has been ripped in places. Only his pants remain intact, but even they are bloody and wet. Maclin, the most talented artist that Terra Convex has never known, stands before the crowd of onlookers bloody, beaten, and shirtless. Humiliated.

I struggle only briefly to reach Mac. The Enforcers have a strong grip on my arms. Still, it as if my heart is in my throat. I feel my airway trying to rebel against me; closing up tight, choking back the anguish that fights to be released. My mind is reeling, replaying images from our childhood, and tender moments that would be meaningless to most but cherished by best friends.

Maclin seems to be searching the crowd, but it is impossible to tell with his face in the state that it is in. Although it is obvious that he has been beaten – his chest bare except for the purple bruises – he seems to have his strength.

A scream to my right causes me to flinch. My eyes are immediately drawn in that direction. I am only barely able to register that the scream originated from Abigail. She has just seen her husband for the first time. She has just seen what the government is willing to do to its citizens if they do not stay in line.

Abigail tries to run to Mac but is instantly stopped, as I was, by two large Enforcers. One of them, I realize at once, is Matlok. His hold on Abigail isn't nearly as gripping as the other that holds tight to her arm. Matlok manages a look in my direction. With a stern yet worried look he shakes his head subtly. I can tell immediately that he is giving me a warning. Still, I struggle against the brutes that hold me.

Abigail continues to scream, and Mac turns his head towards her voice. He begins to mutter something, but at this distance, and against her cries, it is unintelligible.

"This Agitator! This reprobate!" The president bellows to the crowd. "Look at him. He is the one that has misled so many of you. With lies. With hypocrisy. Using your emotions for his own gain. Look at him. He is nothing but a boy, and yet he was able to control you with falsities on simple pieces of parchment."

It is obvious that President DePreist is sending a clear message to the people of Terra Convex. Even through my anguish, I can hear what he is truly saying to his people. This is a warning and Mac is to be the example. I can no longer hold back the tears. They are hot with anger towards the government and sorrowful for what I know is about to happen.

"This could be any one of you." Eyes wide with rage, the president points at Mac. "You have all failed your government by harboring such a miscreant."

For the first time, I actually look at President DePriest. His features are much like everyone else in Terra Convex – blond hair, gray eyes. The only difference is, where we are thin with greasy hair and ashen complexion, President DePriest is well-built and handsome. It's obvious that while his people lived on meager rations and did not have the luxury of proper hygiene, he has been fed well and enjoyed daily grooming. He does not wear a stained or torn uniform like the citizens of Terra Convex. Instead, his clothes are neat and tidy – black pants with a stiff crease running the length of each leg; red shirt with buttons on the front, and a pocket on the left of his chest.

"I forgive you, though," President DePriest says in a much quieter tone. "This young man will take the burden of your sins from you. He will endure the punishment that you all deserve."

Abigail continues to sob loudly. Even though I want to go to her – to tell her that she must remain strong for Maclin - I cannot stand to look in her direction. More than anything, I want to rush the platform and pronounce myself as the one and only Agitator.

Even as the Enforcers hold tight to my arms, I feel a gentle touch on my elbow. I manage to turn enough to see Axel. He has made his way through the crowd and now stands with me. He looks at me with sorrowful, yet perceptive eyes. I feel that somehow, Axel is aware of my desire to charge onto the platform.

As I stare into Axel's eyes, I am only slightly aware of a figure running past me. Turning my attention back to the platform, I see that Abigail has run to her father who stands quietly behind the platform with the other councilmen. She has managed to escape the Enforcers that were holding her. I can't help but wonder if that is partly Matlok's doing. Sobbing loudly, Abigail pleads for her father to intervene.

The president is obviously stunned and irritated by the girl that has disrupted his speech. He approaches Abigail and her father with loud footsteps. Although I cannot hear what is transpiring between the three of them, I am hopeful that Abigail can convince her father and President DePreist to free Mac. There is much discussion, and I am slightly relieved when Abigail's sobbing begins to subside a bit. Relieved, yet apprehensive. It is safe to assume that she is revealing me as the true Agitator. My only hope is that she does not include Axel or Darcy when she begins to list the names of the Defiance.

Abigail runs her sleeve over her nose, attempting to dry her face of the tears that have left her face red. While her father and the president speak to each other a little longer, Abigail glances at me briefly. Her eyes, swollen and sorrowful, look upon me with disdain. I am almost certain that I am about to be apprehended. Abigail's hatred for me will not allow her to conceal my rebellious actions. I find that I am unable to hold her gaze. I allow my eyes to drift back to Mac.

Mac's countenance hasn't changed. He remains standing, arms tied behind his back. There are no Enforcers holding him to that spot, and yet he doesn't try to escape. Not that he could see to get away. Not with his eyes swollen shut. Still, he seems as if he has surrendered to his fate.

Out of my peripheral, I see Abigail approaching me. Although there is still anguish etched on her face, there is also a look of contempt that I know is meant just for me. I feel myself backing up slowly, needing to feel Axel's presence. Knowing he will give me strength for what I am sure is about to happen.

"They have agreed to let me speak with Maclin," Abigail states once she is front of me. Her voice is choked with emotion.

This statement unnerves and confuses me. I was hoping that she had been able to convince Leadership to release him. I feel my mouth working to find the appropriate words.

"Out of respect for Maclin, I asked if you could also have some time with him," Abigail continued with tears beginning to fill her eyes once more.

The look in Abigail's eyes tells me that this is the end, and if I want a chance to say goodbye to Mac, this will be my only chance. I watch as Abigail walks towards Mac. Before I follow her, I turn and look at Axel. His eyes are filled with fear and sorrow. He gives me a slight nod, and I turn and walk towards Mac.

When I reach the platform and step up onto it, Abigail has her arms wrapped around Mac and is crying quietly. Mac's arms are still tied behind his back, so he is unable to return her embrace. Instead, he buries his face in her hair. I can hear their tender whispers to each other but cannot make out the words. The words are not meant for any to hear other than Abigail, so I remain a few steps away, allowing them their precious moment together.

The two finally lean back from each other. It's obvious Mac is trying to see his wife. His swollen eyelids flutter with the effort. He opens his mouth to speak. Abigail's weeping is silent as she concentrates on hearing her husband's voice.

"I would have chosen you," Mac manages to say through the pain, touching his forehead to hers in the customary way that he and I would.

At that moment, I realize that after all this time of despising Abigail, and attempting to exclude her, she really is part of Mac. Although marrying her was not his choice, he grew to love her. She was indeed his bride. In the short time since their betrothal, Mac had found a way to fall in love with Abigail. Somehow, he saw past her conceit and animosity. He managed to chip away at the hard shell of bitterness that she had formed around her, exposing kindness and loyalty. Indeed, Mac would have chosen Abigail.

With Abigail still clinging to him, I hear Mac say my name softly.

"I'm here," I manage with a croak. I can sense the crowd behind me growing restless. The Enforcers are inching closer to us. Our brief time together is coming to an end. For all eternity, I'm sure.

It takes him some time, but Mac finally says, "Nothing that we do, is done in vain. I believe, with all my soul, that we shall see triumph."

His wording confuses me. I am certain that his doom is impending. There is no triumph in this world. Surely, he must sense it too. Before I can clear my head enough to ask what he means, I am drug away from him. Abigail, also, is taken back to the crowd and held by the Enforcers.

In my weeping, I am only slightly aware that President DePreist has returned to the front of the platform. The murmurs of the people are silenced when he raises his arms. When he feels he has the attention of everyone in the room, President DePriest speaks again.

"Out of the kindness and enduring graciousness, I have allowed these two young ladies to speak to the Agitator." He looks directly at Abigail and me with a coldness in his eyes. "Surely, because of this charitable gesture, you realize that I, and everyone else in Leadership, have only good intentions. We in Terra Convex are a gentle and humble people. We wish no harm or ill will to come to anyone." With a subtle nod, the president walks toward Mac. Those known as the Interrogators approach Mac from behind. "Still, there are lessons to be learned from the Agitator."

My head begins to spin violently. I know, before I see, exactly what is about to happen. I am surprised when I hear myself say, "Abigail, close your eyes." For reasons I do not understand, I feel like it is my responsibility to spare her the image of what is about to transpire. I continue to stare forward, though, embracing this as my punishment.

Two of the large Interrogators grab onto Mac's arms. The third stands directly behind him. He takes hold of Mac's hair with violence, causing Mac to reveal his throat. With a swiftness, the man reaches around Mac's throat and swipes across. I don't have to see the knife to know that Mac's throat has just been sliced open with tremendous efficiency. Blood begins to spill from the gaping wound, onto his bare chest.

Abigail did not close her eyes. Her screams echo through the Grand Hall. The Enforcers that held us also seem stunned. Their grip loosens, and I drop to the ground in a heap. Sobs rack my body as I take in the sight of Mac's body staggering and then finally falling into the pool of blood at his feet. Next to me, Abigail also falls, overcome with emotion.

Through the sobs - both mine and Abigail's – I hear the president speaking once more.

"...'As a member of Terra Convex, you shall render unconditional obedience. As a loyal citizen, you shall at all times give your allegiance to Terra Convex. You will be faithful and obedient to the leadership of this community. You will observe the laws and fulfill the duties and mandates assigned to you.'" President DePriest quotes the Terra Convex Proclamation of Existence. Enunciating each word dramatically. "'Consequences for your failures and misgivings will be strict, swift and unwavering. The earth above is a cruel and unforgiving beast that will quickly devour anyone who steps out of these walls. There is no place safer for you and your family than Terra Convex.'"

With that, President DePriest makes an elaborate and unnecessary bow and exits the Grand Hall. The council, interrogators, and many Enforcers follow. The citizens of Terra Convex are left standing in stunned silence, unable to comprehend what they have just witnessed. Before them, lying in thickening crimson, is one of their own. Never in the history of Terra Convex, has their been a public execution. As far as the oblivious citizens of this underground world have ever known, death comes naturally. Not with violence and bloodshed.

"This is because of you," I hear Abigail hiss through her tears.

I don't have to look at her to know that she is speaking to me – accusing me. Rightfully so. This is because of me. Mac's death is my fault. I feel the weight of guilt deep inside of me. I know that I should run from this miserable place. No doubt Leadership is meeting at this very moment, planning who they will execute next. Of course, it is only logical that Abigail and I are now suspected of being part of the Defiance. I imagine, being the daughter of a councilman, Abigail will be spared. I will not be so lucky.

Realizing my fate, I decide what must be done. I make a move to get to my feet, and Axel's hands are on me immediately. With a gentleness I do not deserve, he helps me to stand under the weight of my anguish. Once I am on my feet, and Axel feels like I am able to stand without his assistance, he tenderly brushes my tear-soaked hair from my face.

I'm fully prepared for Abigail to turn me over to the government for my part in the Defiance. When Leadership comes for me, there is only one place I want to be. The only place that matters to me – the window. My hope is that when they come to lead me away to my death, they will see the window and what awaits them above. If just one or two of them feel the same pull as I at the sight of the world above, then maybe they will be inclined to carry on the movement that the Defiance started.

Standing now, I look around at what is left of the Defiance. A pathetic broken group indeed. Darcy sits alone, her head in her hands, sobbing quietly. My sister, Mira, stands nearby with a stunned look of horror on her face. Most likely, she is just beginning to realize what is at stake by being part of the rebellion. Dalen is in the far corner pacing and shaking his head. His face conveys more anger than shock. Matlok stands close to the platform where Mac's lifeless body lies. His fingers are intertwined behind his head as if he is contemplating what he should do next.

I glance up at Axel once more. His eyes are still on me, evaluating my emotional state without asking questions. There is a crease of worry between his eyes, and his dimple is missing. Although he is suffering from the loss of Mac, he is clearly making my response to the horror his priority. I bring my hand up to his face and hold it there. The crease disappears as a look of curiosity replaces the worry. I attempt a smile, but he knows there is no truth behind it and does not return the gesture. His broad hand comes up to his face and rests on top of mine. There are no words for us to say. Nothing can be said that will take back what has happened.

"I feel like I should help Matlok with..." Axel says quietly, his voice drifting off when he cannot find adequate words. "Don't disappear," Axel whispers, reminding me of a time not long ago when I did disappear for several weeks. He is much more intuitive than I realize.

"I'm not," I reply calmly. "You know where to find me." With that, I take my hand from his face and slowly start for the door.

"This is because of you," Abigail repeats with a scream. Her words are shrill. Her voice wild with hate.

Without looking back, I reply, "I know."

Chapter 15

Lukan

An unexpected snowstorm hit Grayson hard. The sky had gone from brilliant blue to dark and menacing within just a few hours. Mother's beckoned for their children to come in as the snow began to spit heavily from the gray sky above. Father's hurriedly brought in firewood before it became wet with snow. Dom and I quickly made our rounds, checking in on the sick and elderly, ensuring they had everything they needed for the next few days. the snow piled up quickly, forcing all of us indoors indefinitely.

The storm lasted eight long days. the end of the storm met us with sorrow. Mr. Monroe – who was neither sick nor elderly – was found dead three days after the storm passed. He had taken his life selfishly, leaving his bloated corpse for us to find and remove from the house.

Even though there is always a sense of bitterness towards those who choose to opt out, Grayson mourned the loss of Mr. Monroe.

As Grayson gathers at the Community Building to Lament the passing of Mr. Monroe, I can't help but stand with my face to the sky. The snow has melted, and the sun is high. I relish its warmth on my face. One of the men from our community is giving a forced speech about birth, life, and death. Some are weeping. However, they weep for those they have lost, more than the loss of Mr. Monroe.

A sound pricks at my ears like a sewing needle on a misplaced hem. I struggle to get a clear sense of what I am hearing because of the man speaking for the Lamentation. Tilting my head towards the direction of the sound, I open my eye and scan for Helix. I find him in the crowd, towards the back, and make my way to him.

I don't have to say anything; he knows I am near.

"Howlers," is all he says and I realize that my instinct was correct.

"All these people in one place could cause a stampede," I say quietly.

"They must be warned," Helix states calmly.

"Come with me," I take Helix's arm and begin making my way to the front of the crowd. The last thing I want is for Helix to get knocked down and trampled if the crowd indeed stampedes back to their homes.

When I reach the front of the crowd, I see the wooden casket that contains Mr. Monroe. The eulogy giver stands next to it. He is obviously confused, and a little agitated that I am barging my way to the front and interrupting the Lamentation.

"Listen, everyone," I start with a calm voice. "Everyone needs to get back to their homes, right now. Howlers are on their way here as we speak."

Gasps and murmurs throughout the crowd.

"They never come during winter," a frightened woman cries out.

"Listen. Listen." I say, hoping to keep the situation under control. I point to four men in the front, "you-you-you-you, take the casket to the woods where the boys hide. Put it out there, and we will finish the Lamenting when the Howlers leave."

"We should get our weapons!" Somebody exclaims from the crowd. I recognize the man in the crowd as Briggs – a man that lives near my family.

"No!" I respond quickly, raising my hands for them to calm down. "That will only make things worse. In fact, go home, and hide your weapons. The only way our plan will work is with surprise."

"Surprise! We have weapons! How about that?" Briggs cries out mockingly.

"Please. No. Just go back to your homes and proceed like you would any other time the Howlers come to town." I am pleading with them.

The four men indeed pick up the casket and begin carrying it to the car cemetery. The boys rush in that same direction. The rest of Grayson quickly but respectfully make their way back to their homes. Just so they can follow the Howlers back to this same spot.

With Helix's hand on my shoulder, we find my family. My mother is obviously fretful, wringing her hands.

"I'm going to go see where they are," I explain, putting Helix's hand on my father's elbow.

I don't wait for an argument. I run to the short rock wall, jump over and crawl up the small hill. The Howlers are near. I can hear their obnoxious hooting and hollering. As they crest a distant hill, I see Gallner leading the pack of madmen. Anger boils up inside me. Like the others, I long to take up my weapon and end him. It takes all of my willpower to stay the course and wait for the right time to attack.

Something catches the corner of my eye, and I turn quickly, startled. Off to my left, sitting in the crook of a tall tree – of all places – is Merritt. She was always too frightened to climb trees when we were younger. Now, in death, she seems to know no fear. I am aware that I am only imagining her there. Still, the thought gives me comfort.

Merritt shakes her head at me and then points back towards town. She wants me to go home. I can almost see her mouthing the words, "Don't be stupid." It makes me smile.

I take one last look at the approaching Howlers before turning to run home and await their arrival.

*****

As is typical for any visit from the Howlers, we can hear them before we see them. Once they are upon us, they break off into little groups and wreak havoc. In the distance, glass panes can be heard shattering. Women are heard screaming. The thuds of fist on muscle can be heard as men are being struck.

My parents, Dom, Helix, and I stand on the front porch of our home. We listen and cringe with every sound of destruction. The sound draws nearer, and I worry what damage we will be left to repair once it is all over. My father wraps an arm around my mom and begins to whisper in her ear. Dom and I exchange a glance. I consider that perhaps we should have hidden Helix away. There could be unanswered animosity between him and Gallner.

Too late. The Howlers round the corner. Like ants who have just had their mounded home kicked over, they scatter throughout our street. None of them seem to have any intent on where they are going or what they are going to do when they get there. They just let the madness guide them.

Except for Gallner.

He heads straight for me. Instinctively, I step to the edge of the porch. Not to challenge him; rather, to ensure that he has to get through me to get to my family and Helix. Behind me, my mother is breathing shallowly.

Gallner eyes me, and a smirk begins to play at the corners of his mouth. The tips of his long mustache are curling up obnoxiously. He stands at the foot of the stairs. One foot on the bottom step, casually. The furs he wears are thick and odorous. His hair is unruly except for a braid with a feather entwined on one side of his head.

He opens his mouth to say something but is cut short when an arrow slices through the air, narrowly missing his head. It lands with a solid thwack in the thigh of another Howler that happened to be standing nearby. The wounded madman howls out in pain and falls to the ground. As one, we all turn to determine where the arrow came from.

Briggs stands in a yard two houses down, bow in hand. There is no denying that he just attempted to take Gallner's life. The man is instantly tackled by several Howlers. Tackled and beaten. no questions asked. Just the sound of grunts and thuds as fists pummel, and feet kick, the man to death. When the fiends back away, breathless and bloodied from the effort, it is clear that Briggs is dead.

Gallner turns his glare back to me. His nostrils flare with anger. His eyes wide with hatred. I feel my chest grow tight as I stare back into his hate-filled eyes. I try to match his glare.

Without taking his eyes from me, Gallner orders his men, "Bring the dead man's family."

Behind me, I hear my mother whimper. Gallner's men storm off. His eyes remain on me, and his smirk begins to crawl back onto his face. Not far away, the screams of Briggs' wife, Laney, can be heard. In my peripheral, I can see the men dragging the poor woman down the street towards where we stand. I know that their sons are hiding in the woods and are not aware of what is happening. Hopefully, the boys will not recognize the screams of their mother and come running to her aid.

Gallner steps away from our porch and walks towards Laney, who is now crouched down in the street in front of our home. She weeps loudly for her dead husband, and probably because she knows what comes next for her. Gallner approaches slowly, his long hair fanning behind him. the woman does not look up. Her face is in her hands, and she attempts to hide from the misery that has fallen onto her in a mere matter of minutes.

Gallner squats down on his haunches and leans in close to her. "Do you belong to this man?" He points in the direction of the bloodied body. His voice is almost kind.

Laney nods weakly and answers, "He is my husband."

I can see Gallner begin to shake his head. His eyes seem compassionate. With a gentle finger, he brings her chin up forcing her to look into his face. "He isn't your husband anymore." A maniacal look erases what had appeared to be compassion. "He's dead." Gallner's voice has turned cold.

Laney begins sobbing loudly once again. Those of us that are nearby can only stand and watch. We do not dare make a move towards the situation. I can sense Dom begin to fidget, ready to get into the battle.

Gallner stands once more and gives his men a chilling order. "Take her. Burn the house."

"Wait," I start down the steps.

Gallner snaps his head around to challenge me. Behind me, still on the porch, my mother gasps and Helix beckons me to come back. It's too late, though. I am already moving forward, ready to beg for the life of this poor woman.

Gallner stomps towards me. "Wait? For what? Do you want to take her place? Or perhaps your mother wants to come with me?" He looks over my shoulder at my mom with raised eyebrows. "No?" Looking back at me, he says with a smugness, "Maybe next time."

He turns away from me. His men have lifted Laney from the ground. They hold tight to her as she struggles to get free of their grasp. Down the street, her house begins to flame. I begin to get an awful feeling that perhaps her boys didn' run into the woods; perhaps she told them to hide in the house instead. My heart sinks as I consider this scenario.

"Every time we visit, you people make it exciting. that's why we keep coming here. Grayson is our favorite place," Gallner announces with a shrill outburst of laughter. The Howlers around us release bellowing howls in agreement. Gallner walks over to Laney who continues to cry and says, "Thanks for the gift."

With that, Gallner raises his chin and howls loudly. All through town, his howls are returned. With one last wink, Gallner walks towards the exit. The rest of his Howlers following.

Once they are gone and can only be heard, I run inside the house and fetch my bow and quiver. Back outside, I leap from the porch. My family, along with many others, are gathered in the street. I begin to run in the direction the howlers went but am stopped quickly by Dom.

"What are you doing?" He asks with wide, frightened eyes. "You can't take them on by yourself."

"I'm not," I reply. "But how are we going to know where their camp is when its time?"

"You're going to follow them," Dom says as he realizes my intent.

I do not answer. Looking past him, I see that more of Grayson is gathering. Most are attempting to battle the flames. The children are reappearing from the woods. Somebody will have to explain to the sons of Briggs and Laney that they are most likely now orphans.

I turn to leave, but Dom grabs my arm. "Let me go with you. You shouldn't be going alone."

I feel my anger coursing through my veins like a poison attempting to change me. I am desperate to go after the Howlers, tracking them to where they lay their heads at night. I imagine running a dagger into their skulls as they sleep, ending our nightmare.

My father must have realized that Dom and I were discussing something of importance. He must have seen Dom holding onto my arm. Must have sensed my desire to leave. I watch him approach. His face is grim.

Before he can speak, I offer, "We have to know where they camp."

My dad nods in agreement and then surprises me by saying, "Track them quietly. When you find their camp, do not tary. Return home and continue training." Looking at Dom, my father says, "Go with your cousin." Before I can argue, he adds, "Map the way to their camp."

In a rush, Dom runs into the house to retrieve his weapon. I have no idea how far we will be traveling. Still, there is no time to gather camping supplies or food. Every minute that passes, the Howlers are gaining distance from us. Dom returns quickly, bow in hand, quiver hanging across his back. He nods at me indicating that he is ready to run. Together, we give my dad one last look, turn and run from the scene of the latest murder.

Chapter 16

Lia

The time immediately following Mac's execution passed slowly. Remarkably, Leadership never came for me. For hours after I walked out of the death chamber (that truly is the only name that adequately represents the room's purpose), I laid underneath the window. I watched the red birds fly through the gray sky above me. Watched as tiny specks of snow fluttered down onto the glass. I waited.

I continue to wait. On my tattered blanket, under the gray sky of winter in the world beyond my reach, I wait for my fate to crash through the door.

Although I try not to think of Mac, the image of his death continues to crash over me with a cruel relentlessness. Alone in the secret room, under the window, I allow myself the opportunity to mourn. For both, Maclin and my mother. The wound left by the death of my mother remains fresh enough that the tears come easily. The cup of sorrow that I carry is filled to the brim – can hold no more heartache – and now runs over onto my face, my shirt, the floor.

After several minutes of continuous sobs - allowing the image of death, and the memory of the stench of blood to resonate freely in my mind – I force myself to remember. I begin to remember Mac as a boy, pulling my braid and squealing with laughter. The time that he had been running through the corridors and fell. He didn't just fall, he slid. Although his knee was a bit scraped, Darcy and I were so impressed with how far he slid through the corridor – on his belly – that he didn't seem to feel the pain at all. He was just pleased that his friends had been impressed.

When my captors come for me, I want my last thoughts to be of the good times with Mac.

As I think back on my time with Mac, I can't help but remember the first time he drew something. He had sketched a tray of food. He brought it to the Hall of Reading to show Darcy and me. We were quite impressed with his talent. Darcy chastised him gently. She was fearful of what would happen if his creative ability were found out by the government. Creativity had been banned many years ago. Just one of the many absurd laws forced upon us by a government detached from its people.

Indeed, his art was found. Because of his young age, his punishment was minor. Still, from that moment, he kept his artistic abilities hidden from his family and his teacher. Only Darcy and I ever saw how creative and gifted Mac was.

And Lukan...

Lukan has seen what Mac could do with lead and parchment...and imagination.

My mind takes me back to the day I asked Mac to sketch a picture of a buck. It was my first form of communication with the outside world. I had no idea what events would transpire after placing that one piece of parchment beneath the window for Lukan to see.

Lukan indeed saw what I had left, and he responded with a bloody arrow. The same arrow that had killed the buck. At the time that the buck was shot above me, I was terrified. I feared monsters lived above. I had never experienced death. Now, I know that in Lukan's world, animals must be killed in order to provide meat for those that live freely in the great expanse.

My mind wanders a bit. Whatever happened to that sketch? Where did I leave it after I wrote my name on the back? In the weeks following, did it get lost in the chaos? I hate to think that I would never see it again. It played such a significant role in what is now known as the Defiance.

Warily, Darcy and Axel enter the secret room where I lay waiting for my punishment, reflecting on Maclin. Quietly, they join me. I had reveled in my time alone but having them with me now, is comforting.

After many minutes of silence, I comment. "They're coming. Abigail won't let Mac's death go unpunished. I am to blame. I am to be punished." As I hear myself saying the words, I realize that they sound much more dramatic than I intended. I become irritated with my self-pity and sit up. "Listen, you two should distance yourself from me."

Sitting up, Axel replies, "If Abigail tells her father that you are an Agitator, she will name all of us as the Defiance – not just you."

Although I do not want to contemplate that outcome, I know that Axel is right.

Changing the subject, Darcy says through her tears, "I wish I had gotten the chance to speak to him."

I have no words of comfort for her. While it was a welcomed gesture to get final words with Mac, there was no consolation in it. Especially now as I reflect back on what he said to me. I replay the words in my head, trying to find meaning in them.

Aloud, I repeat them to Darcy and Axel. 'Nothing that we do is done in vain. I believe, with all my soul, that we shall see triumph.'

Axel is smiling compassionately and nodding. "Sounds like Mac knew what he was dying for. He believed in the Defiance until the very end."

Still, the pain is sharp and without end.

Darcy looks at us with a strange look, as if she is trying to decipher a riddle in her mind. Axel and I exchange a glance. Suddenly, without a word, she jumps up and rushes out of the room.

My heart hurts for the pain that Darcy is enduring. Her love for Maclin runs deep. If not for the Marital Responsibility act, I believe the two would have married. Instead, Darcy had to witness Mac's last few weeks married to a spiteful scamp.

Axel scoots closer, wrapping his arms around me. I concede to his affection, laying my head against his chest. We sit in silence. There are no words that can ease the hurt. His presence helps, though.

Quietly, the door opens again. Matlok and Mira enter hesitantly. Their eyes search mine with tremendous compassion. I imagine they are looking for signs that I am nearing a breakdown. Without a word, I simply nod. Hoping they understand it as a gesture that it is safe to enter. They do.

Without a word, they find a place on the cold floor to sit. I am pleased as I watch Matlok put his arm around my sister affectionately. Although Mac was not part of their lives, they can still recognize the impact that he made on those around them.

I feel as though I need to ask Matlok and Axel what they have done with Mac's body. Honestly, though, I'm aware that I don't need to ask. I already know. His body has been dissolved to ashes just like all the others who find death in Terra Convex. I choke back tears once again.

After some time in silence, the door opens once again. This time with a sense of urgency. We all flinch but are relieved to see that Darcy has returned. In her arms, she carries several books. She is breathless and wide-eyed, with a hint of a smile just teasing at the corners of her mouth.

"What is it?" I ask, alarmed, yet curious.

Darcy closes the door behind her with a kick. In the middle of the room, she gently sets the books onto the floor.

"It's a quote," Darcy announces with slight excitement embedded deep in her sorrow-strained voice.

We all look at her dubiously. I shake my head slightly trying to understand.

"'Nothing that we do is done in vain. I believe, with all my soul, that we shall see triumph.'" Darcy repeats the words Mac spoke to me. "Those words are from A Tale of Two Cities by Charles Dickens."

I'm stunned and a bit skeptical. "Are you sure?"

Darcy's red eyes are wide. "Yes. It's my favorite book. I have read it many times. I am very sure."

"Was it required reading?" I ask, trying to understand why Mac would have read it, and also why he felt it important enough to make it his last words to me.

Darcy rolls her eyes in irritation. While I found my joy in wandering and exploring our tiny world, she has always enjoyed reading. I was able to escape this world and enter the world of my imagination. Darcy's escape was through the words of great literature. It has been the source of many lectures on what I should be doing with my spare time.

"No, I read it because I wanted to. I *re-read* it because I loved it so much," Darcy explains with a slight huff.

"The question is, what significance did that quote have for Mac?" Axel asks. "Why would he say it to you, Lia?"

"I honestly have no idea," I reply honestly.

Darcy's face brightens a bit, and her eyes grow wild with delight. "Because he knew you would carry those words with you. He knew you would eventually repeat them."

Staring deep into my eyes, Darcy hands me a book. Looking down at the hardback, it appears unremarkable. I saw that it was 'A Tale of Two Cities.' I turn it over in my hand, unsure what she intended for me to do with it.

Unable to sit idly by while I try to understand her excitement, Darcy reaches for the book. She doesn't take it from me, though. Instead, she gently opens the front cover.

I am stunned at what I am holding in my hands – A Tale of Two Cities, hollowed out. Inside, folded parchments. Glancing up at Darcy, she smiles knowingly. Tears are starting to form once again. These are not tears of sorrow, though the pain is still evident. No, these are tears of knowing.

Knowing that Mac was successful in his mission to break into the president's quarters and steal the journals. Knowing that Mac's death was not in vain. Knowing that the Defiance now holds the key to the future of Terra Convex.

With a shaky hand, I reach for Darcy. Together, we lean toward each other, touching our foreheads together as we have done since we were children. This is our act of solidarity, and the gesture has always signified our relationship as best friends.

I am aware that Axel, Mira, and Matlok have begun to look through the other books that Darcy had brought in. Each book is a thick novel, written by various best-selling authors throughout the ages. Each book has been hollowed out and now holds the writings of each of the Terra Convex presidents.

In essence, Mac had used books as a weapon against the government. We had discussed this. We had even begun the work. The books that Darcy had brought in, though, are from the Hall of Reading. I hadn't seen them before. I glance over at the small pile of books that we had been cutting into. We have yet to find an opportunity to use them.

"How did he have time to do all of this?" I wonder aloud.

"I helped," a voice says from the doorway, startling us.

Looking up, I am stunned to see Abigail standing there. Her face and eyes, red with sorrow, also reveal the hatred she carries. Hatred for this group, but mostly for me. I feel a tremble as I consider that Enforcers are most likely standing on the other side of the door. Certainly, Abigail would have led them here to imprison, torture, and execute each one of us for our part in the Defiance.

We are all surprised as Abigail sits down and picks up one of the books. It feels strange having her with us, without Mac. She seems like a piece that doesn't fit, and yet somehow does. I imagine that Mac would want us to include her. Yet, I can't help but look over her shoulder at the door. Waiting for Enforcers to crash through.

"This place wants us dead," Abigail says quietly after several minutes of us staring at her. "I know that now. He told me, but I didn't want to believe him." She stares at the hollowed out book in her lap. "The only reason I helped him do this is because I wanted to be part of his world." Abigail looks up. With tears beginning to form, she looks at each one of us. "I realized that if I am to be part of his world, I must be part of yours too."

Feeling the weight of Abigail's words, I manage to choke out, "Abigail..."

"Don't," her eyes are full of fury as she looks in my direction. "Just don't. I hate you, Amelia. I will always blame you for his death. When they come for you...when they do to you, what they did to Maclin, I will not mourn your death." Abigail spits the words out as if they are sour against her tongue.

Even though she means the words to be hurtful to me, they are not. Abigail and I have always felt tremendous malice towards each other. My only concern is the safety of those around me.

"Are they coming?" I ask, ignoring her glare.

Abigail looks away from me and shakes her head. "No, they aren't coming." There is a hint of disappointment in her voice. "I convinced my father that Maclin acted alone. He believed me, as he always does." Abigail manages a coy smile as if she is proud of how she is able to easily lie to her father. "You are all safe. For now."

Lukan

Tracking the Howlers wasn't difficult. They leave a trail of mayhem and refuge. Dom and I run silently, unsure how far ahead the madmen really are. When the Howlers left Grayson, they trekked past the cliffs and caves and then began meandering west. The grass, still withered and brown, was trampled, making it easy to track their direction.

A slight hill came into view. We slow to a walk. Crouching down, we inch our way up the tiny hill. The landscape is silent which gives me a strange sense of unsettled ease. The Howlers were constantly making noise. I couldn't imagine that they would grow quiet out in this vastness. Yet, there are no sounds. The Howlers could be anywhere.

As we crest the hill on our bellies, we are instantly put at ease. No Howlers. Their path remains, however. We are still going the right direction.

"What is that?" Dom whispers, interrupting the silence.

With my one squinted eye, I follow his pointing finger into the distance. It appears that the Howlers have left a pile of clothing on the trail. My heart sinks as I consider the possibility of what I am actually seeing.

"Let's go," I say, attempting to push the possibilities away. Although I know we must walk past the mass, I dread finding out what it is.

As one, Dom and I begin running once again. As we near the mass that we had seen from the hill, we slow to a walk and then are stopped short. My fears are confirmed.

Laney.

There is no way of knowing if the woman from Grayson – the woman who had to stand and watch as her husband was beaten to death – simply became too much of a burden for the Howlers or if she had outlived her usefulness to them in the short amount of time that she was with them. The reason matters little. Her sons are orphans now.

As I stare down at Laney's lifeless body, blood pooling on the ground where her throat had been slashed, I feel tremendous sorrow. Another thought occurs to me though.

"They aren't far ahead," I advise.

"How do you know?" Dom asks.

I do not want to explain to him that there is still steam rising from her wound. The sight and smell of it begin to make me nauseous.

Turning away, I simply say, "I just know."

With that, we begin running again. It doesn't take long before we actually begin to hear them. They howl, and shout, laughing hysterically. Dom and I slow to a walk, draw our daggers, and begin our approach carefully.

The landscape begins to change from wide empty fields to forest. We stand on the edge of the woods and listen. The voices of the Howlers carry on the wind. Among the voices of the men, we begin to hear women and children. Chickens are clucking. If I didn't know any better, I would think we were approaching another community. A town full of people just trying to make the most of primitive living.

Dom and I exchange a confused glance. "Do I hear kids?" Dom whispers. I nod, looking back in the direction of what sounds like a content little community.

"We can't kill kids, Lukan," Dom asserts.

I look at him, stunned that he would allow any Howler to live, "They would not think twice about killing any of our kids."

Dom's eyes widen. "They're just kids, Lukan." His voice is a pleading hiss.

"They're Howlers," I argue.

"You don't know that. They could be kids they have stolen from other communities." Dom's whispers are becoming agitated.

"Laughing? Playing?" This argument is ridiculous, and I am appalled that he desires to continue.

"Surviving," Dom states before clenching his jaws tight.

We remain silent for some time. Listening. Finally, Dom raises his eyebrows, clearly wondering if we are going to proceed further or return home. Although part of me wants to raid the camp and exact revenge for what Grayson has endured, I know that the responsible thing for me to do is to head home. With a sharp tilt of my head, I gesture for us to leave.

Together, we begin to back away from the chatter. The thought of the children scratching at the back of my mind.

Chapter 17

Lia

The end of the world will not come with an explosion or gunfire. No, the end will come with a cough and a fever. Followed shortly by an ache that most will believe to be the flu. The symptoms will prove much more deadly, though, as it will leave each infected person bleeding out in their beds or in the streets. In subways, taxi cabs, and airplanes. Schoolyards and church pews. Capital Hill and the Oval Office. Not one single person in America will be unaffected by the devastation of this virus.

Eventually, the virus will spread to other parts of the world. Entire countries will be destroyed under the wrath of the virus. Nationalities will be erased from the earth. The devastation will be absolute. As the dwindling governments of the world attempt to end the impending extinction of mankind, they will soon realize that their exhaustive efforts will fail.

Although the life of the virus will come to an end, the aftermath will continue on for many years. I believe that there will be a tiny percentage that will have a natural immunity to the virus. These few will witness their loved ones succumb to the outbreak, but there will be no time for mourning.

Catastrophe tends to reveal one's true nature. Mourning will quickly turn to fury. Fury will quickly turn to destruction. Chaos will ensue as those who have kept their psychotic behaviors in check for years finally succumb to the personality that they have hidden from society. It is my prediction that these few will ultimately engage and destroy each other. Leaving the earth free of the true infection, which is us.

It is at that time, after the final scourge of the earth, that she will be able to begin repairing herself from the damage that we, the human race, inflicted upon her. We are the infection that has spread over the earth, and I am the one willing to bring an end to the madness.

M. DePriest – June 28, 2020

*****

The days that followed were filled with a wide array of assorted emotions. The death of Mac hung over us, leaving us feeling drained and hopeless. Even though Abigail assured us that we were not suspected of being Agitators, we each lived with the constant fear that Enforcers could come for us at any time. However, as we studied the journals that had been stolen from the President's Quarters, we began to feel something that could only be described as hesitant hope.

The journals themselves induced emotions in us. In them, the secrets of Terra Convex's past were revealed. As we read through them, we were faced with the brutal reality of the madness behind the devastation of the world above us.

Throughout our lifetime, we have been taught that the virus above was caused by our government. The teachings stated that the men in control of our country had built the virus in a laboratory for the purpose of aiding our military in defeating our enemies.

Only part of that was true.

The virus was indeed created in a laboratory. Not for the military, though. Not even for the government.

It was created by our first president, Marcus DePriest – the man that had Terra Convex built for the survival of mankind. His journals conveyed the true madness behind his intentions.

Somewhere between birth and death, humanity has stripped itself from all decency. We no longer cherish relationships; we conduct them. We no longer preserve the sanctity of life; we sell it to the highest bidder. We no longer treasure our planet; we rape it. The time for watching has passed. the time for action is upon us, and yet we remain seemingly unaware.

As loved ones rot away with cancer that we poured into the waters and sprayed into the air, humanity keeps their faces buried in their technology like ostriches bury their heads in the sand. It is time for the world to find awareness. it is time for their savagery to be met with destruction.

It is clear from the manuscripts that the virus was used to do exactly what it had been created for – destruction of the world. As we searched for deeper meaning in the journal entries, we found that Alayna DePriest – wife of Marcus DePriest – had died shortly after being diagnosed with cancer, leaving him to raise their only child, Webb. Alayna was only 27 at the time of her diagnosis and death. This left Marcus bitter and searching for answers.

Marcus' journals revealed his concerns about cancer and other diseases that he felt could have been prevented if not for man-made chemicals. The entries also spoke of his belief that because of mankind's inability to form meaningful relationships with others, love had become extinct.

Men and women, lost in their own lustful desires, have become incapable of true love. They have fallen in love with themselves. Only because of their natural sexual urges do they even procreate. They reproduce at a much higher rate than anticipated, burdening the earth with overpopulation and loveless affairs. It would be better for our planet, and for the human race, if relationships were governed. Humanity seems unable to form and maintain this aspect of their life.

"So that's why Leadership wrote the Marital Responsibility Act..." I ponder aloud to nobody in particular.

"This entry was written by Webb DePriest," Darcy begins, holding up several parchments. "Apparently, the first few years in Terra Convex, the people had not found a way to overcome their...oh, how did he put it? Here it is, 'their carnal desires.' There was no council at the time, so Webb DePriest enacted that law. On this page," Darcy held up another parchment for us all to see. "On this page, he writes about a rebellion that took place because of the Marital Responsibility Act. Some people were actually killed because of it."

"Oh my," I heard my sister say softly.

In our tiny room, all of the Defiance – including Matlok, and even Abigail - sits together, reading and studying the past of Terra Convex. We have been sifting through the manuscripts for days. Some of the entries are mindless doodles. Some were oddly worded poems that conveyed the true nature of the DePriest family. Most, however, give fantastic insight into the virus, the construction of the expansive compound, and the reasoning for the laws that were placed upon us.

The world above was described as a place of sickness, hate, and selfishness. Governments were corrupt; people were self-absorbed. Obviously, the virus didn't do anything to change the corruption of our government. It did, however, reverse the affects of a self-absorbed population. Instead, all of our individuality was stripped away. Leaving us to roam the corridors, and perform the assigned work, as nothing but mindless drones.

All, so that the DePriest's can live lavishly in their wing of Terra Convex.

I glance at Abigail, monitoring her emotional state. I can't imagine how difficult this is for her. First, she lost her mate. Now, she is discovering just how little our government cares for us. It is probably especially difficult since her father is part of the government. As she reads the parchment that is in her lap, her face reveals nothing. Abigail remains stoic, keeping her emotions hidden away from us all.

"I found it!" Dalen exclaims a little too loudly. We all flinch as he jumps up.

Although the truth of the virus, and the past of Terra Convex, is enlightening, what we have been eager to find is confirmation that the government knows that there is indeed life above ground. With this information, we can convince the rest of the population to revolt and overturn the government. I begin to feel giddy as I consider what Dalen has uncovered.

Dalen cannot seem to sit. Beaming, he begins to pace the tiny room.

"'As expected, and foretold by my father, life found a way. It was reported to me today that a Roughneck, doing his rounds above ground, actually saw life. Even though it was at a great distance, he described what he saw as being monstrous. Although the monsters walked upright like men and communicated with each other like men, they were covered in thick fur and emitted a horrendous howl. I can only assume that these beings are actually mutated from the humans that managed to survive the virus. Because of the panic this revelation could create, I have chosen not to inform the council. Furthermore, to safeguard this new information, I have sentenced the Roughneck to the Isolation Chamber.'" Dalen has stopped pacing. He looks at each of us with expectation.

"Howlers," I comment. "They are monstrous, but they aren't monsters. They're just men that wear thick furs and howl."

"How can you know that?" Abigail asks with fright in her voice and wide eyes.

"Lukan told me all about them? They terrorize all the surrounding communities." I explain.

Abigail huffs, "Then, please somebody explain to me why we would want to live in a world where Howlers are going to be terrorizing us. I thought you said it would be safer above ground." She looks at me with rebuke.

"It will be safe," Axel intervenes. "Lukan is formulating a plan to defeat the madmen as we speak. There is a chance they have been defeated already. It will be safe."

Dalen asks about Lukan. We all patiently listen as Axel recounts the time he spent with Lukan. Our three newest member listen with curious eyes. They look at Axel differently afterward. They are amazed at his bravery – to approach somebody from the outside world without fear or reservation.

Uncomfortable with all eyes on him, Axel redirects the conversation. "So the government knew that life had survived above ground. Even though they were fearful of it, they still could have sent a search party out to investigate. They chose not to. The people need to know this."

"There are so many problems with what you are saying," Abigail whines.

I want to throw her from the room so that those of us that are truly vested in leaving Terra Convex can have a legitimate meeting. However, I know that Mac would not approve of such an action, so I ignore her. "To be honest, I'm tired of hiding and sneaking around. I think the people are tired of seeing the propaganda that we have been leaving in the corridors."

"What are you saying, Lia?" Mira asks.

I consider her question for a moment. What am I saying? I know what I want to do but it is beyond risky. "I want to speak to the people myself." I try to say the words with confidence, but even I can hear the tremble in my voice.

Axel speaks up at once, "No. Out of the question."

"There is no way you can go public with this information," Mira says. "The Enforcers would be on you in a second." She snaps her fingers for emphasis.

"Actually," Matlok begins. He has been mostly silent since joining the Defiance. He looks at me meekly, and I wonder how he ever became an Enforcer. "I know of several Enforcers that despise Leadership. They have seen too much death at the hands of the government. They want real change. Amelia, you're the only one with a plan. They would follow you." His gray eyes look into mine intensely, and I know he is telling the truth.

"Matlok, you're endangering your own life by encouraging her," Mira retorts, obviously displeased with her husband.

"I'm endangering my life just being in this room," Matlok offers. "I agree with Amelia. I don't want to hide anymore. Hiding, and talking, isn't changing anything, and yet people are still dying."

At this moment, I realize why I admire Matlok so much. He has always been kind-hearted. Now, I know that he is logical and brave as well.

"Matlok, do you think you can find out how many Enforcers are on our side?" I ask, a plan formulating in my mind.

Matlok nods, "I think I already know how many. I think most of them are ready for change."

"Lia, please don't," Axel mutters, aware of my tenacity.

Ignoring him, I continue speaking to Matlok. "Talk to the Enforcers. Tell them that the Defiance welcomes them. Tell them to be ready."

"Ready for what, Lia?" Axel asks with obvious worry.

I stand so that I can look each rebel in the face. They need to see me as confident. As brave. Even if I don't feel it myself, I need them to see it. "Soon, the people of Terra Convex are going to learn the truth about this place, why they are here, and what they can do to get out. The people of Terra Convex are going to join the Defiance."

Lukan

When Dom and I return to Grayson, we find that the men are gathered in the Community Building. Some of the women are elsewhere, tending to the body of Briggs – preparing it for Lamenting. Others are sifting through the burned rubble, searching for anything that can be salvaged for the boys that are now orphans.

The air in the large room is thick with remorse and anger. Those in attendance, yell over each other, demanding action. My father seems to have given up on calling order to the meeting. Quietly, with his arms crossed over his chest, he leans against the stage allowing the rant to continue. As soon as the crowd sees Dom and me, they begin to quiet. My father stands and approaches us, relief washing over his face as we walk towards the stage. He embraces us both quickly and gives a quick, subtle scan to ensure that we are intact and have not suffered any injuries.

I whisper the news of Laney in his ear. On our way back, Dom and I had taken the time to quickly build a stretcher out of long branches. We felt it important that she be returned to her sons and to Grayson. I added this information and my father gave a grim nod.

The crowd grows impatient with our whispered conversation and begin murmuring loudly once again. My father turns and raises his arms, quieting them. Instead of returning to the front of the stage, he climbs the staircase and stands where the entire room can see him. Dom and I join, and the crowd grows silent.

"My son and nephew have just returned to Grayson," my father begins. "They followed the Howlers to their camp and have returned." Murmurs erupt from the crowd once more. "They followed the Howlers to their camp and have returned," my father repeats slowly, deliberately. "In less than a day, these two young men followed the Howlers to their camp and returned home. That is how close the Howlers live to our town. That is how close danger is to us every day. Every night while you and your wife and your children are sleeping, the Howlers are near." My father pauses to allow his words to sink into the stubborn hearts of those who are unwilling to defend Grayson.

I grow impatient as the crowd murmurs among themselves. I know many have already taken up arms and begun training. I know they are eager and ready. Now, more than ever, they fidget in their seats. The fight that is growing inside them, ready to burst forth with a vengeance against the Howlers.

"Listen," I begin loudly, tired of the inaction of these men. "The plan is solid. The training that most of you have begun has improved your skills, greatly. In just a few short weeks, Grayson will be ready to end the terror. Today should be proof of what is at stake. Today, we lost two members of our community. A house was destroyed. A family torn apart. I will not judge any of you who do not fight. However, if you do not fight with us, for the sake of all of us, your opinion on the matter is irrelevant, and I ask that you leave this room now so that Kismet may convene without distraction."

I stare through the crowd intently. Some are unable to hold my gaze. They are just too consumed with fear to stand against the Howlers. Slowly, they are the ones that stand and begin to walk out. I am glad to see them go. Only those committed to the plan should stay.

After those lacking bravery have left, I scan the crowd again. This time, I smile proudly at those remaining. They stare back at me with burning determination. These that remain are Kismet. They are eager to finalize our battle plan.

"During the next snowstorm, we attack," I announce.

A look of confusion crosses the faces of those listening. Understandable. Snowstorms are dangerous, and one could easily become lost in the white. Nevertheless...

"We will use the white out to our advantage," I explain. "The Howlers will not expect a siege on their camp...especially during a whiteout. While they huddle in their tents, we will surround them. The goal is that not one Howler makes it out of their tent alive." I pause to let that image sink in. "Go home. Make any needed repairs to your snowshoes. Sharpen your daggers. Get comfortable using it just in case we are forced into hand-to-hand combat. Every chance you get, go to the target practice field. The time will come quickly so be ready."

Chapter 18

Lia

With shaky legs, I crawl up onto the table and stand. As the crowd around me begins to notice the insignificant girl standing over them, they begin to nudge those closest to them and point in my direction. I chance a look at Axel and find that he is now standing in front of the table I am perched upon. He has his back to me and seems to be there to ensure that nobody harms me. Although thankful for his presence, I am no less terrified of what I am about to do.

I'm not sure how long Matlok and the Enforcers will be able to keep Leadership busy. Clearing the fear from my throat, I begin to read from Marcus DePriest's journal.

"'The human race is an infection to this earth that must be eradicated.'" I pause and look at the crowd to see if they had heard me speak. By the curious stares, I can only assume they did. Taking a deep breath, I decide that there is no turning back. I must finish this.

Louder now, I say the words again. "'The human race is an infection to this earth that must be eradicated. Every building that is erected is just another nail in the coffin of this beautiful planet we call home. The automobiles and jet planes that litter our roads and airways are like termites that eat away at the houses we live in.'" I glance up to see if I still have everyone's attention. I do.

"'I feel it is my duty, given the skills and capabilities that I am privileged to possess, to rid the earth of the scourge that the human race has become. To begin the healing process so that the earth may someday be home to a kinder people. To a more loving people. To a people that will cherish the land and not ruin it with overpopulations and poisons.'"

"Amelia! Get down from there this instant!" Ms. Bermingham screeches as she stomps her way through the crowd.

I look down to see Axel bristle, but he stands ready to take the beast on.

It's too late for me to stop, so I continue, "These are the words from our first president, Marcus DePriest. These words came from his personal journal that he brought into Terra Convex...right after he released a deadly virus that killed our ancestors."

I pause, looking around the expansive room. The people are obviously confused. they glance at each other nervously, with quiet murmuring. Ms. Bermingham stands in front of Axel, with her arms crossed over her chest. Her nostrils are flaring, but I try not to let it distract me from the mission.

"The man that created this place," I say loudly, sweeping my arms wide, "did so with one purpose...to live while the rest of the world died horribly because of him. He believed he could reset humanity by killing the majority of it off."

"That is a lie!" Ms. Bermingham shrieks. "Marcus DePriest was a hero for building this place before the deadly virus could kill off every last human on earth. He is your savior."

I consider her words for a second before looking back into the small ancient journal that suddenly feels more like a shield than a leather-bound book. Finally, I find the words I have been looking for.

"'The first shipment of virus-laced bottled water has begun to do the job it was created for. On the news tonight, there was a report of a virus that seems to be ravaging through parts of Africa. By the time the water is distributed throughout America, I along with my most diligent followers will be in our underground world. While the rest of the world bleeds out, we will be tucked safely away.'"

The people around me are clearly distressed with what I have presented them. We have always known that a virus sent us underground. None of us would have ever imagined that our leader orchestrated the virus.

A terrified looking woman to my left finds her voice to ask, "But the virus was created by the government to put an end to war." She looks around warily. "Marcus DePriest created this place and brought his closest friends down when the virus was stolen from the lab. He knew how dangerous it was." The woman, although courageous enough to speak to the strange girl standing on the table, seems close to tears as she considers what has been revealed from the journal.

I know this woman isn't the only one in the room that is being affected by the words of Marcus DePriest. It isn't easy to find out that while our ancestors were allowed to live, everyone else in the world was dying horribly. I glance at Ms. Bermingham. Although she is still fuming, her face has changed. She seems to be listening.

"Marcus DePriest was just a scientist. He was a wealthy man that played around with organisms that could kill. There was nothing special about him. Nothing extraordinary. He had extreme ideas, and he acted on them." I am surprised at how calm my voice sounds while I am still trembling on the inside.

The crowd listens intently. They seem both eager and hesitant to learn more of the truth. As I look into their eyes, their fearful curiosity seemingly gives me the strength to go on.

"Once, our ancestors ruled this world. It wasn't the best. It wasn't. That was no reason to kill them all. No reason for a man, or anyone, to decide who lives and who dies. Whatever was going on in the world ninety years ago, it was better than this."

A man interrupts me this time, "He saved us. We have a good life here. The DePriest's have provided everything we need." His words are followed by several murmurs of agreement from the crowd.

"We don't," Axel interjects, startling me. "Our food supply is dangerously low and has been for some time."

"For some time?" The man in the crowd continues. "Then, we must have enough, or we would have run out already."

"The reason we haven't is because the government, the DePriest's decide who eats and who doesn't. They decide who lives and who dies." Axel explains loud enough for the entire room to hear.

"Have you ever wondered where the elderly go? Where did your parents go? Your grandparents?" I ask the room.

"They go to the Hall of Age Progression where they are treated with kindness until their age takes them." Ms. Bermingham declares, her arms still stiffly folded across her plump bosom. The scowl on her face deeply embedded is now a permanent fixture.

Looking into her eyes, I shake my head slightly and respond with genuine sadness in my voice, "No, they're not. They are taken to the Isolation Chamber. They are given no food or water. No lights. Not even a bed to lay on when they take their last breath." I choke up slightly as I remember holding my mother and feeling her last breath caress my cheek.

The eyes that stare up at me, all across the Dining Hall, are sad but inquisitive. I have their attention. Standing above them, though, gives me a strange feeling. These are my people. I should be standing with them, not above them. Jumping down from the table, I give Axel a slight squeeze on his arm. He flashes me a sly smile that both calms my nerves and causes a fluttering deep in my belly.

Returning my attention back to the people of Terra Convex, I continue, "Have you known anyone that got hurt or sick? Did they disappear? One day they are working next to you, the next day they are gone. You want to ask where they are but you know you can't because questions aren't allowed. Why aren't questions allowed?" I pause, not expecting an answer, but wanting to ensure that the crowd is listening. "Questions are not allowed because too many questions could lead to the truth of this place."

"What's the truth?" A woman that I only know as Shelaine asks.

I walk to her, taking in the sight of her curly hair that I have seen bouncing through the corridors of Terra Convex on many occasions. Although I do not know her well, I remember that she has always been kind to my sister and me. I believe my mother and Shelaine had been friends.

With compassion, I tell Shelaine the truth, and I pray the others listen. "The truth is that we have been lied to. We have been controlled. Our time in Terra Convex is running out, but still, Leadership refuses to acknowledge this fact because if they let us out, then they lose control."

"Out?" Shelaine asks with a slight tilt of her head.

This is it. This is what everything has been building towards. Everything that I have lost, everything that I have risked, is for this moment.

Although I still stand in front of Shelaine, the curious red-head with an abundance of playful curls but incredibly sad eyes, I speak louder so that I am heard throughout the room. "There is life outside of Terra Convex. People are living outside. People are living right above us. Whole communities of people." I can hear the pitch of my voice begin to rise excitedly.

The murmurs in the room intensify. I knew this revelation had the potential of being too substantial. The result of ninety years of oppression has resulted in small minds, unable to grasp the true potential of their curiosity and imagination.

"We should not be living as victims!" I shout over the murmuring. "We have a chance to really live! There is life above us, and we should be living it."

Scanning over the crowd of stunned onlookers, I notice Abigail standing against the wall. Although she has made great efforts to be part of the Defiance in a way that Maclin would approve, her face is set in anger and hatred for me. The animosity she felt for me before has not subsided since the death of Maclin. I remain surprised that their relationship grew so much in their short union.

I try to shake off the distraction, "I know you are afraid. Trust me, I am too. Sometimes, what you are most afraid of doing is the very thing that will set you free. Free to live your own life. Free to marry the person you love. Free to have as many children as you want and to name them whatever you like. Free to create, ask, imagine. You have to know that you were created for more than just this." I sweep my arm across the room dramatically but with purpose.

"It's too dangerous. Leadership will never let us out." I hear someone near the back shout. "What will we do once we leave? It's too much. Too dangerous."

"It could be dangerous to walk away. It will most definitely be scarey. It might even hurt, but that will never compare to the pain of staying. This place has caused too much pain for me to want to stay. I believe that pain is coming for you too. For some of you, it has already. Don't let the fear of the outside and the unknown keep you in this living tomb." I pause briefly. "If you want more proof of the lies of the government, I can take you to the Isolation Chamber. Maybe you will see somebody in there that you know." I add a little more harshly than I intended. "While you are stepping over the decaying bodies of those that are dead and dying, just remember that your time in that place is coming. Unless you leave."

"What can we do though? Enforcers will kill us before we even begin to stand up to the Leadership," a man's frightened voice beckons from the crowd.

I smile knowingly. "Look around you. Look past those standing right next to you. Look past your fear. The doors are being guarded by Enforcers. There is an Enforcer in every corner of this room. There are Enforcers among you. You will be protected by these men. They are no different from you or me. They want change. The stories they have to tell will turn your blood cold. They will enforce a new law. The law of the people."

I watch as the people of Terra Convex scan the room warily. They seem to be noticing the Enforcers for the first time. The realization begins to set in – these men mean no harm to anyone in this room. Fear and confusion seem to fade from their faces. Replaced by curiosity and hope.

"Show us!" Another male voice from the crowd cries out. "Show us the Isolation Chamber." Several join in, demanding to be shown the Isolation Chamber.

I manage to keep from smiling. This is the response we had planned for. I have no doubt that once these people see the horrors of the Isolation Chamber, they will realize the ruthlessness of our government. We had planned for this.

"Very well," I reply calmly. "The Enforcers have cleared the way for you to visit the Isolation Chamber. However, I must warn you. What you will see in there is horrendous. If you haven't the stomach for death, then I suggest you stay behind." With that, I turn and walk towards the exit from the Dining Hall.

In the days since we discovered the gift that Mac left us, in the form of the hidden presidential journals, there hasn't been much rest. Everyone had a job to do. Through the fear, we worked diligently. Always keeping the reward – freedom – in sight.

Dalen assured us that the Roughnecks of Terra Convex were eager to join the fight. They began crafting weapons from pipes, sharp pieces of metal, and anything else they could find lying around the compound. These weapons, once completed, were then smuggled into the Enforcers Ward.

The Enforcers Ward is where the Enforcers gather for shift changes and meetings – lately, meetings regarding The Defiance and how to destroy the rebellious group. It is the place in Terra Convex where the Enforcers store their uniforms, tasers, and helmets. Ironically, it was the perfect place to hide the handcrafted weapons. Each Enforcer has a locker where they store their gear. Those lockers now hide weapons that will be used against Leadership.

My hope is that we will be able to overthrow the government without actually harming anyone. There are many more Agitators now than there are actual people in Leadership. When they see our numbers, surely they will surrender.

Matlok assures me that all of the Enforcers and most of the Interrogators are now part of the Defiance. There are only a few Interrogators that have given true allegiance to the government. I suspect that those few only do so because they themselves suffer from the same madness and narcissism as President DePriest.

As I march through the corridors of Terra Convex toward the Isolation Chamber – Axel beside me; the frightened, confused, curious people of Terra Convex behind me – I am struck with the thought that I could very well be leading them to their deaths. It is possible that the Enforcers do not share my belief that there is life outside. Possible that they have planned an ambush for the Defiance.

In reading the journals, I have learned that Marcus DePriest hand-picked those that were to survive the virus. He chose the ones he felt would bring the most valuable traits to the earth once the virus ran its course. Entire families were given safety from the virus and the world of chaos that ensued. it's possible that because of the rebellion that I created, Leadership is ready to wipe Terra Convex clean and begin again. What better way to do that then lead the enemy to their own death in the Isolation Chamber – where death comes for everyone who enters.

I slow my pace slightly, and Axel instantly notices. Sensing my dread, he takes my hand. "Even heroes know when to be scared," he says quietly before adding. "We're almost to the end."

I'm sure Axel means that we're nearly to the Isolation Chamber – this is where the citizens of Terra Convex will make a choice to fight or die. Possibly, he is referring to the fact that he believes our time buried in the earth is coming to an end. With that though, comes the possibility that the end that is nearing will either be death or freedom. The thought gives me a shudder.

That's what I'm afraid of, I think to myself but dare not say aloud.

Lukan

The days, cold but tolerable, indeed passed quickly. Not a day went by that the target field was empty. Those that wished to fight seemed committed. Not a day went by that another citizen of Grayson decided to join Kismet. All were weary of the pain inflicted by the Howlers. All prepared for that pain to end.

I watched as the skies turned from brilliant blue to gray. The change was gradual. Usually, the graying skies turned moods sour and lethargic. Now, though, the gray skies brought a sense of revolution.

"Your town has changed since I first arrived," Helix says as we sit on the rock wall – me looking out over the brown and withered meadow, he only seeing blackness, yet so much more.

I nod and then realize he cannot see the acknowledgment. "I feel it too."

It had been some time since Helix and I were able to sit alone. I can't help but reflect on the first time I saw him – dripping rainwater from his thick fur coat as I stood dumbfounded inside the cave, fearing that he was a Howler. Although his appearance was intimidating and his voice came out as a growl, his presence put me at ease. I marveled then as I do now, at his amazing abilities without sight.

"I hope to sit with you on this wall again when this is finished, Helix," I say. The words sounded like goodbye even though that was not my intent.

The wind picks up slightly, and a chill runs up my spine. Next to me, I hear the familiar groan of Helix contemplating and I am comforted by the sound of it. I look up at him and realize he appears troubled. A thought occurs to me that I try to push away. The thought persists, and I can take it no longer.

"You aren't staying in Grayson. Are you?" My voice sounds empty.

Helix doesn't have to answer. He purses his lips and then relaxes them as he contemplates how to answer.

"Why not?" I ask quietly.

It takes him a moment to answer. "I'm a Wanderer. You. Your family. All of Grayson has been very kind and generous to me. Still, its difficult for me to stay in one place for too long. It's time for me to keep moving."

Although I hate to think about life without Helix, I understand. Some of my best days have come while exploring the forests beyond the walls of Grayson. I envy a man that can explore the world without actually seeing it.

"I will miss you though, my friend," Helix says clapping me gently on the back. "You have grown into a man since that day we met in the cave." His voice is warm with affection.

I think back to that day once more and realize that I have indeed changed. When we first met, I was hiding from my self-doubt in that cave. When I would jump off the cliffs into the clear blue lake below, I was attempting to rid myself of what I thought was a disability. Now, though, I realize my capabilities. I realize my worth in Grayson.

"You helped with that," I comment. "If not for you, I would have never gone hunting. It was that first hunting trip when I learned that being blind in one eye was not what defined me as a member of Grayson."

Helix and I sit in silence for a little longer. Each of us lost in our own thoughts. I suddenly realize that snow has begun to fall. With the snow comes a new sense of eagerness. The time for action has come.

Chapter 19

Lia

As expected, the people of Terra Convex looked on the scene in the Isolation Chamber with sheer horror. Apparently, the Interrogators that remained loyal to the government had been busy the past few days. The Isolation Chamber is not full - only about a dozen or so dead or dying citizens are scattered throughout the room. Some are elderly – frail, starved, naked, and waiting for death. The rest are just common citizens who had been arrested for some minor infraction that offended Leadership. All were here to die.

The history that I share with this room is too much, and I remain by the double doors while the citizens of Terra Convex slowly begin to meander their way through the bodies. Clearly, there is death in this room. The foullness of the decay is noxious and almost unbearable. There is no air being ventilated into or out of this room. Those that are sentenced to death in this room of putrefaction must endure the smell of rot during their last days.

"Jayda," a hear an elderly man beckon. He repeats the name without getting a response. I watch him as he searches the faces of those lying on the cold, wet floor of urine, feces, and other body fluids. He becomes desperate, and my heart hurts deeply for the torment this place is causing him. That I am causing him by bringing him here. "Jayda," he yells louder as his search continues.

Breaking free from the wall I have plastered myself against, I make my way to the man. He doesn't have to explain who he is searching for. It doesn't matter. It's somebody that he cares for deeply. Somebody that was most likely taken away because of age. Somebody that deserves better than this fate.

"Who are you looking for?" I ask when I reach the man. His eyes are wide with horror. His face is wet with tears.

"My wife. Jayda," the man explains. "They took her three days ago. When the man came to our living quarters, he said that it was time for her to go to a place where she would be taken care of." He looks around in a daze and places his arm across his face. The pungent odor was becoming too much for him.

I have no words for this man. Guilt overcomes me. I should have been more careful about who I brought to this place. The purpose of this trip to the room of death was to spur the people into action. This man, advanced in years, has only found pain here – not a purpose for fighting.

"Will you help me look?" he chokes out. His gray eyes were gentle even while consumed with fear. I shudder, but he doesn't seem to notice. His eyes are fixed on the dead.

I have no heart to tell the man that his Jayda is most likely one of the dead bodies that is littered among the dying. I simply nod. Looking around, I see Abigail close by. There is still tremendous malice between her and I. Still, when she catches my eye, I nod towards the man and she knows exactly what is needed at that moment. With a gentleness I never knew she possessed, Abigail takes the man by the elbow and leads him to the doors. I can hear her whisper words of compassion to him as they walk away.

Quickly, I scan the area for any elderly women. I realize that the old man isn't the only one searching for a loved one. There are people all around trying to find somebody that is important to them. As they search, I can see their faces have gone from disgust to sadness to anger.

Near the door, I see Matlok. He gives me a nod. That is my signal. He has brought the pipes and homemade weapons from the Enforcer's Ward. They are at the door waiting to be utilized. With my eyes, I find Axel who also nods at me. Everything is in place – including the emotions of the people of Terra Convex.

"I know this place is difficult to take in," I begin with as much courage as I can muster. "I know you don't want to believe that your government has a place like this for people like you or your loved ones." I pause, looking around – meeting as many eyes as possible. "This place – this room - isn't the end for the dead. Once a week, the dead are cleared from here, and they are burned to ashes."

All throughout the room, I can hear gasps. It is difficult for the people of Terra Convex to fathom that their bodies will be reduced to ash whenever the government deems it necessary. Although painful, this is the reaction I had hoped for.

"We can put a stop to this madness, though. You! You can put a stop to all of this. Even if you don't want to leave Terra Convex, surely you want a better life than this. A more dignified death than this." I sweep my hand through the air, gesturing towards those that lay all around us. "Push down your fear and accept the task that has presented itself to you. Every moment of inaction is cowardice in this tomb of oppression."

"I will fight," I hear a man roar from somewhere in the large room.

"I will fight," another yells with fervor.

One by one, sometimes with their voices intermingling, the people of Terra Convex spoke up. They were ready to put an end to the oppression. I feel a small smile begin to work the edges of my lips.

With a nod, I walk to the door where the weapons wait. The people let me pass by. Their faces are etched with anger, horror, and anticipation of a battle that they had not planned on fighting when the woke this morning.

At the door, I pick up a pipe that had been crafted into a lethal weapon. The pipe looks large in my tiny hands, but it actually fits just right. The deadly end has been fashioned with sharp blades of metal protruding, making it quite menacing. I turn and face the people. Their faces reveal that they are just now realizing that this is indeed happening. They are on the precipice of something tremendous and daunting.

"Sometimes what you're most afraid of doing is the very thing that will set you free," I say with a calmness in my voice that surprises me. Those closest to me began to pick their weapon. There were some that were tending to the injured in the Isolation Chamber.

Matlok is at my side, brandishing his taser and a handmade weapon. Axel is on my other side – his face set in determination.

"This is for freedom. This is for all those we have lost to this room." I catch Abigail's eyes and add, much quieter, "This is for Mac." Louder once more, "All those the government has taken from us." I yell exuberantly.

The angered crowd before me raise their weapons in unison and bellow loudly. With that, we turn and exit the room. With that, the course has been set. I can't help but fear that some will be lost. There are still plenty of Interrogators, as well as the President's security guards that we will have to go through to see victory over oppression.

Lukan

The snowstorm seems to have turned into a blizzard. The wind howls fiercely against the windows and walls of my home. Curled warmly in my bed, I bring the thick blankets over my head to drown out the noise. Eventually, sleep finds me, and I find rest.

Hours later, I wake groggily to the screams of the wind continuing to whistle through the slightest of cracks in the windows of our home. Tossing, I press the blanket tighter against my ears. Still, the shrieking of the wind continues.

Begrudgingly, I rise from my bed. I grab a shirt that I had thrown onto the floor and walk to my window. I hope that by placing the shirt firmly against the window sill, the sound will cease. At the window, though, I am met with horror.

Flames writhe violently with the wind, burning through homes all throughout Grayson. The home next to ours is fully engulfed. Its occupants stand huddled in the street, the wind and snow blowing their bedclothes. Just as I am turning to get dressed so that I may go help, a menacing figure appears in the street. Running towards the sobbing family, a Howler hunts.

Quickly dressing, I sling the quiver of arrows across my back and grab my dagger and bow. The Howlers are attacking Grayson, and I must get out there to help protect our town. Opening my bedroom door, I am immediately met with hot flames. I stand in my doorway watching the walls of my home burn.

"Mom! Dad!" I cry out, listening for their voices over the fury of the fire. "Dom!" I begin to choke on the acrid smoke. Shutting the door hard, I begin shoving all of my clothes and blankets against the bottom of it in an attempt to keep the smoke out. My mind is frantic with worry for my family. Outside, I can hear the screams of Grayson and the howls of the fiends who are attacking us.

I go to the window once more. There are bodies in the street. My neighbors. My heart sinks as I realize that the Howlers have set Grayson on fire and now wait for its occupants to flee their homes. As the people run from the flames, they are being murdered in the streets. Is that what happened to my family? Did they run?

I scan the yard near my bedroom window. It appears clear of Howlers. I open the window and climb out carefully. Behind me, my bedroom steadily fills with smoke. When I am out, I chance a look in that direction and get the eery sense that smoke is hunting me just as the Howlers are hunting.

Crouching, with my back against the wall, I sneak toward the corner of my house toward the street. The screams of the people are heinous. It's obvious they are enduring unspeakable tortures. As I peak around the corner, I see that the street is clear. All that remains are the bodies of those the Howlers have already slain. Frantically, I search the street for any sign of my family. Hopefully, Dom was able to get them to safety before it was too late.

I rub my face, trying to decide which direction to go in search of my family. Screams come from every direction. The fire that consumes own house swells and I am forced to move away from the fracturing structure. I decide that they probably would have gone toward the woods. The Howlers have never gone in that direction.

The street seems too dangerous, so I begin my trek towards the woods by going through the backyards of my neighborhood. Every house is ablaze. I wonder briefly if I should check for survivors in each home but decide that finding my family is my priority right now. I can only hope that others have successfully fled.

There is a loud explosion somewhere behind me causing me to flinch and cover my head instinctively. I am rattled by the sound of it and distracted when I am knocked to the ground with violent force. Wrestling to get out from underneath the brute that has tackled me, I am stunned when a fist punches me in my right jaw. Immediately, I am met with a shrill ringing in my ears that I attempt to shake off. All while continuing to wrestle.

The fiend that straddles me is especially pungent with the odor of the dead animal he wears. He leans up just enough that I can see his face in the light of the flames of the home burning beside us. His face is scarred horrifically, and for a brief second, I wonder if those scars were inflicted by other Howlers trying to show their dominance. He has several missing teeth, and the rest are black with rot. I try not to gag at the sight and smell of the beast.

As he adjusts his position to get a better angle for punching me, I manage to get my hand on my dagger that rests in my belt just waiting its turn for action. The Howler does not seem to realize his mistake until he feels the smooth slice across his belly. Stunned, he reaches a hand to the area. When he brings his hand back up, it drips with blood.

I take this moment to end him with a swift slash across the throat. Immediately, I am coated with the monster's blood. I buck once. Twice. Three times and he falls off of me. We are both blood-soaked, but I am the victor. This time.

In the distance, I hear my name. I listen intently, hoping it is just my memory of Merritt beckoning me. Again, I hear the voice. It is a woman's voice, and she is screaming.

My mother.

Running now, I rush in the direction of her anguished voice. Beside me, houses and yards burn furiously. People lay dead. Children scream in the shadows.

As I near the Community Building, I immediately come to a halt. On the stage, I see my mother on her knees. She is bloody and bruised. She sobs and I can tell that her cries are not for her. Glancing around, I see the reason for her tears. My father lays dead just off to the right of her. Dom too. My heart rips violently in my chest, but anger soon replaces the heartache.

Behind my mother, Gallner stands. His hand is full of her hair, and he holds a knife to her throat. The image is eerily similar to the way he held Merritt before he murdered her. I take a slow step forward.

Although I am angry, I plead for the life of my mother. "Please Gallner. Don't do this. Take me instead. Let her go."

Gallner only smiles coyly. He loves people to beg, so I continue, inching forward slowly. His smile remains, and to my horror, with a slow, methodical motion, his knife goes cleanly across my mother's throat.

Screaming, I wake. The room is dark except for the glowing lantern that sits on my bedside table. My mother sits over me with a look of both concern and compassion. Seeing that she is alive and unharmed, I wrap my arms around her neck, surprising her. She must realize that my nightmare had been about her. Releasing her, I look into her eyes. They sparkle with a tenderness that only a mother can give her child. She doesn't ask me about the dream that woke the house. My mom knows that such things are best forgotten and never spoken of.

Dom appears at the door of my room. "Well, since we are all up. Let's finish this."

"How long did I sleep?" I ask, rubbing a still shaky hand over my face.

"Three hours," my mom replies.

The attack on the Howlers is set for the morning. The plan was to try to get two or three hours of sleep during the evening and then leave an hour after dusk. We would trek to the camp through the night and attack at first light.

If I had any trepidation about attacking the Howlers, it is erased now. Perhaps my mind knew what I needed to fuel my hatred for them. I glance at my mother once again. She gives me a nervous and loving smile. She understands what must be done.

"I will see you soon," I promise her.

"I know," she acknowledges, standing from the bed. She heads to the door and gives Dom a pat on the shoulder on her way out. "I will see you soon, too."

Dom and I exchange a knowing look.

Time for action has come.

Chapter 20

Lia

Our footfalls are thunderous in the narrow corridors as we march towards the Presidential Quarters. Our loud approach will not be a surprise to the guards that have sworn to protect Leadership at all cost.

I have no way of knowing how many are following me to what could be our demise. I dare not chance a look behind me for fear of losing my balance and being trampled by what has now become an angry mob intent on revenge.

These that march with me are doing so with a different passion than my own. Their pain is fresh. The ache of loss; the sting of a lifetime of lies. Raw. When they woke this morning, they woke as loyal citizens of Terra Convex – content with their life of oppression in the name of freedom. I have been aware of the lies told by the government for some time.

Because they know the way, Matlok and several other Enforcers take the lead. Axel and I are behind them. Although I know many are still scattered throughout the compound, it sounds like all of Terra Convex is behind me.

I hear commotion far in front of me. A man is yelling; obviously, he is startled at the sight of several Enforcers stomping towards him. There are thuds and grunts somewhere at the front of the pack. I have no doubt that Matlok and the Enforcers that are leading the way have engaged the guards.

Although I know it is impossible, I struggle to stand on the tips of my toes and strain my neck to see what is happening in front of us. There are still Enforcers that remain with the group. They stand defensively with their weapons in front of them. I can feel myself being drawn to the skirmish that is happening beyond my field of vision.

I feel a hand clamp down on my arm. Looking up, I see Axel standing over me, clinging to me. His eyes are narrowed; his brow creased with annoyance. "You will see the fight soon enough, Lia," he warns.

Before I can respond, the Enforcer in front of us announces, "We're moving again."

I look at Axel once more as we indeed begin to move forward but his eyes are distant, anticipating the fight.

As one unit, we snake our way through the many twists and turns that lead to the Presidential Quarters. We pass by four men who lay in a heap upon each other. Their faces are bruised and bloody. Beside them, Matlok and another Enforcer wait. As soon as Matlok sees me, he rejoins our march.

"Are you all right?" I ask even though he doesn't seem harmed in any way.

"They were surprised to see us," Matlok explains as we walk. "They were easy to take out. I don't imagine the rest will go as quickly." He keeps his eyes steadily gazing ahead, ready for the next ruckus.

The corridors in this area of Terra Convex are much different than the ones in the heart of the complex. There is no muck covering the walls and floor. In fact, the walls and floor shine bright and clean. Leadership does not live surrounded by cold, damp concrete. The lights are even better - bright and warm.

I can feel those behind me begin to notice the affluence as we proceed through the corridors. They respond with hostility, pressing forward with murmurs and complaints. Just as I am about to shout for them to stay focused, something catches my eye. Stepping out of the mob and toward the wall closest to me, I feel my chest constrict.

Slightly confused, the crowd slows to a stop. They stare at the walls with wide eyes of amazement and awe. The murmuring has ceased. I feel Axel next to me. He gently takes my hand, as I fight back the tears of sadness and anger. I scan the wall from the direction we came from and the direction we are going. Every direction, the walls are the same.

Art.

The walls leading to the Presidential Quarters are covered with beautiful artwork. Masterpieces of exquisite creativity, each one speaks volumes to the elegance and refinement of a long ago time. Staring up at the paintings, I feel tears of regret begin to fall. Regret that Mac wasn't able to see this. He loved art. Loved to create beauty from nothing on a piece of parchment.

He did see it though.

He had to have come through this corridor when he was sneaking into the Presidential Quarters. Which means, he would have passed by all of these pieces. I begin to wipe my tears as I realize that Mac was able to view such creative beauty before his life was taken.

Another thought occurs to me, and my anger begins to rise once again. Aware of the people around me gazing at the various pieces of artwork, I realize that this also their first time at seeing such beauty. Creativity was banned in Terra Convex. Every sketch Mac ever created, he had to throw away or risk being punished mercilessly. Yet, Leadership has an entire corridor just for their art display.

Just as I turn to gather the people for our final push forward, screaming comes the back of the group. I begin to move toward the sound, but Axel still has my hand in his. I look at him, confused.

"We have to keep moving," he explains with urgency.

"But they are being attacked," I argue. "Somehow, they have managed to come around behind us."

Axel nods. "Our fight is this way, though. The guards think that we will run towards the screams to help those at the back of the pack. While we do that, there will be more guards coming at us from the other direction. We have to move forward." His eyes are intense, and I feel as if I hardly recognize this part of Axel. Still, even though it seems rather heartless, I know Axel is right.

Behind him, Matlok yells, "He's right, Amelia."

With a nod and a lump in my throat, I begin to run the opposite direction of the shouts and screams. There are fewer of us running this way. Most of the mob went towards the pleas of their neighbors. Only Axel, Matlok, and a few Enforcers maintain our course to the Presidential Quarters.

Ahead, a security guard stands his ground. He holds his taser in front of him as if he can fend off all of us with the one weapon. I hate to think of it, but I know that one of us will have to be the one to take the jolt of electricity while another uses the opportunity of distraction to gain control of the guard violently, only so that the rest of us can continue on. I am only slightly relieved in knowing that the pain from the taser will be temporary.

The large guard shouts for us to halt. We do not. Our pace doesn't slow at all. His taser hand sweeps back and forth as he tries to decide which of us will be receiving the shock. The enforcers that run with us – I feel a tinge of guilt for not knowing the names of everyone that is fighting beside me – maneuver themselves to the front of our small pack. They have decided to take the hit for those of us bringing up the rear. A sense of ease comes over me as I realize that the taser strike will not be nearly as painful – if at all – since the Enforcers wear thick uniforms.

Just as I think this, though, I hear the taser discharge and see a large Enforcer fall to the ground. The other Enforcer that had been running beside the fallen one does not break stride as he runs straight into the guard, knocking him to the ground and disarming him.

"Don't stop!" I hear Matlok shout to me, somehow sensing my desire to render aid to the fallen Enforcer. I heed his shouts, though, and continue running.

I do chance a glance in the fallen Enforcers direction though. He clutches at his throat and writhes on the ground. Apparently, the guard was aware of the Enforcer's thick uniform. He had aimed at the exposed skin of the man's throat. the other Enforcer stands over the guard, kicking him violently.

"How many more?" Axel asks Matlok as we run.

"Not sure," he answers. "I imagine the rest are coming up behind us now."A shiver snakes up my spine as I fight the urge to look behind me.

"We're almost there, though," Matlok adds, giving me a strange sense of relief and unease.

Relief because the fight will be over soon. Unease because another fight will soon begin.

Next to me, Axel screams out and falls to the ground, the metal pipe he had been carrying clanking loudly onto the hard floor. His body convulses violently. I run back to where he has fallen and realize that he has been shot with a taser. The sharp barbs are buried deep in his back.

"Amelia, get out of here," Matlok shouts, pulling me from Axel and nearly throwing me down the corridor.

Angry tears wet my face as I am torn between finishing this battle once and for all or staying with my love. I am aware, however, of the other Enforcers running towards where Axel lays. I realize that they are running to protect him from further harm. It is now up to Matlok and me to end this. An unlikely pair, for sure.

"Here!" Matlok says, taking a sharp left that I would have missed if he hadn't told me where to go. The shine of the walls made it nearly impossible to distinguish where one wall ended, and another began.

The left turn is the end of the line for us. There is nowhere else for us to run. At the end of this short hallway, stands a grand door.

The Presidential Quarters.

Like the corridors leading here, the walls and floor are made of some sort of extremely shiny material. Not gray or black like the rest of Terra Convex, but a bright, clean cream color. The door is made of the same material and the same color. I can see our reflections as we slowly approach.

There should be guards, I think to myself. Just as I do, the grand door opens, and two men step out. Larger than the rest, the brutes are clearly there to ensure the president's safety when others fail. They are the last line of defense, and we are the first to test them.

One Enforcer. One rebellious teenager girl.

I feel panic stab at my belly. Closing my eyes, I revisit my darkest memories – holding my mother as she breathed her last; watching the blood pour from Mac. Memories that I would not have if not for President DePriest and the Council. the panic subsides. Only to be replaced with purposeful malice.

I glance over at Matlok and am pleased to see that his face conveys only determination. If he is afraid, his face does not betray him. He must feel my eyes on him. With one subtle motion of his head, he nods. He puts his taser away and grasps the pipe with both hands.

Refocusing my attention, I also gain a tighter grip on the pipe that I chose as a weapon. I hold it in front of me, and as one, with a shriek, Matlok and I race toward the sentries. They seem slightly taken aback at the spectacle racing toward them but gather themselves quickly, standing their ground, tasers at the ready.

At the last minute, Matlok reaches for his taser and brings it up. With a fluid motion, he engages the taser, shooting one of the guards in the throat, while bringing his thick metal pipe down onto the head of the other. While the tasered man writhes on the floor, Matlok brings his foot down onto the man's head. Both men are rendered useless immediately.

Breathless from the brief burst of energy, I can do nothing but stand over the two men. I hadn't had to do anything. Matlok seemed to have it planned exactly the way it played out.

Behind us, somewhere in the winding corridors, there is a battle taking place. The sounds of it echo through the pristine hallways. There is no way to tell who has the upper hand. I worry for Axel's safety. There is a large part of me that aches to return to the fight; however, I know that I have my own battle to face, just on the other side of the magnificent door.

"This is it," Matlok states. "You ready?" His blue eyes bore into mine as he reaches for the door.

I bring my weapon back in front of my chest and hold it with two hands. I cannot seem to find my voice, so I just nod. Matlok jerks the large door open and we both step in.

The room we have stepped into is roughly the size of the living quarters I share with my sister and Matlok. The walls are burgundy with intricate gold designs spaced evenly across. There is lush carpet on the floor, and an obnoxious light with many prisms hangs from the ceiling. On the absurdly patterned walls, hang pictures of the presidents and their families. Matlok and I take in the scene before us with a mixture of amazement and nausea.

Without warning, Matlok's body jerks violently into the wall behind him. His head hits hard, and he topples over onto the floor. That's when I see taser prongs. They are embedded into the side of his neck. Unconscious, his body twists silently as the electricity courses through him.

In an instant, I bring my weapon up and strike at the perpetrator who has taken down Matlok. The pipe slices fluidly across the man's face, leaving a nasty gash as he falls helplessly to the thick carpet. His blood turns the beige to red.

The sentry had snuck up on us from a room to our right. We had been so enamored with the gaudiness of this space that he was able to get the upper hand. Either Matlok's frame had hidden me from the man's view, or he simply didn't think that a young girl would be capable of landing such a blow. The reason for his hesitancy with me doesn't matter. When he wakes, he will have a scar to remind him of the moment he underestimated a young girl from the lower class of Terra Convex.

I check on Matlok. He is still now. Unconscious but breathing steadily. The taser prongs remain in his neck. I dare not pull them out. They are hooked at the end, making removal a painful and dangerous procedure. He will have to see a physician.

Glancing around, I try to decide what I should do. I hadn't counted on being the only one in this room. There are more of us than there are of them. This should have been an easy battle to win. Yet, we are scattered, and I am alone.

As I lean over Matlok, I look up. The room that the guard had been hiding in is open. There is a large desk in the middle of it.

The Presidential Quarters.

Taking Matlok's weapon, I stand. Now I have two weapons. Still, my confidence level doesn't match my tenacity. Moving toward the room, I scan the area to make sure that there are no other guards lying in wait. As I cross the threshold, I see him.

President Reid DePriest.

Just a man, really.

Nothing fascinating or intriguing about him.

He stares at me dumbfounded. He stands behind his desk, his fingertips resting comfortably on the wooden surface. His clothes are as fancy as his living quarters. They are clean, and without wrinkle. His skin, however, is quite wrinkled - paper thin and nearly translucent. I'm not sure of his age. Honestly, I don't care.

I can't hide my smirk as I take a careful step towards him. "You're time is coming," I say with an almost maniacal chuckle.

His face changes from that of bewilderment, to that of authority. "Time for what, child?" He tries to hide it, but there is fear in his voice.

I lean forward slightly and say quietly, "Time for you to burn, old man."

His eyes grow wide, and I notice him flinch slightly.

I am nearly to the desk now. To be honest, I have no idea what I am going to do. I'm hoping that Matlok will regain consciousness, or one of the citizens will come in and take control of this situation. I thought I knew what I wanted. I thought I wanted to kill the president and free everyone. Now, I am just hoping that maybe he will...

His hand suddenly reaches under his desk, and I am on alert. When it comes back up to my field of vision, it is holding a revolver. As far as I knew, there were no guns in Terra Convex. Not even the Enforcers carry guns. The only reason I am aware that this is a gun is because of an antique magazine that had been found in the Hall of Reading before being confiscated by Leadership.

The aging man points the gun at my head with a smirk of his own. His crooked thumb pulls back the hammer, and I hear the clicking as if the timer of my life is ticking off the seconds I have left.

Without thinking, I take two running steps towards the desk – and the gun. Leaping, I land with one foot solidly on the desk and kick with the other. The gun makes a tremendous thundering boom as my foot finds its mark, kicking it from the old man's withered hand. Before the president can react, I swing around dramatically, bringing both pipes across President DePreist's face. First one, and then the other. Both impacting him solidly and sending a spray of blood over me and the desk, and then finally the floor when he lands with a thud.

Although I believe him to be dead, I immediately jump down from the desk to retrieve the gun. There are still council members to deal with, and I have no idea where the remaining security detail is. As soon as I land, severe pain in my left leg nearly sends me to the floor. I cling to the side of the desk and survey the area of pain. I only have to glance at the area to realize that I have been shot in the leg. Two symmetrical tears in my pants reveal the wounds. Just on the outer part of my left thigh, there is an entrance and exit wound. A wave of nausea comes over me, but I fight it.

With blood seeping steadily from both wounds, I hobble to where the gun rests and then back to the president. I roll him over onto his back and survey his wounds. His face is mangled. His eyes are open. The president is dead. I am the one that killed him.

I take a moment to ponder that. The president is dead. I am the one that killed him.

There is no time to celebrate. No time to harbor regrets. There is more to do. Ripping at his elaborate clothing, I manage to tear a strip of the cloth and tie it around my thigh. The pain is intense, but the bleeding starts to subside slightly.

I know that if we are to be truly free, the council members will also need to be dispersed. My strength is waning though, and I'm not sure if I can do any more on my own. Slowly, and with tremendous pain, I make my way to the outer room where Matlok lies. He is just beginning to stir when I reach him. His hand reflexively goes up to his neck where the prongs wait to be removed. He sucks in a sharp breath and then sees me leaning against the wall.

Jumping up awkwardly, Matlok rushes to me, pulling the still attached taser along with him. "Amelia. What's happened?"

With a slight jerk of my head, I gesture towards the next room. Matlok looks past me and then back into my face.

"The president is dead. I killed him. He shot me though." I can hear my strength draining. I'm not sure if it is the blood loss or just a reaction my body is having from too much adrenaline in a short amount of time. My vision becomes clouded, and then blackness seems to inch in from the edges, intent on taking me with it.

My body begins to slide down the gleaming wall. I can feel Matlok's hands try to steady me as I give in to the darkness that beckons. With tenderness, he lays me on the floor. I feel no more pain. I feel no more hate or fear. I only feel the lush carpet on my face.It makes me smile.

Chapter 21

Lukan

Kismet marched. The group of men and women proudly left Grayson a little after dusk, as planned. Even though we hiked in darkness, the moon was full and bright above us. Only I used a lantern as I led the way. The rest of the group followed along silently, watching for the tracks of snowshoes of the one in front of them.

With such a large group, I feared that we would make too much noise as we traipsed through the snow. I was quite surprised with our stealth. Pleased even. Only the soft thump of the snowshoes in the thick snow could be heard.

We marched through the night. Each one replaying the plan in our minds. Each one thinking of what is at stake if we fail. I imagine there were many quiet conversations between husbands and wives the evening before. Many tender moments spent with sons and daughters.

We celebrated the lives of Briggs and Laney yesterday. The people of Grayson attempted to make the Lamenting tender and light-hearted for the sake of the boys left behind. Their new life as orphans was still in turmoil. They needed to realize that the loss of their parents was difficult for all of Grayson. They needed to see that we will continue to rally behind them and support them however needed.

In the distance, I can see the forest looming like a black wall. The trek didn't take near as long as I thought it would. Or perhaps, my thoughts were so tangled that I hadn't considered how much time it was taking.

Stopping, I signal to the one behind me to do the same. He signals to the one behind him, and so on and so forth until the last one. There is no need for me to explain what is happening or what will happen next. We have gone over the plan many times. Each person knows their task. There are still a couple of hours before daylight. Time for everyone to get into place.

Dom had drawn a map of where we thought the camp was inside this forest. We realize now that we should have explored further. Still, I believe we still have the element of surprise on our side. The forest is quiet. The Howlers remain in their beds.

It will be much darker once inside the forest. Even without leaves, the moon will struggle to light our way. I take the hem of my fur coat and cover the lantern twice, signaling that we are about to enter the forest. Stealth is key from this point forward.

In a long line of nearly one hundred people, Kismet quietly treks into the forest. We hike slowly, making a wide arc around the oblivious camp of Howlers. Once in the woods, I put the fire in the lantern out. Because we are walking in the dark, and we are trying to do so quietly, it takes us some time to fully encircle the camp.

Through the trees, the camp is before us. The moon shines down on it as if pointing it out to us. From my vantage point, I can see several tents, a chicken coop, and a sty for pigs. The Howlers remain unaware. I wait several minutes. It is important that everyone be in place and ready for what comes next.

During our last planning meeting, I told the town about the sounds of children that Dom and I had heard coming from camp. Although my opinion on the matter remained the same – mostly – I felt it important to be honest with those who were going to be fighting. Since there really was no way of knowing where the children were in the camp, we decided on a plan of attack.

Helix was instrumental in the plans. Because of his time living with the Howlers as a child, he was able to help us write out a crude map of the layout of their camp. It had been many years since his time in their camp, but it was agreed that the Howlers were not keen on change. Nothing in their methods of terrorizing the communities has changed in decades. With the information that Helix provided, we felt fairly certain that we could move forward with our original attack plan. Of course, everyone realized that there was no way to attack without risking the lives of the children.

Time for action has come.

Briefly, I am reminded of the time that Helix and I sat on the edge of the cliffs. He had surprised me by sitting in the very spot I would normally jump from. I had marveled at the fact that he hadn't fallen over the cliff in his blindness. That is the day he told me the story of Lukan, the archer who defeated an entire village of pillagers, much like the Howlers.

Helix had asked me if I was ever scared when diving from the cliff into the blue lake below. I assured him that I enjoyed the feat very much, but admitted that the scariest part about it was taking that first step from the cliff.

"'Ah, yes. That first step. Taking that first step towards a free fall of unknowns. That is always the scariest thing. But once you do, once you take that first step...that leap, there are no more unknowns. Because after that one step, you are staring at the end result full-on. It's just a matter of getting from the first step to the goal,'" Helix had said to me on that day.

At the time, I felt like he was trying to say something important to me. I struggled to grasp it. Now, though, standing on the edge of the Howlers camp, ready to take that first step towards true freedom, I realize that everything he has ever told me, every conversation we have ever had, has been leading to this moment.

Now, much like Lukan the Archer, it is up to me to take that first step. Out of my quiver, I pull an arrow for just this occasion. It has been wrapped tightly in cloth and drenched in rendered fat. I open the lantern and place the cloth wrapped end of the arrow into the smoldering ember that remains. It quickly lights. Nocking it, I point the arrow high into the sky, pulling the string back with two fingers. Just as I release the string, I breathe out one word. "Merritt."

As my flaming arrow flies, I hear bows all around the camp releasing their arrows. Mine is the only one that burns. Once the arrows reach their maximum altitude, they will begin to plummet back down to the ground and hopefully into the tents of sleeping Howlers.

Each person nocks another arrow, immediately after their first has been fired. We do not want to use them all in the first few minutes of the battle. Just a few to keep the Howlers cowered down or hopefully mortally wounded.

Many of the first arrows find their mark. Screams and shrieks of pain begin to fill the camp. The first arrow, my arrow, remained lit as it flew through the air. It now burns brightly as its tip is embedded deeply in a pile of what appears to be clothing and furs. A Howler races from his tent, the fletching of an arrow sticking from his side. In his confusion and pain, he runs into the burning pile, and he himself catches on fire. His howls of pain are horrific.

All throughout the camp, Howlers are fleeing their tents. Many are bleeding and run around in a blind rage of confusion. The sun is beginning to peak through the trees giving us just enough light to see the chaos.

This is not the time for watching the mayhem. This is the time for action. We had agreed to fire three arrows into the camp before using our daggers. After my third arrow flies, I count to twenty. I want to give the rest of the soldiers time to fire their third arrow before I go running in to finish off the camp. I don't want to get shot with a Kismet arrow that was meant for a Howler.

On the count of twenty, I grab my dagger from my belt. With a shriek that resembles madness, I rush toward the scene of death and chaos. The circle of men and women that make up Kismet push in from all sides, closing around the camp with their owns shrieks, their own daggers, and their own madness. the Howlers, already disconcerted with arrows landing amongst them, seem to lack the wherewithal to realize that they are indeed under attack.

Strangely, the first thing I notice when I run into the camp is that the snow has turned red with blood. The second thing I notice is a woman, dressed in stinking furs, sprinting towards me with a look of lunacy etched on her face. She is screaming shrilly. Above her head, she holds a dagger. her intent is obvious. I hadn't thought about what it would be like to have to kill a woman. However, as she nears me, I know that this woman is pure Howler. There will be no talking her out of her intentions.

At the last second, just as she is nearly upon me, I drop down to the ground. Spinning in the snow, I bring my left foot out abruptly. She hadn't considered this action and immediately trips over my outstretched leg, her face landing in the snow and hand releasing the dagger that had been meant to kill me. Without giving her time to recover, I bring my dagger down into her back where I imagine her heart to be. I feel the life leave her. The feeling gives me no satisfaction, and a thought occurs to me that I will be haunted by this day for the rest of my life.

Quickly, I grab the woman's dagger, placing it in my belt. All around me, Kismet and Howlers battle. I see some from Grayson that are injured. Still, they continue to fight.

Running through the camp, the sun rising quickly upon us, I find the place where Helix said the captive women and children would be. In a cage-like contraption made from trees, several women and children cling to each other desperately. There are no guards. I had assumed there would be. As they see me approach, they cry out for help. When I reach them, I count roughly eight women, fourteen children, and one man. The presence of the man is puzzling, but he doesn't wear furs, so I don't believe him to be a Howler.

I begin to cut the simple knot that keeps them in the cage. Suddenly, one of the children screams shrilly, pointing behind me. Turning, dagger already in my hand, I see a Howler rushing towards me. Clearly, they do not want to see their prized possessions escape. He is determined to stop me.

The Howler is quite large – as most are – and I worry, as he approaches, that I will not be able to defeat him in the same manner as I did the woman. Dropping my dagger, I remove my bow from across my chest and nock an arrow. Because the Howler is large, he lacks speed, and I am able to draw back and release the arrow before he can maneuver away from the impact. The arrow strikes him solidly in the chest, and he falls immediately. The snow beneath him turns red in a melting pool of slushy blood.

Grabbing my dagger from the snow, I return my attention to the captives, cutting the knot and opening the cage door. There is no time for the thanks they seem intent on giving me. More harshly than I intend, I push them off and scream for them to run, while pointing in the direction of Grayson. They realize the dire circumstance and begin racing away. As the man exits, he lingers as if he doesn't know where to run. His mouth moves, but he cannot seem to find his voice. His plain clothes are unlike the other captives. They seem familiar, but I do not linger on why. The battle wages on and I must return to it. I push the man in the direction he needs to run if he is to find safety.

Now that the women and children have escaped, I know that no Howler remaining in this camp will be left alive. Slowly, methodically, I make my way through the camp. When I see a Howler on the ground, I check for life. Most that I encounter have lost their lives to Kismet. Those that have not succumbed to their injuries are quickly eliminated. Many of Grayson's soldiers are doing the same as me. They check the ones that are down, dispatching those that are near death.

I begin to think that we have won this war. As I search the dead and dying, I realize that I am looking for something. Someone. Gallner. Before we leave this place, I must see Gallner dead. My search becomes somewhat frantic and discouraging, but I continue on.

The camp is chaos. Smoke billows. The injured and dying wail. Tents burn. Those of us that continue to fight have kicked off our snowshoes. Now, we wade through crimson snow that has begun to melt under the heat of the battle. As I search the camp, my feet quickly become soaked in the bloody mud.

Still, I continue to search.

When I round one of the tents, I am surprised to see Gallner standing not far away. He didn't run. Didn't hide. As I stare at him, and him at me, I am met with the realization that Gallner has been looking for me for the very reason I have been searching for him. This is our fate. Our Kismet.

"Is this because of the girl?" Gallner asks, yelling over the chaos around us. "Do you seek my death because of the love you lost?"

How dare he mention Merritt. Anger swirls inside me. I maintain control of my emotions, though. My lips remain pressed tight. I do not dare answer, for fear that he will realize my act of bravery is just that – an act. Although Gallner appears, at times, to be just a mindless Howler, he is quite maniacal. I am aware that his words are meant to cause me to react in such a way that will end up with me dead and him the victor.

An evil smile spreads across Gallner's face. The sun is coming up, breaking through the gray clouds, slicing through the trees. With it, the breeze awakens, and Gallner's long brown hair – with the feather in the braid – begins to sway in a way that is eerily peaceful. He begins to walk toward me. In his right hand, a dagger that is meant for my death.

I do not take my eye from the madman. Reaching behind me, I retrieve an arrow. I nock it in the bow that I already hold in my other hand. The gesture doesn't seem to phase Gallner. His smile remains, and his pace towards me quickens. He has anticipated this day as much as I have. Still, my heart thumps violently inside of my chest. I have to match his confidence, even though I do not feel confident.

As our pace towards each other quickens into a jog, Gallner raises his dagger. I point my bow just a little to his left and release. The arrow streaks past his head, causing him to flinch away and take his eyes from me. Just as I had planned, Gallner is distracted, giving me the opportunity to take advantage.

In the brief second that Gallner flinches, watching the arrow fly past him, I quicken my pace. I race towards him. When his eyes come back to me, I am upon him. With wide eyes of surprise, Gallner is knocked to the ground. Obviously, he hadn't expected for the one-eyed boy to have the upper hand. Quickly, I straddle the Howler. I have never fought anyone with my fists. Never fought anyone at all, to be honest. The first punch I land on Gallner is excruciating. For me.

Gallner anticipates the blow and begins writhing under the weight of my body. Anger courses through my body and without realizing that Gallner's head is slightly turned, the punch that was meant for his nose, lands solidly against the side of his head. The cracking of bones, and a shockwave of pain reminds me that I didn't really know how to form a punching fist.

The pain in my hand is intense. I attempt to push it away. With my other hand, I grab for the dagger that is in my belt. Gallner writhes and bucks. His small-framed, but muscular, body is more than I can handle and somehow I end up underneath him. I anticipate that he will punch me and brace for the pain in my face or belly. Instead, he latches onto my right fist – the one that is badly damaged because of my poor punching technique. Gallner squeezes and twists, causing me to scream out in pain.

The pain is distracting, and it takes me a minute to realize that I still have another hand that works perfectly. A hand that is holding a dagger ready to strike. I have had this knife for many years. It never seemed important until I began hunting. When I realized how long it took to skin out my first kill, I began sharpening it on a regular basis. It has become as important to me as my eyepatch or my shoes. Because of its incredible sharpness, Gallner barely realizes that I have slid the knife through his side, between two of his ribs and into his right lung.

Gallner continues to twist on my injured hand until he realizes that his breath is coming in short gasps. With a cough, he spews blood that startles him and causes him to cease his assault on my injury. Laying beneath Gallner, his blood splattered across my face, I see the moment he grasps his predicament. He releases my hand and slowly places his hand on his side. I do not wait for him to comprehend what is happening. I jump up, throwing him off of me. Gallner coughs again, blood dousing the snow around him. He doesn't come for me. He remains on his hands and knees, stunned by the sudden turn of events.

I approach Gallner slowly. Crouching in front of him on one knee, I look into his face. Death is coming for him. His face begins to gray as he struggles for each breath. Gallner looks up at me with pleading eyes. He realizes his time is quickly coming to an end.

As I stare at the Howler that has caused me so much grief, I begin to see something familiar. He blinks slow, and I begin to see tears forming. His thin lips and long mustache are coated with blood. His chin is sharp. Familiar. I stare into his eyes for several seconds as he gasps for breath and coughs blood into the snow. Suddenly, I realize – I see Helix in Gallner's features.

I had never noticed before. Never got the chance to really look into the man's eyes when they were not filled with hate. Now, with death approaching, Gallner's face softens, and the madness seems to disappear. Without the malice, I can see clearly that Gallner resembles his brother, Helix.

Feelings of sorrow begin to build inside of me. Not for Gallner, but for Helix. He wasn't able to save his brother from the fate laid on him by the Howlers when he was just a child. I am reminded suddenly of what Helix said as we sat on the rock wall back in Grayson right after he told me that he would be leaving to wander.

"Are you going to be angry with me when I kill Gallner?" I had asked Helix. "Will you think differently about me?"

Helix had groaned softly, as he always does when pondering. "My brother was lost to me long ago. The Howlers stole his freedom when they stole his soul. There is only one way for Gallner to find freedom. I just wish I could have told him that I'm sorry for the life he had. I hope he can forgive me, as I have forgiven him."

I remain crouched on one knee in front of Gallner. Unafraid, I reach forward with my uninjured hand, placing it behind his head. He flinches slightly, uncertain of what kind of pain I am going to unleash. Surprising him, though, I lean forward until our foreheads are touching.

His putrid breath is coming in ragged gasps now. His time is short. Quietly, I say to him, "It wasn't just for the girl. It was for everyone who deserves freedom." I pause briefly. "Even you, Gallner."

Gallner doesn't speak. He only nods. I lean back to look into his eyes. The light is leaving them quickly. Blood coats his lips, and he falls over into the snow.

"Her name was Merritt," for reasons I do not understand, I add this bit of information before whispering, "Helix forgives you."

Gallner stares at me until a blankness fills them.

Kismet.

Chapter 22

Lia

Time does not stand still for those that mourn. Nor does it heal. Time has no affection for the wounded or sick. It has one purpose – keep moving forward. Relentlessly. Because time waits for no one, we spend our lives attempting to maintain a steady pace with it. Until our time comes to an end.

In the days following the death of President DePreist, the people of Terra Convex made their demands of Leadership. The time of oppression was over. The time for a rebirth had come. The people were like young children – no plans, no ideas. They had been given the gift of true freedom but didn't know what to do with it. They had never been given gifts. They had never known freedom. The two concepts were foreign to them.

Those that fought and survived found and captured the council members. They had been hiding in various places throughout Terra Convex. One had actually tried hiding in plain sight – he had heard my speech to the people and then accompanied us to the Isolation Chamber.

When Marcus DePriest built Terra Convex, he created a secret passageway in the Presidential Quarters. It was built in case of a revolt. After the councilman watched us leave the Isolation Chamber, he ran to the passageway and warned the security guards. That is how they were able to attack the back of the group.

That councilman was made into an example to the rest of Leadership. They were forced to watch as he was questioned. Only one question.

What is the code to the hatch door?

He remained tight-lipped. Adamant in his stance. There were Enforcers present that were more than willing to extract the information from him. Emotions ran high for those wounded and lost. The councilman died with the code still locked inside him.

A second councilman was brought forward. The code was not as valuable to him. He relinquished it quickly. He was spared. It was never the intention of the Defiance to murder the councilmen. Or anyone, really. The code was the key.

Still, it was not time to exit. Winter was in full force above Terra Convex. The people would need to take the next few weeks to prepare for the exodus.

"I will let you know when it's time," Axel explained to the eager, yet nervous, crowd.

With murmuring and head shaking, they accepted this. The people had never lived a life where they had not been told what to do with every aspect of their life. They accepted this and began their preparations.

*****

Time might not heal emotional wounds, but it does tend to heal physical wounds.

Although my leg still aches at times, even weeks after being shot, the pain is tolerable. The pain has not hindered me from preparing to leave this underground world. The physician did a fantastic job cleaning and stitching the wound.

As I lay under the window now, I can't help but wonder about Lukan. I worry about him and his group. Worry about what they must be enduring in the cold and with the Howlers. Sometimes, I feel an incredible pull to walk out the hatch door and go find him. Perhaps, together, we could defeat his enemy. Other times, I am perfectly content to stay here.

After I had healed and could make the trek to the secret room – we kept its location secret from the rest of Terra Convex only so that the original Agitators could have their space – Axel suggested we take an afternoon for ourselves. I was giddy on the way to the room. It had been too long since I looked up at the sky.

When Axel opened the door and stepped aside for me to enter first, I gasped. In the middle of the floor, nearly taking up the entire room, was a thick mattress covered in fine linens. There were thick pillows at one end that seemed to invite me in.

Axel explained that he and Matlok had confiscated it from the Presidential Quarters. They felt that I deserved a better place to lay while looking up through the window than that old tattered blanket.

"I'm not sure how you feel about laying on a mattress that the president used to lay on," Axel admitted.

I hadn't considered it like that. As I gazed down on it, all I could think of was that it used to belong to the most powerful person in Terra Convex. Now, an Agitator will be laying her head on it.

Beaming, I say, "It's perfect."

Now, as I lay here under the window, watching the clouds roll by in the blue sky above, I know that the heart of winter is passing. Time in Terra Convex, for me at least, is coming to an end. I lay alone. Everyone has a job to do.

Axel is somewhere helping Dalen repair a piece of vital equipment.

Although Darcy loves books, she no longer feels the need to monitor the Hall of Reading – people are allowed to come and go as they please, enjoying the other worlds that reading brings. She has found a new passion – researching the artwork left behind in the corridors of the Presidential Quarters.

Mira's belly has begun to show signs of new life growing inside her. Matlok beams with pride every time he glances her way. They say that if the baby is a girl, she will be named Marcella – after our mother. What if its a boy, I asked. They are adamant – it is a girl.

Abigail has mostly avoided the rest of the Defiance since the revolt. Sometimes, we see her helping in the Dining Hall. She has taken it upon herself to help sort and count out the food stores. When I see her, I smile, and she smiles back.

I cherish my time under the window. I relish my time alone. It gives me a chance to think and to imagine.

Above me, just out of view, the grass moves in a way that startles me. The snow has long since melted. The grass, brown and lifeless, lies matted onto the cold ground waiting for the spring air to revive it.

The grass moves again, and then Lukan appears. He stands above me. He seems different than the first time I saw him. Certainly, he has gotten taller, but there is something else about him that seems altered. I can't quite figure out what it is.

Lukan's mouth spreads into a delighted smile, and he bends his legs under him. I sit up and stare at him, returning his smile. From his pocket, he produces a parchment. He lays it on the window for me to read.

SAFE NOW. COME OUT.

My eyes begin to burn with tears as I consider the words. I realize that I can no longer hide inside this place that I have tried to escape for so long. It's safe now. Time to come out.

Lukan

Somewhere in the act of justification, I had to come to terms with the fact that I had taken human lives. The thought weighs heavily on me. I feel the judgment from all of those in town. Can sense it with every whisper that blows by on the breeze. My family assured me that the only reason people look at me differently now is because I was the only one brave enough to stand against the Howlers. The people of Grayson were thankful for what Kismet accomplished on that bitterly cold, snowy day. Thankful, yet sorrowful.

We lost a dozen of our own in the war on the Howlers camp. Twelve citizens that fought bravely against an enemy that no other community dared to stand against. Three women. Nine men. All, regarded and buried as heroes. We mourned their loss and celebrated their lives.

Elvin was one of those who perished in the raid. He fought bravely to the end, even killing four Howlers all on his own. Still, he was lost in the fight. We buried him next to his wife, Myna, who had died just a few years earlier.

Those that we freed found their way back to their own communities. The women and children had come from several different towns near ours. In the days that followed, these communities visited Grayson, bringing gifts and food for what we had done for them. Each time someone new would visit to give thanks, it was obvious that a new sense of kinship had formed between communities.

The man that we freed never spoke. He seemed lost and unaware of what exactly had happened. He didn't seem to have a community. The clothing he wore seemed odd but familiar. One night, just as I was drifting off to sleep, it occurred to me where I had seen clothes like that before. Even though it was dark, and I was in my nightclothes, I hurriedly put on my coat and ran to the house where the stranger was staying. He had been given one of the empty homes to stay in until he decided where he was going to go. Although he never spoke, he seemed thankful to at least not be locked in a cage any longer.

I barged into the house. It was late at night, and the man jumped up out of his bed. He stood rigid in the corner. Eyes wide with fright and trembling, he stared at me.

I apologized hastily and asked, "Did you come from below? Are you from Terra Convex?"

The man opened his mouth to say something. He seemed surprised and confused that I would ask such a question. I could tell that I had said something striking to him.

"Please. I need to know. Is Lia all right?" I continued with my questioning.

The man's face changed. No longer surprised. No longer confused. A look of resolution came over him. He climbed back into his bed and covered his face. Obviously, he knew what I was talking about, but he had no intention of speaking to me.

The next morning, the strange man was gone. He left a note on the kitchen counter that simply said, 'thank you.'

I could feel my time with Helix coming to an end. He had begun gathering what he would need to make a long journey. I tried to spend as much time with him as possible. On the rock wall, he and I, along with Dom, sit contemplating our new life without Howlers.

I told Helix about my final moments with Gallner. He was sorrowful for the loss of his brother but pleased with the tenderness I showed when I didn't have to.

"That's called integrity," Helix groaned pleasantly. "That's the sign of a good man."

I chuckled slightly, embarrassed at the compliment. "I was just hoping to be like Lukan the Archer," I said.

This time, Helix chuckled. He leaned into me and said, "You are Lukan the Archer, my friend."

Dom and I looked at each other with confusion.

"The story I told you about Lukan the Archer was just that – a story.' Helix explained.

I am dumbfounded. "He didn't exist? It was a make-believe story?"

"He didn't exist," Helix said with a wink. "But now he does."

*****

Every day, I wonder about Lia. I know she is facing her own challenges right under my feet. Perhaps, now that the land is free from Howlers, Lia can figure out a way to escape and live peacefully above ground. When I spoke to her friend, Axel, I had told him about the Howlers and the danger they pose to our survival. I realize that Lia isn't aware of their demise.

The sun is shining bright and warm. Although the air still carries a chill, and the ground is still saturated with water from the melted snow, the sun feels good on my face as I walk to the window. It has been quite a while since I last visited, and the excitement from going back helps to hurry me along.

As I walk, I think of all that has happened since the first time I saw the window hiding in the tall grass. I think of how my life has changed – how I have changed. At the time, I was absorbed in feeling as if I was of no use to my community. I was bitter and ashamed for only having one eye. Now, though, I know that what I thought was a disability was never anything more than just a good story to tell the kids.

"Girls love guys with scars," Dom liked to tease. Especially after gaining his own scar during the battle with the Howlers. He likes to tell the story of getting the scar across his left cheek. Every time he tells the story to one of the neighborhood children, there are a few more details that I have never heard before. I always smile.

When I reach the window, I am surprised and pleased at what I see.

Lia.

She stares up at me from a thick mattress with lots of pillows around her. Although she appears quite comfortable, she also seems weary. I smile down at her. A warm smile spreads across her face. Crouching down onto the window, I reach into my pocket. I had planned on leaving this parchment for Lia to see. It pleases me that I am able to watch her face as she processes the words. I read it once more before laying it on the window.

SAFE NOW. COME OUT.

I watch Lia's face as the meaning of the words become clear to her. Being able to see her face while she reads it makes the moment much more special. Tears of gladness begin to pool up in her uplifted eyes. I watch as she closes her eyes in what appears to be relief. She opens her eyes and looks at me. Nodding, I know that I will see her soon. Outside.

Chapter 23

Lia

The crowd presses me towards the hatch door. The people of Terra Convex are eager to breathe their first gulp of fresh air. Everyone felt it appropriate that I be at the front of the group. I should be the first to experience the sun on my skin.

I had envisioned this moment for so long. I had dreamed of running through the grass and climbing trees. Now that the door to that dream is opening, however, I feel a pang of anxiety and sorrow.

A whoosh of air startles the people behind me as Dalen opens the door and stands back for me to exit. We stare into each other's eyes and something personal passes between us. I step aside. The people are confused, but they begin to file out one by one. Axel stands next to me. He doesn't push me to exit. I'm sure he realizes my pain.

The people continue to amble past us. Through the door. Up the steps. Into the new world.

Abigail. Darcy. Mira and Matlok. They all pass by with nervous smiles and giddiness.

As the last of them pass by, I look up to see Axel gazing at me compassionately.

"I always envisioned this day," I start. "I just really wish my mother were here."

Axel nods. "She is." He presses his hand to my chest. "She's here. She's with you for all time."

I look over at Dalen. He is nodding. Then he looks out the door and walks up the steps.

Hesitantly, I take Axel's hand in mine. We exit Terra Convex and walk up the steps.

At the top of the steps, I look around at the people of Terra Convex. Some are weeping. All are breathing deep. The children are running and laughing. The air is cold, but the sun is high in the sky.

"Lia?" I hear a voice come from my left.

I scan the area to find the source. Then I see him. The boy that showed me life is possible even against all the odds. He has become a man since that first encounter. He stands taller. There is confidence in his smile. Somehow, through all of this, he found his place. Found his purpose.

I approach him with a smile.

"Lukan."

Lukan

Helix was eager to return to the wilderness. He seemed to gain a new sense of freedom when the Howlers were decimated. I do not begrudge him for wanting to fulfill the need he has to explore. Truth be told, I wish I could join him. Perhaps someday. For now, my duty is to stay here and continue training the people of Grayson, and the surrounding communities, to defend themselves. We should not be so naive to think that the Howlers were the only fiends that roam the countryside. Everyone needs to be ready to defend their homes.

Unable to stall Helix any longer, the people of Grayson hold a feast and celebration for our friend. The whole town has grown fond of the blind Wanderer. Everyone is sad to see him go. Helix is embarrassed but gracious.

Dom and I walk with Helix. Past the cliffs. Past the cave.

"I have noticed something," Helix comments.

"What's that?" I ask.

"No more death smoke," Helix breathes in deeply.

I realize that I haven't smelled the acrid smoke either. I can't remember the last time I did smell it.

"Perhaps I will begin my journey near the hatch," Helix muses.

It seems a strange place to start, but I have learned not to question the wise man. We change our path slightly and continue on.

As we near the area where the hatch door lies hidden down the short staircase, we are met with something odd. Sounds emanating from the forest. Children running and laughing. Men and women talking excitedly. I hasten my pace and quickly realize the source of the noises. The people of Terra Convex have emerged from the underground.

I think to myself - This is what it looks like when somebody sees the sun, trees, birds for the first time. First time breathing natural air into their lungs. First time to feel the cold on their skin.

I look over at Helix and Dom. Helix, although he cannot see what Dom and I see, is smiling broadly. I hear him chuckle as he listens to children laughing as they chase each other past us. Dom is also smiling. The people from Terra Convex do not seem to notice us standing here watching. They are completely engrossed in the world around them. A world that has been hidden from them for ninety years.

As I turn in a circle to take in the scene, I see her. She stands at the top of the steps, holding Axel's hand. She is pleased with the reaction of her people. I walk towards her, but she seems oblivious to my approach. Her eyes are on her people.

"Lia," I say her name softly, and she looks my direction.

For the first time, I see a smile of contentment on the girl from the underground.

Chapter 24

Lia

"I have to go with you, Lia," Abigail chokes out.

I'm not sure if the words are difficult for her because the pain of losing Mac is still so fresh or because the thought of leaving the only world she has ever know, with her sworn enemy, is completely terrifying to her. I can sense what a struggle it is for her to say my name the way Mac would have. The thought of her hatred following me across the broken landscape of this new world somehow seems like the proper self-imposed punishment for all the hurt I have caused.

"Think long and hard about this. I don't even know where I'm going...or if I will ever be back." I respond after considering her request. "There are too many unknowns in the wilderness, and I'm honestly not sure you are ready to say goodbye to this place." I continue, gesturing weakly in the direction of the door that leads back down into Terra Convex.

I can see the pain in Abigail's pale eyes. She nods and lowers her eyes slowly. I start to think she has decided that I am right and her place is here, with these people. I am just about to turn away, ready to be done with this uncomfortable conversation with a girl who, not that long ago, declared her eternal hatred for me. Abigail's gaze returns to me, and I can see the turmoil in her eyes, but especially in the tightness of her jaw.

She stands just in front of me and gently places her hand on the back of my head. Not long ago, I would have withdrawn from her touch. I probably would have shoved her away. Today, though, I allow her the moment she needs. Her eyes close as she pulls our heads together until our foreheads are touching. She sucks in a deep breath, seemingly to steady herself against the memory of watching this same gesture that her lover and I had shared as best friends. My eyes begin to water at the tender gesture she is trying to recreate.

"I will go wherever you go." She whispers with our foreheads still touching.

Her words are not lost on me. I can sense that she is trying to make amends for her own sins. I have my fair share, also. Too many. Even though the weight of those killed in our fight for freedom weighs heavily on me, I imagine her pain and regret is incomprehensible.

My strongest desire, since walking out of Terra Convex, is to rid myself of the pain of loss. The brutality of our government has left its mark on each of us. I am ready to leave the underground and begin a new life with Axel, exploring our new world. This moment with Abigail, though, makes me realize that perhaps leaving our hatred for each other in Terra Convex is a great step toward a brighter future.

I reach up and embrace the back of her head to complete the embrace, just as Mac and I would have done. It seems, at this moment, Abigail understands the task that she is undertaking by joining Axel and me. I'm not entirely convinced that the animosity that she has always had for me is completely gone. Still, this feels like the proper way for us to begin on the path of forgiveness and reconciliation. Mac would be proud. We release each other and stare into each other's eyes. I wonder if I look as scared as she does.

With a nervous tremor in her voice and a shy smile, Abigail asks, "When do I get my own name?"

I know what she is asking. Abigail is ready to be free from the uniformity that Terra Convex forced upon us all. She wants to be different.

I smile tenderly and answer, "Whenever you are ready."

Abigail is thoughtful for a few seconds, and a smile spreads across her face. It's the first genuine smile I have ever seen from her. I realize how lovely she really is. Her pale eyes are clear, and I can see hope in them.

Quite proudly, she gives me her new name. "Gail. I want to be called Gail."

Smiling through my tears, I realize that Abigail has been thinking about this for quite some time. She did not just pick the name Gail randomly. I wonder if it is something that she and Mac had talked about.

"It is a pleasure to meet you, Gail."

Lukan

The breeze warms steadily as winter is pushed away by the spring. With the new season, comes a renewal. A rebirth. An awakening. Just like those that emerged from Terra Convex. Just like Grayson rebuilding both physically and emotionally after defeating the Howlers.

Just like me as I try to discover my new role in this larger world. A world without Merritt. A world without Helix. Both very important parts of my life. One dead. One wandering. Both still vital.

As I sit on the cliffs, I am reminded of the time I was leaving Grayson to do the very thing I intend to do today – cliff-dive. I couldn't fool Merritt with my intentions. she knew me all too well. I believe, even though I never said the words to her, she knew that I loved her. Still love her. Always.

That day, when I arrived at the cliffs, I was surprised to find Helix sitting there. It was almost as if he was waiting for me. That was the day that he told me the story of Lukan the Archer. Of course, that story turned out to be just a fictional tale to embolden me to rise up against the Howlers. the story, and his friendship changed my life forever.

Helix has been gone for several weeks. The day that Lia came up out of the ground was the day that Helix walked into the forest. I considered pleading with him to stay. That was for my own selfishness though. I knew that he is perfectly capable of taking care of himself, even in his blindness.

Lia left shortly after Helix, taking Axel and another from Terra Convex with her. I did plead with them to stay. There was much they didn't know about this world. Too many unknowns and dangers that they hadn't considered.

To be honest, though, I wanted to go with them. Or Helix. There was a huge part of me that would love to wander through life, discovering this new world without Howlers. That was a dream that I had with Merritt, though. It didn't seem right to leave if I couldn't leave with her.

The sun breaks through the clouds. Closing my eye, I raise my face into the sunshine. I relish the warmth after so much cold. I am reminded of what I came here to do. A shiver crawls up my spine as I begin to consider how cold the water below is going to be when I dive in.

Standing, I remove my shoes and most of my clothes. When I am climbing back up the steep hill, I do not want to be weighed down by cold, dripping clothes. As I toss my shoes towards some rocks to my right, I see her.

Merritt.

I know she isn't really sitting on the rocks smiling at me. Still, I smile at my imagination for bringing her here for me to see. The breeze picks up, blowing her dark hair across her face. Merritt's hair always smelled like lavender. Breathing in deep, I imagine that I can smell it even now.

My Merritt illusion stands and walks gracefully to the edge of the cliffs. In life, Merritt would have never gone close to the edge. She would have been unnerved by the height of it above the lake below. Now, she stands with her toes just over the edge. With a mischievous smile, she looks over her shoulder at me and winks. I approach the edge, without taking my eye off of her.

On the edge of the cliff, the blue lake below, Merritt and I stand together for what I know is the last time. Although her memory will stay with me for a lifetime, there is no reason for me to continue to imagine her with me.

Returning Merritt's wink, I take the step off the cliff. I have this step from this spot many times. Each time is exhilarating. Diving through the air, I position my body so that I will slice through the water with my hands. My body whistles through the air as I plummet towards the lake. I feel my hair flying behind me.

As the blue lake approaches, I glance over to see Merritt free-falling beside me. Her dark hair flows behind her, hints of red teasing subtly. She smiles broadly, just like I knew she would if she had tried this in life.

Just before I breach the surface, just before I suck in the last breath before going under, I say, "I love you, Merritt. Always."

Epilogue

Four years later...

Lia smiles up at Axel as they near the place where they emerged from the earth. They are met with the sounds of a thriving community. Children laughing. Dogs barking playfully. Lia and Axel smile at each other as they are welcomed with sounds of progress coming from what used to be a tomb to them.

Like ants, the people of Terra Convex scattered across the land when they surfaced. Many found it impossible to crawl back into the earth after tasting freedom in the fresh air of the world above. As Lia suspected long before the Defiance, those citizens found determination deep within them. They studied the ways of Grayson and learned how to live in a world where hard work is rewarded with a full life of contentment.

Darcy remained at Terra Convex. She took it upon herself to maintain order inside Terra Convex. The pain of decades of lies from the government left the people naive, childlike. Although Darcy and Lia were best friends, she didn't share Lia's eagerness to explore their new world above. Darcy was perfectly content to stay behind and help rebuild a new life for those of Terra Convex.

The new Terra Convex was now not only what remained below but had also expanded to the land above. With the help of the citizens of Grayson, homes were constructed, the people were taught how to source water from the ground and purify it. Dom taught the people how to hunt for their meat and gather their herbs. His aunt, Luetta, helped them plant and tend gardens. the people of Terra Convex were indeed like children – learning, failing, learning from their failures.

Inside Terra Convex, Dalen worked on restoring the aging living quarters, air purification system, and solar panels. the Isolation Chamber was scrubbed clean and turned into a true Grand Hall. There, weddings were held. Weddings between two people that actually chose each other to be life partners. All of the laws of Terra Convex were discarded. People actually married out of love and compatibility. Children were born from love. Citizens realized their true potential by working jobs they enjoyed and cherished. the heavy weight of intrusive laws no longer crushed the spirits of the people.

Mira and Matlok also decided to stay. Matlok became head of security in Terra Convex. He, along with Abigail's father, was instrumental in writing the new laws of Terra Convex. Laws that were actually meant to protect the people and not oppress them. In the four years since the emergence, Mira and Matlok had two children. Their daughter was born a few months after Lia departed. They named her Marcella just as they planned. Two years later, Mira gave birth to a son. They named him Slayton. Healthy, happy children born out of love and not duty.

Lukan, revered by all of the surrounding communities as a hero, also proved instrumental in the building of the new Terra Convex. He aided Dom in teaching the people how to hunt. Even though the Howlers were decimated, he felt it wise to train the people how to fight and defend their homes. He knew that there was always a chance that another group like the Howlers, or even worse, could rise up. The towns will be ready if that happens.

Helix had spent two years wandering. When he returned, he spent many hours telling of his journey. He told Lukan about the distant towns he had visited. At each one, he told them the story of the true Lukan the Archer. Lukan's face would blush as Helix spoke of him with such regard. If Helix mourned his brother's death, he never revealed it. He never spoke of it, and Lukan never discussed it either. Although Helix wouldn't take any of the empty houses, he seemed perfectly content with his new life in Grayson. He built a crude structure in the antique car cemetery to live in. This caused Luetta to fret and Avis to plead with him to come into town to live, but Helix maintained that he at least be allowed to live as a wanderer even if he wasn't roaming the land. We were all just glad to have him nearby, so we let him live in the manner that pleased him.

Lia, her excitement growing as her little group nears their former home, takes Axel's hand. He gives her hand a slight squeeze and asks if she is alright. Lia instinctively rubs her swollen belly. smiling, she answers that she feels great. Axel nods. His eyes, warm and affectionate. Lia looks over her shoulder at Gail who walks a little further back. Gail's eyes are on her child. With blond hair and sparkling blue eyes, the child looks like any other from Terra Convex. It's the shape of his nose and the sharpness of his chin that sets him apart as Maclin's.

Indeed, Mac would have chosen Gail, just as he said. He did choose her. Gail had just realized that she was harboring her own secret when Mac had been caught by the Interrogators. As he faced his execution, she whispered the news of her pregnancy in his ear. "I will always be with you. This child is proof of that. Show him a mother's love and a new world," Mac had whispered in hers after finding out that he was to be a father to a son he would never meet. Gail named the child Audrik.

Gail's eyes meet Lia's, and she smiles. The friendship between the two has changed dramatically in the four years since leaving Terra Convex. What once was hatred and animosity has evolved into love and admiration. Both had endured the presence of the other in honor of Mac. Now, though, they cherish each other.

Lia is surprised to see what the people of Terra Convex have accomplished and built in the time that she has been gone. They have expanded far beyond the area where they all emerged from the hatch door. The field where her secret window lies is now a flourishing garden full of vegetables. Lia beams at the pride she feels for what the people have learned to do in such little time.

In the distance, Lukan and Helix stand near the edge of the forest. They seem to be discussing the garden. Lukan looks up at the sound of the small group's approach. Smiling, he says something to Helix that Lia cannot hear. She's sure that he is telling the blind man that the Terra Convex Wanderers have returned.

Lia's little group approaches the two men, embracing them warmly. They speak briefly. Axel comments on the size of the garden. Lukan gives the credit to his mother and Darcy. As the group converses, Gail remains quiet. She keeps her eyes on her son. Always.

A tug on Lia's shirt does not distract her from the reunion with her friends from Grayson. Without a word, she lifts the tugging-tike, placing her on her hip. Lukan takes in the sight of the auburn hair child and is reminded of the girl with auburn hair that he adored but was lost to him. He smiles at her, and she hides her face in Lia's hair.

"Ehl, there's no reason to be afraid. This is our friend, Lukan," Lia explains to the child. To Lukan, Lia says, "Her name is Marcella, after my mother. We call her Ehl, though."

"She's beautiful. I knew somebody with hair that same color once," Lukan replies. "Your sister also has a child. Just a little older than yours. Her name is also Marcella."

Lia chuckles softly. "Before I left, Mira told me that she was going to have a daughter. She just knew it. She also said that her name would be Marcella. That's why we call our daughter Ehl."

They speak for a little longer. Axel, Lukan, and Helix discuss the rebuilding and other topics that men enjoy speaking about. Lia places Ehl near Gail. The child and Audrik immediately start playing together. Lia gives Gail a gentle squeeze on her shoulder and walks away. There is something she must see before they leave the field.

Lukan watches Lia as she walks into the field. He reflects on his first time seeing her when he was in that field. At the time, she was an anguished girl bearing the weight of too much heartache. Now, he thinks, Lia is a woman at peace with the life she created for her and her people.

As Lia stares through the dusty glass, she smiles. She smiles as she remembers all the time she spent in that spot, looking up. Hours looking up. Waiting. Hoping to see someone looking down on her just as she looks down on the empty room now. As Lia thinks back on everything that has happened, she realizes that what she was looking for - hope, strength, and a future. Often times, however, the only thing Lia could see was the reflection of a young girl full of curiosity, determination and unwavering loyalty to what she knew to be true. Lia smiles now, as she realizes that everything she had longed for was in that reflection – hope, strength, a future. Now she sees clearly. Hope, strength, and a future had been in her all along.

Always.

This book is dedicated to all those with wandering minds and the spirit for exploring. May the burdens of this life never become so heavy that you cannot carry them into the forest and release them from your soul.

CPSIA information can be obtained
at www.ICGtesting.com
Printed in the USA
FSHW021259281218
54737FS